"…too dangerous…no backup…can't allow it…another way…against policy…irresponsible if I…"

Finally he ran out of steam. Or so I thought.

"Lacie, you're smart and perceptive and you know your stuff. I wouldn't mind spending more time with you. Professionally. Or personally. But there's no way I'm going to let you risk your life for this case."

I stared at him, taken off guard by his admission. But I wasn't about to let my emotions get in the way of my better judgment. Or doing the work I was committed to.

"I'm going to do this," I said quietly. "You can help me. Or you can cut me loose. Like it or not, Anthony, I have the perfect cover."

Dear Reader,

We're new, we're thrilling, and we're back with another explosive lineup of four Silhouette Bombshell titles especially for you. This month's stories are filled with twists and turns to keep you guessing to the end. But don't stop there—write and tell us what you think! Our goal is to create stories with action, emotion and a touch of romance, featuring strong, sexy heroines who speak to the women of today.

Critically acclaimed author Maureen Tan's *A Perfect Cover* delivers just that. Meet Lacie Reed. She'll put her life on the line to bring down a serial killer, even though it means hiding her identity from the local police—including one determined detective.

Temperatures rise in the latest Athena Force continuity story as an up-and-coming TV reporter travels to Central America for an exclusive interview with a Navy SEAL, only to find her leads drying up almost before her arrival. That won't deter the heroine of Katherine Garbera's *Exposed.*...

They say you can't go home again, but the heroine of Doranna Durgin's first Bombshell novel proves the *Exception to the Rule*. Don't miss a moment as this P.I.'s assignment to guard government secrets clashes with the plans of one unofficial bodyguard.

Finally, truth and lies merge in *Body Double,* by Vicki Hinze. When a special forces captain loses three months of her memories, her search to get them back forces her to rely on a man she can't trust to uncover a secret so shocking, you won't believe your eyes....

We'll leave you breathless! Please send me your comments c/o Silhouette Books, 233 Broadway, Suite 1001, New York, NY 10279.

Best wishes,

Natashya Wilson

Natashya Wilson
Associate Senior Editor

Please address questions and book requests to:
Silhouette Reader Service
U.S.: 3010 Walden Ave., P.O. Box 1325, Buffalo, NY 14269
Canadian: P.O. Box 609, Fort Erie, Ont. L2A 5X3

A PERFECT COVER

MAUREEN TAN

Silhouette®
BOMBSHELL™

Published by Silhouette Books

America's Publisher of Contemporary Romance

SILHOUETTE BOOKS

ISBN 0-373-51323-2

A PERFECT COVER

Copyright © 2004 by Maureen Tan

This edition published by arrangement with Harlequin Books S.A.

® and TM are trademarks of Harlequin Books S.A., used under license. Trademarks indicated with ® are registered in the United States Patent and Trademark Office, the Canadian Trade Marks Office and in other countries.

www.SilhouetteBombshell.com

Printed in U.S.A.

MAUREEN TAN

is a Marine Corps brat, the eldest of eight children and naturally bossy. She and her husband of thirty years have three adult children, two grandchildren and currently share their century-old house with a dog, three cats, three fish and a rat. Much to his dismay, their elderly Appaloosa lives in the barn. Most of Maureen's professional career has involved explaining science, engineering and medical research to the public. To keep her life from becoming boring, she has also worked in disaster areas as a FEMA public affairs officer and spent two years as a writer for an electronic games studio. Maureen's first Bombshell book, *A Perfect Cover,* is set in New Orleans and recounts one woman's fight to save Vietnamese immigrants from a serial killer.

For my family and friends, who make it all worthwhile.
And for Peter, the love of my life.

Prologue

I never knew my mother. She was probably a prostitute. Or perhaps she was just a woman who loved the wrong man. In either event, she was most likely dead.

There was panic in the streets of Saigon when Ho Chi Minh's troops poured into the city. Barefoot, ragged soldiers carrying AK-47s streamed from hidden tunnels. The Cholon district was in flames. South Vietnamese soldiers were stripping off their uniforms, trying to blend in with the population. And the Americans—caught off guard by the swift fall of the city—were fleeing the embassy's rooftop by helicopter, abandoning their friends and allies.

Abandoning their children.

That day, an American soldier—a black man in a torn and charred Marine sergeant's uniform—burst into Grandma Qwan's home. He interrupted a dozen orphaned children and Grandma Qwan as they knelt in prayer, saying the Rosary out loud, petitioning the Virgin for her protection.

The soldier's hands were badly burned, Grandma Qwan told me later, but still he held a blanket-wrapped toddler tightly in his arms.

"Her name is Lai Sie," he said in Vietnamese as he put the child gently on her feet and placed a silk-wrapped bundle on the floor beside Grandma Qwan.

Stunned into silence, Grandma Qwan simply stared at the soldier. His hair was singed, his eyes were bloodshot, and tears streaked the gray soot that coated his dark face. Later that night, Grandma Qwan discovered enough money and jewelry among the little girl's clothing to support the orphanage for years.

"Please. Keep her safe for me," was the soldier's only request. "I'll come back for her."

Then he'd disappeared into the chaos of the smoke-filled streets.

I waited for years, but my American father never returned. And no young Vietnamese woman stepped forward to claim me.

Grandma Qwan loved and protected me as she did all of the children in her care. But my coloring and features, inherited from my parents, made me an outcast in my own country. I was *bui doi*. Throughout my childhood, I heard the curse shouted by pedicab drivers, spat out by old women in the marketplace, muttered when soldiers knocked me aside, used as a taunt by playmates.

Bui doi. Dust of life. *Bui doi.* Child of dust.

Chapter 1

I was sitting in darkness, waiting to be rescued. Or to die. As were we all. More than fifty of us, trapped inside the long, battered trailer of an eighteen-wheeler. Men and women, young and old. A few adolescent children. But no infants. Yet.

All around us were splintery shipping crates, large and small. They filled the trailer top to bottom and front to back, with just enough room left between the rows to conceal a human cargo. Shipping labels, stenciled in black paint, said the crates contained an assortment of machine parts destined for America. We, too, had been destined for America. But the truck that pulled us was long gone, its trailer and its cargo—human and machine—stationary. We were locked in and abandoned. And the heat was becoming unbearable.

Beside me, Rosa groaned—a deep, harsh sound with surprisingly little volume to it. I leaned in closer to her, my hand brushing the sleeve of her light cotton dress, then moving to find a thick braid, a soft cheek and, finally, her forehead. It was damp with perspiration. From the heat. And from her labor. I stroked Rosa's hair back away from her face, murmured pleasant, soothing nonsense and tried to give comfort where none existed.

Rosa groaned and tensed again. My wristwatch was gone, stolen. But I had counted the seconds between her contractions, confirming what we both already knew. Soon, Rosa's child would arrive. And I wished I could stop the inevitable.

I'd met Rosa weeks earlier. As the sun rose over the lush green of the jungle, a group of desperate and excited strangers had gathered on a hill, close enough to the Actuncan Cave to feel the cool, damp air flowing from its mouth. We had each paid a life's savings to smugglers called *polleros*— chicken herders—for a few forged papers, the promise of a minimum-wage job and legal citizenship for any of our children born on U.S. soil.

"Me llamo Rosa Maria Martinez," Rosa had said. "I go to America. To New York City."

"I am Lupe Cordero," I replied in Spanish that was touched by the distinctive accents of rural Guatemala. "From Chichicastenango. I am fifteen and go to live with my sister in Houston."

Lies. All of it. My real name was Lacie Reed. I was twenty-seven, an American citizen, and I had no sister. But there was nothing about my appearance to make her doubt me. My hair was dark and curly, my skin unwrinkled and golden-brown, my almond-shaped eyes dark. And I was tiny—small-boned and just a breath over five feet tall. Like Rosa and the others, I was dressed to travel in nondescript clothing that would draw little attention.

This wasn't the first time I'd lied for my Uncle Duran. I was Special Assistant to the Right Honorable Senator Duran Reed, a position that covered an amazing variety of activities. This time, it meant being part of an interagency task force that included Mexico's National Immigration Institute and the U.S. Immigration and Naturalization Service. The INS.

For two weeks we traveled together on foot, by car and by rickety open truck, making our way from Flores to Tapachula, Mexico. Then two days by freight train brought us to Veracruz. We spent that night in a warehouse, on a dirty concrete floor surrounded by fifty other exhausted refugees.

The United States government wanted these people stopped. These and many thousands like them. A flood of illegals from Central and South America passing through Mexico on their way to the U.S. But even as the government of Mexico cooperated with the U.S. to solve the problem, corrupt officials grew rich extorting the immigrants.

If organized traffickers were brought to justice, the danger for those who continued traveling along Mexico's underground highway would be lessened. But that required the testimony of a reliable witness. And immigrants who cooperated with the authorities had a bad habit of disappearing or dying.

That was where my skills came in.

In the dim yellow light of a bare overhead bulb, in the layer of grime on the warehouse floor, I used the edge of a plastic cigarette lighter I found in a corner to draw the faces of two National Railway workers I had seen taking bribes that day. It didn't matter if I used a pencil on a sketch pad, a piece of chalk on a blackboard or a stick on a smooth patch of ground. If I drew what I saw, I could remember it and reproduce it accurately. Always. Faces were easy. As were diagrams and numbers. More than that, the very process of drawing objects and people freed my intuition, enabling me to make connections that weren't apparent when I merely observed a situation.

And so, that night, I added more descriptions to my mental catalog of incidents and faces. My sketches at journey's end, along with my recollection of dates, locations and times, would enable both governments to identify and arrest traffickers. Then I would testify against them.

The sun was just rising when we loaded into the truck. We went willingly, ducking beneath an overhead door that had been raised only a few feet from the trailer floor, moving as quickly as we could into the shadowy interior. We squeezed through a maze of claustrophobic aisleways created by shipping crates, occasionally crouching low to avoid a load bar. When our progress through the trailer was briefly stalled by a large, slow-moving man from Honduras, I looked more closely at one of the bars. A ratcheting mechanism telescoped the tubular steel bar outward until it spanned the width of the trailer. Swivel rubber pads at each end wedged the bar tightly into place, creating a strong, temporary, horizontal barrier.

At the far end of the trailer was an open area large enough—barely—to accommodate all of us. Rosa and I settled down in a cramped corner as a *pollero* announced that the drive would be long and uncomfortable. But it would end in America. In Laredo, Texas. In the meantime, we could relieve ourselves in the buckets he'd placed inside the trailer for us. Then he closed the door with a thud and I heard a heavy lock drop into place. The truck lurched its way out of the freight yard and picked up speed on the roadway.

We were still moving when the narrow pinpoints of daylight coming through small scars in the trailer's aluminum shell faded to darkness.

In the middle of the night, things went terribly wrong.

It started with sirens in the distance. As the sound came closer and caught up with us, conversation stopped inside the trailer.

"*Uno. Dos. Tres.*" Rosa counted under her breath as the sirens resolved themselves into at least three vehicles.

The truck slowed and the surface beneath the tires roughened. The floor beneath us sloped slightly to one side as the driver pulled the rig onto the shoulder of the road. But he kept the truck moving.

The sirens blazed past. The red lights of emergency vehicles glanced off the trailer, throwing shattered fragments of light into the interior. Then the light was gone. And the sirens were lost in the distance.

But the driver must have panicked. The truck pulled back onto the highway, continued along at high speed, then abruptly braked and downshifted to make a right turn. More time passed and the road deteriorated. The movement of the trailer became increasingly violent. We were thrown like rag dolls, bouncing against each other and into the unyielding shipping crates.

Then, abruptly, the terrifying ride stopped.

For a moment, except for the sound of the engine, there was silence. Then male and female voices erupted, shouting in Spanish, cursing the driver in the vulgar colloquialisms of Mexico and Guatemala and Honduras and El Salvador. We threatened him, demanding that he open the trailer door and let us out now. But the driver didn't respond. Instead we felt the jolt as he freed the truck from the trailer. Then he drove away, abandoning us to the desert heat.

Despite the exterior lock, a dozen sets of bare fingers and straining backs and shoulders tried to pull the trailer door upward. The heavier men and a few of the women threw their shoulders against the door, trying to shift it outward. We climbed up the stacked crates, grasped the overhead track for the door and tried to yank it from the brackets that mounted it to the ceiling.

We were still working to escape when the pale beginning of a new day gradually found its way in through the tiny holes in the trailer wall. The heat inside the trailer grew worse. As each escape attempt was revealed as futile, activity inside the trailer slowed. An hour past dawn and those inside the trailer were quiet. Deathly quiet.

Rosa cried out again.

Her contractions were now coming in waves, one after another, barely giving her time to rest in between. For the first time since her labor began, she began crying. Quiet, hopeless weeping. Heart-wrenching, inconsolable weeping.

"Never give up, little one," I murmured.

Only after I had spoken did I realize that I'd said the words in Vietnamese, repeating them exactly as I had first heard them. Rosa was too preoccupied to notice, but the words brought back memory, still vivid though two decades had passed.

I was eight when Grandma Qwan put me on a fishing boat crowded with people fleeing Vietnam. The men she'd paid had assured her that I would be safe. And perhaps they'd believed that. But we were intercepted midvoyage by Thai pirates. From my hiding place beneath a pile of rotting nets, I listened to the screams as they murdered the men, raped the women and stole everything of value.

Fourteen of us were left alive—cast adrift on a ruined boat without food or water. Thirteen women and one scrawny, mixed-race orphan who reeked of fish guts and filth. Days passed. One by one, the others died. Some of thirst and exposure. Some quietly, hopelessly, casting themselves into the sea. Until just one young woman and I remained. Though I was just a child, I had seen enough death to know that she would not live much longer.

That night she had held me close.

"Never give up, little one," she had whispered in Vietnamese, as if she were telling me a precious secret.

When I awoke, she was gone. And I was alone.

I did not despair. I did not give up.

I had come too far to die today.

I stopped thinking about the imminent arrival of Rosa's

child. Using an edge of the cigarette lighter against the vertical surface of a nearby crate, I imagined that I was drawing with a nicely sharpened charcoal pencil on paper torn from an expensive vellum pad. I drew the exterior of the trailer, its only door solidly locked, and surrounded it with desert. A blazing sun hung in the sky. Mentally, I set that drawing aside. Then I drew the interior of the trailer.

I began with a rectangle with six solid walls—back and front, sides, ceiling and floor. I sketched the details of a door that pulled upward to open, that rode on tracks mounted parallel to the ceiling. Between the tracks and the ceiling there was at least a foot of space. I added crates. And refugees. And load bars that ratcheted into place...

The load bars could be moved!

I stood and began dragging at one of the horizontal bars as I described my plan to the others. Within moments, I had help. We freed the bar, set it on its end and ratcheted it upward until it pressed against one of the tracks from which the trailer door was suspended. Then the big, slow-moving man from Honduras, who was the strongest among us, continued working the stiff ratchet. He lengthened the load bar one inch at a time until there was so much pressure against the track that it buckled and bent.

Though the door remained on its track, it sagged at a top corner, bringing in a triangle of bright sunlight and a hot desert breeze that was fresher and cooler than the stale air inside the trailer. The space between the door and its frame wasn't very large. Even the weight and strength of the man from Honduras failed to make it larger. But the gap was enough that a very small, athletic woman from Vietnam could squeeze herself through.

I pushed myself through headfirst and on my back. Head and shoulders escaped the trailer and above me I saw the brilliant blue Texas sky. Cloudless and beautiful. Breathtaking. But the thrilling moment of rebirth was immediately quashed by more practical concerns.

Grabbing finger and handholds wherever I could find them, I hauled myself upward until my entire body was free of the trailer. Then I hung for a moment, catching my breath, taking advantage of the trailer's height to look off into the distance. As far as I could see, there was nothing but clumps of scrub, spiny cactus and an occasional thorny tree. And lots of rocks. The largest of which I tried not to land on when I pushed away from the trailer and dropped to the desert floor.

The landing was inelegant, but relatively painless. I picked myself up off a patch of dusty earth, spent a moment prying a large dry thorn from the palm of my right hand and dusted the back of my pants. Then, using a solid-looking rock, I tried to dislodge the padlock that locked the trailer door down. Spurred by cries of encouragement coming from within the trailer, I bashed and pounded at the lock until my hands were bloody, until the rock split in two.

Then, though no one could see me, I shook my head. Beating at the lock was wasting time and eating away at my remaining energy. Adrenaline helped, but it was only a temporary cure for dehydration and heat exhaustion.

"Take care of Rosa," I shouted in Spanish. "I will go find help. And I will come back. I swear."

Then I turned my back on the trailer, focusing on a single goal. I had to find help. For everyone. I began following the truck's tire tracks. I wanted to hurry, to run, to push myself to my limits. Instead, I walked. Slowly, steadily, concentrating on my breathing.

I was already tired and thirsty. It didn't take long before even the ruthless beauty of the desert held no appeal. Thoughts of how I would go about capturing its arid vistas with pen and ink faded. I began cursing the cloudless blue sky, the thorns that pierced my clothing and my skin, the rocks and sand that filled my shoes, and the relentless late-morning sun. My head throbbed in rhythm with every step, with every painful breath.

My attention drifted, back to the trailer, back to Rosa, back to our travels through Mexico and Guatemala. I saw myself walking in the streets of Flores and Veracruz and Tapachula. I stumbled on a rock and fell hard onto my hands and knees. A dry black branch tore a jagged furrow in my leg. Pain brought concentration back with a snap. Ignoring the warm trickle of blood down my left calf, I stood. And made a horrifying discovery.

I had wandered away from the tire tracks.

I tried not to panic, tried not to think of dozens dying because I had gotten lost. I took a deep breath, then another, and carefully reoriented myself. The tracks had been heading north and I had followed them, keeping the rising sun on my right. Now I was facing directly into the sun. I turned slowly, looking for evidence that a truck had recently passed that way. Several dozen yards to my left, I spotted a crushed cactus and a brittle, skeletal tree whose spindly limbs were smashed on one side. I walked in that direction and rediscovered the tracks.

I walked on.

I am in Texas, I repeated to myself. In Texas. Near Laredo. And I must find help. I concentrated on the pattern of tires in the dust. On the details left by the tread. On the texture of the plants crushed by the truck's passing that way not once, but twice. On the tiny brown lizards that skittered frantically across my path. On insects so small that the track's grainy texture shaded them.

I walked on.

The tire tracks led to the barest hint of a road. I followed it, head bent, eyes downcast, focused only on the scars that passing tires had laid on the desert floor. I traced each scar with an imaginary stylus, wove each detail into an imaginary length of rope stretching between me and the main highway, between me and the help I needed.

I walked on.

Soon nothing mattered but the heat. The dreadful, pounding heat. And the imaginary rope. I held on to it with my mind, with all the strength that remained in me, watching closely as it gradually twisted, turned and changed. It became a fishing net, worn but still strong, tossed into the sea by the sinewy brown hands of Thai fishermen. Thrown to a child who drifted, helpless and alone, in a battered boat on the South China Sea. Pulled on board by hands that eagerly pressed a tin cup of water to a child's parched lips.

I walked on.

Suddenly there was a blaring horn and squealing brakes.

America! I thought as I heard a woman shouting at me in English. I've made it to America!

More lucid thoughts quickly followed, snapping me back into the present.

I had emerged from the dirt road, stepped into the highway and owed my life to the quick reaction time of a middle-aged woman with bleached-blond hair driving a shiny blue pickup truck. She rolled down her window to get a better look at me, stopped shouting, and scrambled from her vehicle. Her arms around my shoulders supported me as we staggered back to her truck.

I need help, I thought, but the words came out in Spanish. I saw her incomprehension, forced myself to concentrate and managed a language I hadn't spoken for many weeks.

"Please," I said in English, "Do you have a phone I can use? To call the police."

She listened, openmouthed, as I offered the dispatcher enough information to convince him that the situation was beyond urgent. Then I disconnected. And my rescuer stopped me from walking back into the desert alone.

I sipped the bottle of lemon-flavored water she offered as I counted the minutes. A lifetime seemed to pass before the police arrived, before I could lead a convoy of police cars and ambulances to the abandoned trailer.

Within that lifetime, no one inside the trailer died.

Within that lifetime, a baby girl was born.

Chapter 2

Uncle Duran had arranged his desk to take full advantage of the window in his office. A man of upright posture, powerful build and impeccable taste, the senator sat with his back to the expanse of glass, fully aware that the view from the trio of wing-backed chairs facing his desk was a postcard image of the nation's capitol. Seen from a height and distance that softened detail and muted noise, visitors to his office saw stately monuments, manicured lawns, cherry trees and the orderly movement of pedestrians and traffic along wide boulevards. It was Washington, D.C., at its most picturesque.

Framed by the window as he sat in his leather-bound chair, the senator looked positively presidential.

Not only did he look the part, but he wanted the role. Because he was a man who knew the right people and did the right things, the Beltway press was already speculating that he was a strong contender for the Democratic party's nomination. Although it was too early in the election cycle for

Uncle Duran to make a public announcement, he had begun talking privately and often about his ambitions. Mostly to people who counted. Occasionally to me. Before I'd left for Mexico, he'd wondered out loud if being President would inhibit his ability to act as he saw fit, then smiled as he told me that my job was to be sure that it didn't.

It was only when he stepped away from his big window and massive desk that first-time visitors realized how big Uncle Duran was. At six foot seven and a muscular three hundred pounds, he dwarfed not only me, but most of his constituency.

It was his size that had terrified me as a child when I first saw him in the Songkhla refugee camp in Thailand. Though I wanted desperately to go to America, I shrank back as this burly, big-voiced man and his entourage approached. Only a camp worker's tight grip on my hand kept me from running to hide in my bed.

Most Americans I had met had large noses, but this man's was *very* large and crooked. His face was craggy, with a tall forehead, a jutting chin and thick eyebrows. Like a fairy-tale giant, I thought as I stared at him. Without hesitating, he leaned forward and scooped me up, lifting me far from the ground. I trembled when I saw that his eyes were like pale pieces of silver. And that his teeth, when he smiled, were large and very white. I had wondered if he ate children.

Then he turned to those who were with him and spoke. My English was not good enough to understand what he said, but the camp worker whispered a translation. As cameras flashed and pencils scribbled on small notebooks, the senator explained that I was special to him. Because he could not locate my father, his brother and his wife would adopt me. I was the first of the needy children that the loving, generous citizens of America would rescue. He intended to find placements for hundreds of children like me—children who had been orphaned by war and who dreamed of America.

Now, almost two decades later and just months past his six-tieth birthday, Uncle Duran's dark hair had turned the color of brushed steel. But his rich baritone voice and gentleman's charm still won hearts and even votes on the campaign trail.

Unfortunately, Uncle Duran was not being charming now. Nor was he smiling. The argument that we were having across his centuries-old desk had boiled down to a few simple truths. It didn't matter that I had worked for him long enough to prove that my professional judgment could be trusted. And it didn't matter that I was his brother's only child. It only mat-tered that I was defying him.

As I stood behind one of the wing-backed chairs, my fin-gers digging into its cushioned sides, my face impassive, I watched him clamp his unlit cigar between his front teeth and slowly shake his head. Then he rolled the cigar back into a corner of his mouth to speak again.

"Though I warned your parents against him long ago, I've overlooked your friendship with Tinh Vu, even tolerated your addressing him as 'uncle.' I tried to accommodate a child's need to rediscover her roots, to embrace the familiar. But you are no longer a child. And you're more American than you are Vietnamese. Damn it all, Lacie. When was the last time you actually *spoke* Vietnamese?"

"It's been a long time," I admitted. As a teenager, I'd tried to become part of the Vietnamese community in Chicago, but quickly discovered I didn't belong. Even Uncle Tinh and I had, for many years, conversed in English.

Uncle Duran nodded, smiled around his cigar. But if he thought I was going to back down, he was mistaken.

"Does it matter how Vietnamese I am?" I said. "Or how American? I'm a good mimic and a quick study. As you've often pointed out, I can fit in anywhere I want to. All I am asking is to be allowed to do a job that I'm trained to do. That's all *Uncle Tinh* is asking."

Uncle Duran's smile disappeared.

"And *I* am asking you—no, I am *telling* you—that I will not authorize this venture. I have been part of your life longer than Tinh Vu has. *I* was the one who found you, who gave you a family and a job that *means* something. Can you so easily dismiss my decision about this?"

Tears welled in my eyes. I didn't want to defy him, to hurt him. But it was because of him, because of the values he'd taught me, that I had made the only decision I could when Uncle Tinh called.

"You've told me often of your work for the senator," Uncle Tinh had said. "Can you come down to New Orleans right away? On business, Lacie. Please. My people…our people…need you."

How could I say no?

I looked directly at Uncle Duran, lifting my chin for emphasis.

"I'm sorry, Uncle Duran," I said. "This is something I have to do."

He moved the cigar away from his mouth, put it down on the clean crystal ashtray on his desk. When he lifted his head, our eyes met and I braced for what I knew was coming.

"You're fired," he said clearly. "Effective immediately."

I had chosen.

And so had he.

I went back to my adjacent and more functional office. Determinedly dry-eyed, I packed my personal belongings into several cardboard boxes as Uncle Duran stood in the doorway and watched, unspeaking. Then he helped me carry my possessions downstairs and load them into my car. But before I turned the key in the ignition, he leaned into the open driver's side window.

"Even if I approved of Tinh Vu, which I don't now and never have," he said, "I cannot risk having anyone in my employ so closely associated with organized crime. I know what your feelings are on this subject, and I've tried to spare them by waiting until now to bring this up. I have evidence, Lacie. Recent evidence that Tinh Vu is actively involved in the production and distribution of breeder documents. You, of all people, should know what that means."

Then he stepped back from the car. But he spoke, once again, before I'd completely rolled up the window.

"Should you ever find the courage to face the truth about your Uncle Tinh, call me. We can revisit the issue of your employment."

That gave me plenty to stew over as I sped down the Beltway toward the studio apartment I rented. Uncle Duran's suspicions about Uncle Tinh's ties to organized crime were all too familiar. But a specific accusation and talk of evidence were new.

Even though he had never even met him, Uncle Duran had never made a secret of his dislike for Uncle Tinh. It seemed to me that his dislike grew to the point of near obsession when Tinh's City Vu opened in New Orleans. After that, Uncle Duran had taken every opportunity to point out that great food and impeccable service were not the reasons the restaurant thrived. Impossible, he said any time an opportunity presented itself, that an immigrant could parlay a storefront restaurant in Evanston, Illinois, into a landmark twenty-room hotel and restaurant just a block from the French Market in New Orleans. Tinh Vu could not have achieved this merely through hard work.

I agreed. And so did Uncle Tinh.

Even when he still lived in Evanston, Uncle Tinh had catered to those who wanted to keep their business dealings private. It was not unusual for businessmen, cops, politicians, criminals and, I suspected, individuals who combined two or more of those avocations to meet over a meal in the little storefront. Uncle Tinh always managed to arrange that such meetings were undisturbed. In New Orleans he'd taken the concept a step further. He claimed proudly that if you were to ask any journalist in the Big Easy where the city's power brokers met, their list would include the quartet of small dining rooms on the mezzanine level of Tinh's City Vu. Those rooms, I knew, were swept daily for listening devices.

That did not make my adopted Vietnamese uncle a criminal.

Supplying false documents did.

A few years earlier I'd helped the INS break up a documents syndicate in Los Angeles by locating a storage facility that, when searched, yielded two million "breeder" documents. Such documents—counterfeit social security cards, resident alien cards, U.S. birth certificates and more—established legitimate backgrounds for illegal immigrants. They proved legal residency in the U.S. and were used—bred—to obtain genuine documents such as driver's licenses, student ID cards and insurance cards. Counterfeit documents were big business. The stash I'd discovered was worth forty million dollars on the streets. And those who produced such documents were closely tied to those who exploited illegals once they arrived in the U.S.

In the past I had dismissed Uncle Duran's periodic accusations about Uncle Tinh, thinking that he was unnecessarily suspicious. And, perhaps, jealous. But now, as I turned onto the ramp down to the garage beneath my building, I wondered whether I should return to Uncle Duran's office and examine the evidence he claimed to have.

Did I have the courage to do that?

The tears that I'd so successfully suppressed for most of the afternoon began to creep down my cheeks as I pulled into my parking spot. I killed the engine, lay my arms across the steering wheel and rested my forehead against them. For a few minutes I sat that way, unmoving, as I considered my options.

Though I owed much to my Uncle Duran and I had worked

hard to make him proud of me, Uncle Tinh was my oldest and dearest friend. He and I first met when my new American parents took me to a little campus restaurant in Evanston, Illinois, for *pho*. As I attacked the noodle soup with chopsticks and a deep ceramic spoon, Tinh Vu had nodded approvingly, then come over to chat with us. In doing so, he gave my parents a means to communicate with a nine-year-old girl who had lived with them for just a few weeks. My parents spoke only a few words of Vietnamese; I knew only the broken and often crude English spoken by street-smart teens at the refugee camp.

Over the years I ate in the restaurant's tiny kitchen frequently. Beneath a colorful poster of the kitchen god, Ong Tao, Uncle Tinh and I talked about our lives and our problems and our dreams as we ate steaming bowls of *pho* or nibbled chopsticks full of *do chua*, a spicy-hot fermented pickle. About the time I went off to college, Uncle Tinh sold the campus town restaurant and moved to New Orleans. But despite busy schedules, we kept in touch. My last visit to the Big Easy had been just five months earlier.

I trusted Uncle Tinh with my life. Did I trust him not to lie to me?

I lifted my head from my arms and sniffled as I dug around the glove compartment for a tissue. I blew my nose, then looked at myself in the rearview mirror. My own very serious dark eyes stared back at me.

I knew what I was going to do.

I would go to New Orleans. Uncle Tinh would explain the current crisis in detail and, if it was within my power, I would stay and help the Vietnamese community. At the same time, I would observe and interact with my Uncle Tinh not only from the perspective of someone who had grown up loving him, but as the adult I now was.

When I had done all I could, I would return to Washington. There, though the thought of it made my heart ache, I would examine Uncle Duran's evidence. If it had substance, I would confront Uncle Tinh, giving him a chance to convince me of his innocence.

And if I discovered that Uncle Duran's accusations were true?

I took a deep breath as I stepped from my car. I squared my shoulders, straightened my spine and lifted my chin. For the second time that day, I made the only decision I could.

If Uncle Tinh was a criminal, I would dedicate myself to bringing him to justice.

Chapter 3

A week later I checked into the room that Uncle Tinh had reserved for me at the Intercontinental New Orleans. The luxury high-rise hotel was conveniently located in the Central Business District and offered impeccable service along with the anonymity of almost five hundred guest rooms.

My flight was an early one so, as we'd agreed, once I'd settled into my room, I joined Uncle Tinh at the Old Coffee Pot. His restaurant—Tinh's City Vu—was a dinner place, so the Old Coffee Pot was our long-time favorite for a quiet, relaxed breakfast.

Uncle Tinh was already sitting at one of the little tables in the restaurant's tree-shaded courtyard when I arrived. Before he realized I was there, I stood for a moment watching him sip his coffee and, once again, I found it impossible to believe that this man could be a criminal. I walked over to stand beside the sun-dappled table.

"Hello, Uncle Tinh," I said.

He smiled broadly as he stood and hugged me enthusiastically. Then he held me briefly at arm's length, his dark eyes sparkling as he asked about my flight. I looked back at the man who was the bridge between my two worlds, my only connection to my birthplace and its culture.

Although he was almost sixty, Uncle Tinh looked much the same as he had the day I met him. He had a round, unlined face, a body kept strong through the practice of martial arts and was tall for a Vietnamese man—almost five foot eight inches. His head was shaved clean and his hands, as always, were beautifully manicured. He wore a white dress shirt that was unbuttoned at the collar, a pair of gray trousers and his trademark leather sandals. His favorite Rolex watch—a bit battered from hard use—rode on his right wrist, accommodating his left-handedness.

"You look lovely as ever, *chère,*" he said as we settled into our chairs. "Fit, certainly. But maybe a little too thin."

I laughed. No matter how much I weighed, Uncle Tinh complained that I looked too thin. In the past month, I had, in fact, regained all the weight I'd lost in Mexico. Which put me at my usual one hundred and five pounds. And I was sure that the bulky blue cotton sweater and jeans that I wore made me look several pounds heavier.

"One of your desserts will remedy that, I'm sure," I said.

"Ah, that reminds me. Since your last visit, I have created a new dessert. It will be a favorite, I think. But you are my most honest critic. So I wait for your approval before adding it to the menu."

I had never yet disapproved of one of Uncle Tinh's desserts.

"I will sample it at the first opportunity," I said.

Uncle Tinh waited until I'd taken my first bite of the *callas*—crispy Creole rice cakes smothered in hot maple syrup—before telling me that he'd arranged for me to attend an evening gala in the Garden District. It was being given by the Beauprix family.

"Anthony Beauprix is the son of an old acquaintance of mine. He is a policeman and a friend of the Vietnamese community here in New Orleans."

Uncle Tinh, it seemed, had already decided to contact me when Beauprix had come to him for help. Beauprix had told Uncle Tinh that without someone inside the Vietnamese community, his investigation was hopelessly stalled. That was when Uncle Tinh had told Beauprix about me. Uncle Tinh laughed as he related that part of their conversation. Or, more correctly, he laughed in reaction to my expression.

"No offense, sir," Beauprix had said to him. "but I was hoping you could recommend someone who lives or works in Little Vietnam. Someone who'd be willing to pass relevant information on to me. The last thing I need is some gal from up north coming down here and playing cop. I don't doubt she's good at her job—she sounds like a fine little actress. But this is police business, always best handled by the police."

I didn't know Beauprix and hadn't worked with the New Orleans P.D., but the attitude was all too familiar. And I knew from experience that my size would make it even easier for him to underestimate me.

"For this," I asked Uncle Tinh pointedly, "I've disrupted my life?"

"Patience, *chère,*" he replied. His accent, like his restaurant's food, mixed the French of upper-class Vietnam with the Creole accents of New Orleans. "If I had the means to aid the Vietnamese community without involving you or the police, I would. Certainly, many in Little Vietnam would prefer it that way. But I have only wealth and the guilt of one who did not suffer as many of my countrymen did. This situation *requires* the intervention of outsiders. Anthony Beauprix is doing his best. But whether he likes it or not—whether he knows it yet or not—he needs you. That means convincing him to accept your help. I have already laid the groundwork. So now I will tell you how it can be done…."

* * *

I spent the rest of the day shopping and, by midafternoon, put a dent in the expense money that Uncle Tinh had given me. I was pleased with the purchases I carried back to my room in an assortment of boxes and bags. I now had a suitable dress, appropriate undergarments and matching shoes to wear to the gala. I shed my clothes in the dressing room—a luxury I'd longed for in my small D.C. apartment—and took a long soak in the deep marble tub.

I submerged myself so only my face was above water and considered my future. Unlike Uncle Duran, I was not independently wealthy. Thanks to Uncle Tinh, my stay in New Orleans would cost me nothing and I had enough savings to coast for a while. But eventually I would have to support myself.

If Uncle Duran's evidence was nothing more than malicious speculation—and I felt that it likely was—I would seek a new job among organizations that already appreciated my diverse and, by most standards, peculiar skills. Past assignments had given me contacts within an alphabet soup of government agencies specializing in national security: CIA, FBI, ATF, DSS, INS. One of them would probably hire me. But the appeal of my job with Uncle Duran had been the commitment to the immigrant community that he and I shared.

As I made circles in the bubbles with my toes, questions about my future ran through my mind. Would I ever again be able to work for Uncle Duran? Did I even want to? Would he blackball me, making finding another job in Washington impossible? What impact would conflict with Uncle Duran have on my parents?

So many questions. No answers.

My mind flashed to the poster that hung in my adoptive mother's office, and I smiled. Her favorite movie was *Gone With the Wind.*

"I won't think about that now," I said out loud in my best Scarlett O'Hara imitation. "I'll think about it tomorrow."

I splashed enthusiastically just for the hell of it, spent a moment blowing bubbles with my head beneath the water and my hair splayed out around me, then practiced my New Orleans accent by reciting Dr. Seuss's *Green Eggs and Ham* out loud until the words echoed off the bathroom's glossy white-tiled walls.

Out of the tub, I thought about slipping into one of the cushy terry-cloth bathrobes supplied by the hotel, realized that one-size-fits-all wasn't created with me in mind and, instead, wrapped myself in a thick, white bath towel. Then I sat on the upholstered bench in front of the lighted vanity, carefully applied my makeup, fixed my hair and slipped on my new clothes. I was a vision in basic black.

"Ah, the belle of the ball," I said as I turned slowly in front of the room's full-length mirror. Then I laughed and added, "Not!"

Unlike Scarlett, I wasn't dressed in dusty velvet drapes. But I doubted that Beauprix would fully appreciate my wardrobe choice. At least, not tonight. I took the elevator downstairs and was pleased to note that few eyes turned in my direction as I made my way through the lobby.

I could have taken a cab, but this was New Orleans and I loved the romance, if not the Spartan nineteenth-century amenities, of the city's arch-roofed streetcars. The St. Charles line ran past the front of the Intercontinental, at the No.3 stop. I got on, carrying the exact change required, dropped my five quarters into the box and felt like Cinderella going to the ball.

Unfortunately, my teal-green coach was crowded with tourists and commuters, and all the reversible wooden seats were occupied. So I stood toward the back, congratulated myself on selecting new shoes that were actually comfortable, and enjoyed the New Orleans scenery sliding past at nine miles an hour.

About twenty minutes later, I stepped down from the coach

at stop No.19 and walked for two blocks. The umbrella I'd taken as a defense against the light drizzle was almost unnecessary—live oaks formed living canopies along the residential blocks above Louisiana Avenue. The house I was looking for was on Prytania and Seventh, just a block below the free-standing vaults and above-ground crypts of the City of Lafayette Cemetery.

The Beauprix home was a double-galleried Victorian gem with a first-floor living area that even the bodies and voices of several hundred guests didn't fill completely. Inside, the huge open spaces of the first floor were a swirl of color and texture, of light and sound. Everywhere, tall crystal vases spotlighted by tiny, intense lights overflowed with pink and violet varieties of roses, lilacs, irises and gladiolas floating in clouds of baby's breath.

Unfortunately, I couldn't at the moment fully appreciate the beautiful decor, the sounds of celebration or the smell of fresh flowers. Because within a few minutes of my arrival through the back kitchen door of the lovely house, I had ended up standing at a stainless-steel counter, surrounded by the bustle and din of food preparation and reeking of fish and onions.

I wrinkled my nose and tried not to breathe too deeply as I finished dusting a large silver tray of pale-pink appetizers with a sprinkle of red caviar and finely chopped chives. Grateful that the smell was not necessary to my disguise, I wandered across the kitchen to the sink, carefully washed my hands, then rubbed them dry on the front of my bibbed apron. Beneath the black apron was a black rayon uniform that hung limply below my knees. Beneath that, there was enough padding to make me look forty pounds heavier and distinctly barrel-shaped. Once my hands were dry, I briefly tucked my right hand into an apron pocket, assuring myself that the tiny electronic device I'd hidden there was still safe. It was one of a handful of specialized items I'd collected over the years and brought with me to New Orleans.

"Olivia!" the caterer said loudly. "Take that tray out to the dining room, please."

I counted to ten slowly before looking up, deliberately slack-jawed and blank-eyed, from my contemplation of the heavy support hose and the sturdy black shoes I wore. For the gala, carefully applied makeup had changed my complexion from golden to dusky and I had braided my hair in deliberately thick, uneven corn rows. The wax forms that thickened my cheeks and made my upper lip protrude also distorted my voice.

"Yes, ma'am," I said slowly.

Ignoring the direction of the woman's pointing finger, I picked up the silver tray nearest the sink. It was littered with a few limp pieces of parsley, a half-nibbled radish and a few abandoned olives.

The caterer—a tall, middle-aged black woman whose presence seemed to calm the chaos of the busy kitchen—was destined to be a saint. She spent only a moment rolling her eyes heavenward before stepping in front of me, taking the tray from my hands and returning it to the counter.

"This one, honey." She gave me a filled tray, then corrected my hands so that they held it level. "Now be careful, Olivia. Don't spill."

"No, ma'am."

I offered her a smile enhanced by a gold-capped front tooth, then walked to the dining room down a short hallway lined with glass-fronted shelves stacked with fine china and polished silver.

I slipped behind the long buffet table and carefully set the tray down at the far end of the table, in an open space beside a huge arrangement of irises. The thick petals looked like velvet and were a shade of purple so deep it was almost black. I tucked myself behind the arrangement with my back into a corner.

Slowly, with an air of intense concentration, I began lifting each stem, turning it slightly and settling it back into the vase, as if to make sure that each flower was shown off as beautifully as possible. Except that the flowers I was arranging were at the back of the vase. Either the caterer didn't notice or she'd given up on keeping the most dim-witted of her employees busy. And I wondered what favor Uncle Tinh had called in to saddle her with such a useless worker.

From behind my curtain of flowers, I peered out at the party through my thick-lensed glasses, genuinely enraptured by the graceful patterns that formed and reformed as guests sought out acquaintances and made new contacts. Laughter mixed with the murmur of voices and the rustle of the leathery leaves of the magnolia trees that overhung the open gallery windows. A live, six-piece band wove it all together with a soft, bluesy melody.

This was New Orleans at its best. For a moment I regretted mightily that Lacie Reed wasn't making an appearance as herself at the party that Anthony Beauprix had thrown for his father's eightieth birthday. Briefly, I considered how I could capture the evening in pen-and-ink washed with the faintest suggestion of colors. Then I sighed and considered what Uncle Tinh had told me about my host, Anthony Beauprix.

Besides being a cop who desperately needed my help but was too chauvinistic and anticivilian to accept it, Beauprix was wealthy beyond most people's wildest dreams. That, Uncle Tinh had told me during breakfast. The Beauprix family was old money, their fortune tied to a history of sailing ships, bootleg rum, smuggled guns and an uncanny ability to end up on the winning side of any war, no matter which side they'd started on. In New Orleans, that knack earned them as much respect as their money did.

Perhaps inspired by a public hanging or two—the citizens of New Orleans also having no problem executing those they respected—the Beauprix family gradually shifted their attention to more legitimate enterprises such as shipping and oil. Which was what made Anthony stand out among the current generation. A maverick, Uncle Tinh said. A beloved black sheep. Unlike his younger brother and sister who'd earned M.B.A.s at Tulane or his engineer and lawyer cousins, Beauprix was a detective in the New Orleans Police Department. A job, Uncle Tinh noted, more suited to the morals and attitudes of the founding members of the Beauprix clan. Certainly in his attitude toward women and his unlikely friendship with Tinh Vu, he was a throwback.

Then Uncle Tinh had shown me a black-and-white print of a photo of Anthony Beauprix that the *Times-Picayune* had on file. It was a candid shot taken as he'd accepted the police department's award for valor. The caption taped to the back of the photo mentioned a hostage situation and no one dying. Thanks to Beauprix. From the grainy photo, I could tell that he was taller and slimmer than the mayor, dark-haired, and had his eyes, nose, mouth and chin in approximately the right places.

More guests arrived and the area around the table became crowded, blocking my view of the room. The caterer, who still looked unharried, swept past me, switched out a nearly-empty tray of white-chocolate-dipped strawberries for a full one and disappeared back into the kitchen.

In a halfhearted attempt to keep Uncle Tinh in her good graces, I spent a few minutes brushing crumbs from the linen tablecloth before busying myself with the irises again. I had just finished stuffing a particularly gooey stem back into the vase when a nearby male voice said "the flowers" with the slight rise in tone that usually implies a question.

I lifted my head and slid my eyes in the direction of the voice.

Standing on the other side of the vase, staring in through the flowers, was a man in a tuxedo. He was perhaps six feet tall with olive skin, well-cut dark hair and hazel eyes. He was smiling with a mouthful of perfect teeth.

My first thought was that this was Anthony Beauprix. My second was to wonder who he was smiling at. My third thought was that there was only one possible candidate.

I looked quickly at my feet.

"Do you like the flowers?" Beauprix repeated.

I nodded.

"And strawberries," I muttered thickly and for no particular reason, except that I'd always believed that distinct characteristics and a personality quirk or two were essential to creating a believable persona.

"What's your name?"

"Olivia," I said, wondering why he could possibly want to know my name. Impossible to think that he had seen through my disguise. Perhaps he was planning to complain to the caterer about her useless staff.

I was wrong.

"You're doing a fine job, Olivia."

He flashed me another smile, put the plate he was carrying down on the table, picked up several dipped strawberries from the tray and added them to the bounty on the plate. Then he frowned and looked back at me.

"If you wouldn't mind, would you fetch me a paring knife from the kitchen?" he said.

I nodded, went on the errand and returned fairly promptly.

I watched him slice each of the strawberries on the plate into quarters, wondering at the task.

"Thank you, Olivia," he said.

I nodded, carefully not making eye contact, and didn't look up until he'd picked up the plate and turned away from the table. Then I lifted my head and watched him, admiring the fit of his formal wear as he moved across the crowded room, pausing to speak with one guest, then another. He had the muscular build and awareness of body and space that brought to mind a dancer. Or a street fighter. I'd met a lot of cops in the past couple of years, so there was no doubt in my mind: plainclothes had never looked so good. Though it probably helped to have a millionaire's wardrobe and a personal tailor.

As the crowd parted to let Beauprix pass, I saw that an elderly man—Beauprix's father, I guessed—had joined the party. He was sitting in a wheelchair in the center of the room, surrounded by a knot of people whose coloring and bone structure marked them as family. Beauprix joined them, leaning down to place the plateful of food carefully on his father's lap. As the elder Beauprix smiled up at his son, I noticed that the right side of his face remained stiff and expressionless. When he picked up his food, he used his left hand awkwardly and chewed each small piece slowly and methodically.

I kept a close watch on the family group, remaining behind the serving table, but periodically shifting my position so that I could see them through the crowd. My job was easy. They stayed together in the same spot, chatting and laughing as their guests moved forward to greet the elderly gentleman. Periodically, Anthony would lean in close to his father and murmur something that made the old man smile.

After I'd been watching them for about ten minutes, I saw Beauprix nod and smile at his brother and sister. He signaled to the white-suited waiters to provide everyone with a full glass of champagne. While the waiters did their work, he chatted amicably with his family. Then he knelt, put his arm around his father's shoulders and lifted his champagne glass with the other.

"To a good man, our dear friend, and my lifelong hero. Charles Beauprix."

Anthony Beauprix wasn't a handsome man by any conventional definition. But I doubted there was a woman in the room who wasn't aware of him, who didn't feel her pulse quicken as he walked past, who couldn't imagine his hands and lips on her body. Certainly, I wasn't immune to such thoughts. Nor was I oblivious to the effect that Beauprix was having on my libido. But I had more pressing things to think about. Such as where I was going to set a small, very dramatic fire.

A large cake, lavishly decorated with fresh and spun-sugar flowers, had been baked to celebrate Charles Beauprix's eightieth birthday. It was several layers tall, rested on a silver-plated wheeled serving cart, and looked like it might serve a hundred people.

Beside the cart was a linen-clad stationary table that supported several large silver trays holding more dessert—dozens of uniform *petit fours* arranged in soldier-straight rows. Each tiny cake was covered in a smooth layer of marzipan, decorated with a single sugar rose and a pair of fresh violet blossoms, and topped by a small candle.

Toward the end of the evening, the catering staff began the task of lighting all the candles on the cake and the *petit fours*. Then most of the lights on the first floor were switched off and the large cake was wheeled to the center of the living room, where the Beauprix family was gathered. I stayed behind, lingering near the table that held the *petit fours*.

The crowd sang "Happy Birthday," the elder Beauprix worked on blowing out the candles on his cake, Anthony Beauprix stood with his hand on his father's shoulder and I surreptitiously dripped globs of gel fuel between rows of *petit fours*. As the last bits of whistling, cheering and applause faded, I tipped a lit candle into the silver **tray and** quickly stepped away from the table. A heartbeat or two later, there was a satisfying roar.

Someone shouted, "Fire!"

While everyone's attention was focused on the flaming pastries, I made my way around the perimeter of the crowded room. Before the overhead lights came on, I was racing up a sweeping staircase whose grandeur reminded me of my adoptive mom's favorite movie. Just call me Scarlett, I thought as I reached the hallway.

"His room has paintings of ships hung on the walls," Uncle Tinh had told me. "Anthony once told me about his collection. Appropriate, don't you think, for the descendant of a pirate?"

The second door on the left opened into the room I was looking for. Downstairs, I could hear shouting and the sounds of a fire extinguisher being discharged. That noise was muffled as I pulled Anthony Beauprix's bedroom door shut behind me.

Time was short, so I gave the room only a sweeping glance. His queen-size bed was covered with soft bedding in shades of cream and tan, the dresser and desk were polished mahogany and the desk chair and love seat were covered with a nubby brown fabric. Tall bookcases were built in against one wall. Opposite, ceiling-to-floor guillotine windows flanked by sheer curtains in a surprising shade of tangerine let in the night air from a second-floor gallery. Paintings of tall ships and battles at sea hung on the walls, and a scale model of the *U.S.S. Constitution* graced the fireplace mantle.

Neat and comfortable, I thought as I crossed the room to Beauprix's bed and knelt on the pillows. Hanging above the headboard was a gilt-framed oil painting of the *Constitution* defeating the British frigate *Guerriére* in 1812. I admired the artist's use of blue, ochre and crimson as I swung the painting aside, revealing a vintage wall safe. The safe's location and Beauprix's habit of keeping his "piece" locked in the safe when company was in the house was information Uncle Tinh had provided. Information obtained from the Beauprix housekeeper's adult daughter, whose husband liked to play the ponies. In exchange for the information, Uncle Tinh had arranged for a gambling debt to be canceled.

From my apron pocket I pulled out the electronic device. It was the size of a quarter and attached by thin wires to a pair of ear buds. I put the tiny black pads in my ears, placed the device against the safe, turned the dial slowly and listened. Right. Click. Left. Click. Right again. Click. A quick tug at the safe's handle and the job was done.

I ignored everything else inside and went for Beauprix's gun, a Colt .45 semiautomatic compact officer's model. Uncle Tinh had suggested that it was exactly the item needed to get Beauprix's attention. After returning the bullets to the safe, I tucked the unloaded gun securely between my belly and the corset-like padding I wore. Before closing the safe, I left a handwritten note inside. An invitation, of sorts. Then I went out the gallery window, shinnied down a vine-wrapped drainpipe and ran around the house to the kitchen door.

The kitchen was bustling with clean-up activity. The caterer, apparently unruffled by a mere fire, was calmly giving directions to her staff. As her back was to the kitchen door, I slouched in through the doorway. My apron was wet and soiled from my encounter with the drainpipe, so I picked up the nearest littered serving tray from the counter and tipped it toward me, adding a smear of discarded party food to my apron. Then I began scraping the remainders of crackers smeared with paté and thin brown bread topped with a pink-flecked spread into the garbage.

The caterer turned, saw me working hard, and nodded.

"Good, Olivia. Very good."

I couldn't help but smile.

The phone call I was expecting came near midnight. There was no warmth or humor in the deep male voice on the other end.

"City morgue," Anthony Beauprix said. "Six a.m."

Then he disconnected.

Chapter 4

The ringing phone and cheerful female voice that was the Intercontinental's wake-up service pulled me out of bed at four forty-five the next morning. Between bites of a room-service breakfast of crusty French rolls dipped, New Orleans style, in rich strong coffee, I dressed for my meeting with Anthony Beauprix.

I pulled my hair back into a French twist, applied makeup to emphasize my high cheekbones and the shape of my eyes, and put on khaki slacks, a black top and dress boots that added a couple of inches to my height. A glance in the full-length mirror mounted in the room's tiny foyer confirmed what I already knew: I looked as unlike the slow-witted Olivia as was possible.

A taxi dropped me off in the lot adjacent to the city morgue where Beauprix was already waiting. He wore dark slacks, a blue-on-cream pin-striped shirt that definitely wasn't off the rack and a silk tie that probably cost more than my entire outfit. He was leaning against one of the three cars parked in the parking lot at that ungodly hour. It was a standard police-issue unmarked four-door sedan, the kind that any street-savvy twelve-year-old with halfway decent eyesight can pick out from half a block away.

Beauprix's legs were crossed at the ankle and he was smoking a cigarette. He didn't bother moving, but watched with his head tilted as the taxi disgorged me near the entrance to the small lot.

I walked over to his car.

"Ms. Reed, I presume," he said.

His voice was too hostile to be business-like and I suspected he wouldn't shake my hand if I stuck it out. So I didn't bother. I kept my own tone moderate.

"Yes, I'm Lacie Reed. Tinh Vu suggested I might be of some help to you."

Beauprix threw his cigarette onto the pavement and ground it slowly beneath the toe of a very expensive leather shoe.

"I didn't ask for your help," he said. "Last night, you took something that belongs to me. I'd like it back. Now."

Beauprix sounded like a man very used to having his own way. And his expression was clearly intended to make it difficult not to give him what he wanted. Dark, straight brows angled down over narrowed, hazel eyes; an angry flush of color underlaid his olive complexion and stained his broad cheekbones; his full lips were pressed into a thin, hard line.

Spoiled brat, I thought. But I smiled pleasantly as I replied.

"Returning your property before we talk would make it awfully easy for you to walk away. And that would make Uncle Tinh unhappy. So maybe I'll hang on to it for just a little longer."

"Maybe you don't understand, little girl." He spoke just above a whisper, and though his accent softened his vowels, he was unmistakably furious. "This is not a game and I have no intention of talking with you. If you don't return my stolen property, I *do* intend to arrest you. Charge you with breaking and entering—"

There was no doubt in my mind that when he and his police buddies played good cop/bad cop, he always got to be the bad cop. Not that intimidation or bad temper was going to work on me.

"I didn't break in," I said matter-of-factly. "I walked in. I even spoke to you. Last night, you were charming."

He forgot his anger for a moment as he stared at me assessingly, focusing exclusively on my face. Comparing it, I was sure, with the faces of any strangers he'd met the night before. Most people remembered features that could be changed readily—height and weight, eye and hair color, the appearance of teeth, the shape of a nose. Only the visually astute or the very well trained noticed the shape and placement of ears, eyes and mouth.

Beauprix was talented or well-trained or both.

"Flowers. And strawberries," he said slowly, searching. "A homely woman. Kinda backward. And shy." Disjointed detail became coherent memory. "Olivia!"

He snapped his fingers, almost shouting the name as a look of triumph and, perhaps, the slightest flicker of admiration swept his face. But his expression hardened almost immediately as his voice turned accusing.

"You! You set that damned fire! Not to mention, you scared my daddy half to death. So maybe we'll just add arson and property damage to the list of charges—"

I lost my patience. And my temper. It was too early for such nonsense. Besides, I hadn't had nearly enough coffee that morning. I stuck my arms out toward Beauprix, thumbs touching, wrists limp and hands palms down.

"Go ahead, *Officer.* Cuff me. Read me my rights. See how far *that* will get you."

At that point, the sheer absurdity of the situation must have struck Beauprix. He snorted, gave his head a quick shake and waved his hand in my direction. The gesture was, at best, dismissive.

"Oh, hell, little girl!" he said. "You proved your point. And your uncle won his bet. Just give me back my damned piece and let me get back to work."

When Uncle Tinh had suggested I remove Beauprix's gun from his safe, he hadn't mentioned any bet.

"Bet?" I said as irritation gave way to curiosity. "What bet?"

Beauprix seemed surprised that I didn't know.

"The bet he and I made," he said. "When we were arguing about whether I needed your help or not. Which I don't. And whether you were as good as he said. Which I said you weren't. And, well, maybe I was wrong in that regard. But, in any event, he said you'd leave a personal message for me. At my home. During my daddy's birthday party. He said that I was naturally inclined to be pigheaded and it was worth five thousand dollars to him to prove me wrong."

The old scoundrel, I thought. He'd used me. And it took some effort to keep my expression serious.

"You took the bet," I said.

He nodded.

"Yeah."

"And lost. Not only five thousand dollars, but your damned gun."

"Yeah."

Then I took a guess.

"And now you're pissed. Not over the money, which is probably going to some local charity, but because the foxy old bastard outsmarted you. Again."

He began to nod, then looked at me and grinned instead.

"Yeah," he said, and almost laughed. "Real pissed."

He looked down at the pavement again and gave the mangled cigarette a poke with his shoe.

"I used to have a pack-a-day habit. Now I only smoke when I'm pissed."

I smiled back and revised my opinion of him.

"With a temper like yours, might be better if you cut back to a pack a day again."

He thought about it for a minute, found the joke and actually did laugh. Then he stepped away from his car and began walking toward the morgue. He didn't slow his pace to accommodate my shorter stride, but turned his head to talk to me over his shoulder.

"Come on," he said. "I might as well show you what I'm dealing with. Then you can return my gun, pack your bags and head back up north where you belong."

The autopsy room was cold and smelled of decay and disinfectant. Pale green ceramic tiles covered the walls and a concrete floor slanted to a drain in the room's center. Several stainless-steel gurneys—each holding a shrouded cadaver—created an island in the center of the large room. From the doorway where Beauprix and I paused, I could see the cadavers' feet sticking out from beneath the white sheets. Manila tags dangled from every other big toe. The two walls that ran the length of the room were lined with double rows of shoulder-width, stainless-steel drawers. At the moment, all of the drawers were closed.

We'd come in through a foyer and walked down a short hallway to the autopsy room. Just steps inside the door where we'd entered, there was a battered gray desk where a very thin Caucasian male in a white lab coat was sitting. He was bent forward over the desktop, which gave visitors a top view of thinning, slicked-back hair that was Grecian-Formula-44 dark. At one corner of the desk, nearly at the man's elbow, was a tower of wire baskets. A basket labeled In was half empty, as was the Out box. The contents of Pending were overflowing onto a folded, greasy paper sack that served as a plate for a half-eaten ham sandwich. A soda can anchored one corner of the sack; dozens of crushed, empty cans filled the wastebasket.

Mayonnaise and yellow mustard had stained several of the papers on the desk, including the one that the man was furiously writing on as he noisily chewed the food in his mouth. He started when Beauprix cleared his throat, looked up quickly to reveal a narrow face and a blob of mustard at one end of a dark, pencil-thin mustache. The movement must have included inhaling a piece of sandwich because he spent the next minute or two choking, sputtering and finally sneezing into a tissue. He looked at Beauprix with teary eyes and I noticed that the tissue had also taken care of the mustard.

"Damn you, Anthony," he said. "You almost give a man a heart attack."

He began struggling up from the chair, but Beauprix stopped him.

"Don't let us interrupt you, Joe. I know the way. If I need you, I'll just give a shout."

Joe flashed Beauprix a smile as he settled in his chair and went back to his paperwork.

Beauprix picked up a small blue jar of Vicks from the corner of Joe's desk. He twisted off the metal lid and put in on the desk before using his little finger to dip into the jar's gooey contents. I watched as he put a smear on the inside edge of each nostril. Then he casually tossed the jar to me. I caught it, followed his example, then screwed the lid back on before returning the jar to its spot.

"You won't need these," Beauprix said, snatching a pair of disposable gloves from a box that was weighing down the contents of the In basket. He pulled on the gloves as he walked around the clutter of newly arrived corpses, moving along the left wall as his graceful strides carried him quickly through the room. He stopped in front of a drawer in the top row, second from the far wall.

I followed more slowly, taking in details. Each drawer had a preprinted number and was sequentially numbered, with *1* prefixing the upper row and *2* prefixing the lower. Most of the drawers also had a more temporary index card with the victim's name scrawled on it in indelible black marker. The drawer that Beauprix stood beside was labeled 15/Nguyen Tri.

Beauprix looked at me and, when he spoke, his voice was in some middle ground between concern and challenge—a male cop struggling to figure out how to relate to a woman who is not his mother, sister, lover or a hooker or a perp.

"Sure you can you handle this?" he said.

"I'm not a rookie," I said, implying that my experience with corpses was recent and professional. Certainly the memory of those who had died around me on a small boat in the South China Sea remained vivid.

"All right then," Beauprix said.

He pulled the drawer and it slid noiselessly open, releasing a draft that briefly intensified the cold and the smell in the room. Inside the drawer was a corpse shrouded in a dark green sheet.

Beauprix grasped the edge of the sheet, folded it back and revealed the face of a young man. Waxy yellow skin. Blue lips. Darkly hollow eyes. An angular face with a thin growth of long, silky hair on the chin and upper lip. Largish ears. Dark, straight hair clumped with dried blood.

Suddenly the autopsy room was airless and much too warm. And everything seemed to be slowly rotating....

A strong hand grasped my arm.

"Don't you faint on me, little girl," Beauprix said.

His voice made it a challenge.

Anger cleared my head and I pulled away from his support. I lifted my chin, swallowing the bitter liquid that had pooled at the back of my throat, and took a deep breath. The sharp whiff of menthol made it possible for me to ignore the smell that accompanied the oxygen.

"I'm okay," I said shortly. "Get on with it."

"Nguyen Tri," Beauprix said. "Five foot five. One hundred

twenty-five pounds. Body found below the I-10 bridge on the east side of the Inner Harbor Canal."

He said the words as if he was reading from a clip board, as if the boy was nothing more than a number on a toe tag. I wondered if the fate of this child was nothing more to him than a job. Curiosity compelled me to lean forward and turn my head so that I could look directly into Beauprix's face. Our eyes met.

"Tomorrow, we're releasing the body. His family will be burying him on his eighteenth birthday," Beauprix continued without pausing. But I knew, without a doubt, that his indifference was feigned.

I looked away, refocusing on the boy's face. But some detached part of me was still thinking about Beauprix. About what I had glimpsed in his eyes. Could I capture that suffering, I wondered, with pen and ink? And that thought led me to wonder if I wasn't the coldhearted monster in this vignette.

"The trauma to the head—" I began and was surprised when the words emerged as a whisper. I cleared my throat. "The trauma to the head," I repeated. "Was that the cause of death?"

Beauprix used a gloved hand to part the young man's longish hair.

"You see how little blood there is here, in spite of the relatively large wound? That's an indication that the blow was delivered after the time of death. Judging from this mark here, he was struck with a sharp—"

"What killed him?" I interrupted.

"It isn't going to be pretty…."

"I need to know."

He pulled the sheet away.

"He was tortured. Then dumped."

Beauprix's voice mixed oddly with the ringing in my ears. I saw brown-encrusted punctures and slashes. Distorted hands with mutilated fingers. And a deep wound just over the heart.

My head throbbed, my cheeks and ears burned, tears blurred my eyes. Bile rose in my throat, filled my mouth. I gagged and turned blindly away, seeking escape.

I felt Beauprix's hands on my shoulders.

"Hang on," he murmured, and there was nothing but sympathy in his tone. "Bathroom's just around the corner." He guided me through the door near Joe's desk, across the foyer and into a tiny rest room. "Go ahead. Throw up. You'll feel better."

Chapter 5

I entered Uncle Tinh's hotel through a locked door on a narrow alley. The word Private was stenciled on the door, which was just a few feet removed from the entrance to the restaurant's kitchen. During my first visit to New Orleans, Uncle Tinh had given me a key to the private door.

Unlocked, the door swung open to reveal a small foyer and a smooth wall of marble hung with two simply framed photos. One photo was in color, taken of Uncle Tinh standing in front of Tinh's City Vu. Matted in the same frame was a newspaper article about the hotel's recent renovation and the restaurant's grand opening.

The other photo was older, black-and-white, and looked like a candid shot. In it, a middle-aged Vietnamese man, who I recognized as Uncle Tinh, sat at a sidewalk café sharing a meal with a group of American soldiers and journalists. He wore a uniform shirt, but the camera angle made it impossible to see his rank. Everyone in the photo was laughing or smiling.

The photo had been taken just weeks before Saigon fell to the Vietcong, Uncle Tinh had told me. Uncle Tinh was among those taken by chopper from the rooftop of the American embassy to an aircraft carrier bound for Hong Kong. From there, he had immigrated to the U.S. and settled in Evanston, Illinois. In all the years I'd known him, I had never heard Uncle Tinh speak of who or what he'd left behind.

To the left of the foyer entrance was a highly polished wood panel that, at the push of a button, slid silently open to reveal an elevator large enough to accommodate two people comfortably. I tapped a five-number code onto the keypad inside, the elevator door closed and I was taken upstairs to Uncle Tinh's apartment—the entire fourth floor of a seventeenth-century Creole town house.

Uncle Tinh and I sat in a pair of upholstered, high-backed chairs at one corner of the long dining table. It was just past noon but, as was Uncle Tinh's custom, he ate his primary meal before the start of his busy business day. Downstairs on the first floor, in the bistro atmosphere of Tinh's City Vu, he worked nonstop and was completely devoted to serving his customers. But in the privacy of his home, he indulged himself. That meant having a live-in staff, including a chef. As far as I knew, Uncle Tinh rarely stepped into his ultra-modern kitchen except to pour himself a cup of coffee or a glass of wine.

The meal was, by Uncle Tinh's standards, informal. I had dressed appropriately in a simple black sheath topped by a red linen jacket and wore the string of pearls that Uncle Tinh had given me on my twenty-fifth birthday. Tiny silver clips just behind my temples anchored my long, unruly hair back from my face. Uncle Tinh wore a white shirt, tan slacks and leather sandals. Despite the simplicity of his outfit, the quality and cut of the fabric made me wonder if he and Beauprix shared the same tailor.

A uniformed male servant I didn't recognize from my last visit carried a large silver chafing dish into the dining room

and brought our conversation to a halt. With a quick bow—
first in Uncle Tinh's direction and then in mine—the servant
placed the dish on the table.

"Thank you, Vin," Uncle Tinh said in Vietnamese.

Vin reached to lift the chafing dish's lid, but Uncle Tinh
stopped the motion by laying the fingers of his left hand
lightly across his wrist. Vin stiffened at the unexpected touch
and his eyes widened. Uncle Tinh casually moved his hand
and lifted the linen napkin that lay beside his plate.

"My niece and I will serve ourselves," he said as he carefully arranged the napkin in his lap. "I will call should we
need anything."

Vin, who now held his arms rigidly at his sides, bowed
again, this time only to Uncle Tinh. And his fear made me
wonder anew if Uncle Tinh was, as Uncle Duran had often
insisted, the *anh hai* for the central region of the United
States. *Anh hai* was a traditional title of respect that Vietnamese gangs had co-opted for their most senior leaders.

As the kitchen door swung shut behind Vin, I said in English, "He's new. And obviously intimidated."

I raised an eyebrow, making it a question, wondering if this
would lead prematurely to the questions—the confrontation—that I dreaded. It never crossed my mind that Uncle
Tinh would lie to me.

But Uncle Tinh's long-suffering sigh hinted at an explanation that had nothing to do with crime—organized or otherwise. I found myself swallowing laughter that was directed
not only at Uncle Tinh, but at myself and my suspicions.

"Lee Leng hired him because she felt Odum was too—I
think her words were 'coarse and common'—to wait at table.
Odum splashed soup on her dress."

Lee Leng was my uncle Tinh's mistress. She had glossy,
raven-black hair, large, dark, almond-shaped eyes set above
high cheekbones, a slender nose and a delicate, rosebud
mouth. A dozen years my senior, she had been educated at

one of France's most prestigious finishing schools and, in her best moments, was disarmingly sweet and charming. In a different time, spilling soup on one such as Lee Leng would have been punished by death.

"What happened to Odum?" I asked.

"He now assists Cook."

I bit my lip, but couldn't keep a chuckle from escaping. "I'm surprised he still has a job."

Uncle Tinh sat up very straight and lifted his chin.

"*I* say who works and who doesn't work in this household." Then he slumped into his chair and shook his head sorrowfully. "Unfortunately, I say it quietly so as not to offend my beautiful young mistress."

Then, I did laugh.

Uncle Tinh sighed again, then reached over to lift the lid of the chafing dish. A waft of ginger and pineapple scent accompanied the sight of a whole red snapper resting in a nest of pale white scallops and surrounded by a sauce that was colored with slivers of vivid pea pods, toasted almonds and bright carrots.

"Ah, I see Cook has outdone himself," he said with great dignity. "Shall we eat before the rice grows cold?"

"What about—"

"We will continue *that* conversation after dinner. For now—because my lovely Lee Leng is shopping in Paris this week—I will take the opportunity to describe the difficulties of living with such a woman. You will listen sympathetically and offer advice, my dear Lacie."

Lie. See. As always, he spoke my name as no one else in America did, emphasizing both syllables equally, making it sound much like Lai Sie, the Vietnamese name from which my American name had been derived.

We resumed our more serious conversation as we sat in a pair of deep leather armchairs in the study. Behind us, French doors opened onto a balcony that overlooked the manicured front lawn of the Old Ursuline Convent. Between us was a low, leather-topped table. At the moment it held an open bottle of wine and two nearly full glasses.

"So, I embarrassed myself by getting sick at the sight of the body. *That* went a long way toward proving to Beauprix that he was correct. I might be good at cloak-and-dagger stuff, he said, but I was obviously too refined for the reality of street crime. Especially murder. He suggested—politely, mind you—that I go back to Washington where I belonged."

Uncle Tinh's eyes widened momentarily. Then he shook his head and reached past the table to briefly pat my hand.

"Obviously, I misjudged the man. Without his cooperation…" As he shook his head, Uncle Tinh raised his hands, palms upward. A very American gesture of hopelessness. "I apologize, *chère*, for dragging you into this. I will call Senator Reed, thank him for your services and ask him to bill me for any expenses incurred on my behalf."

I hadn't told my Vietnamese uncle about my American uncle's suspicions. Nor had I told him that agreeing to help him had cost me my job. Fortunately there was still no need to bring up either subject.

"Actually, Detective Beauprix has agreed to work with me. For a time, anyway."

"That's very good news," Uncle Tinh said. He looked less surprised by my success than he had when it seemed that I'd failed in my mission. "Please, explain how you accomplished this miracle."

"After the bathroom…incident…I returned Beauprix's gun and he offered to drop me off at my hotel. I agreed, intending to use the time to convince him that I *could* help. But his cell phone rang before we left the building. As he talked, I stood waiting in the hallway near the entrance, trying not to eavesdrop. And I found myself thinking about the dead boy. Recalling details."

I paused, wondering how best to explain what I'd done. The hollow ticking of the clock on the mantel above the fireplace filled several minutes.

"And?" Uncle Tinh prompted.

I sighed and lifted the delicate wineglass. The multicolored facets of an ornate Tiffany lamp were reflected in the pale liquid the glass held. I took a sip, swirled the Chardonnay in my mouth, savored its grassy, slightly astringent taste and swallowed.

"So much that is bright and beautiful to build a lifetime around," I said softly. I set the glass aside, searched my uncle's face. "And yet—"

"And yet the dark and grisly holds a certain appeal," Uncle Tinh said matter-of-factly. "I assume you went to look at the body again."

I nodded.

"Uh-huh. You know that I always carry a drawing tablet and pencils with me...."

Uncle Tinh didn't bother answering. Instead he swept his hand toward the opposite side of the room, in the direction of a series of matted and framed drawings hanging behind his desk. All studies of Uncle Tinh. All done by me. They ranged from an early and very childish sketch of him frying a duck in a deep wok to a formal pen-and-ink portrait I'd drawn a few Christmases earlier.

"Well, I walked back down the hallway to the morgue and grabbed a pair of latex gloves as I passed Joe's desk. He looked confused, but didn't try to stop me. I remembered which drawer Nguyen Tri's body was in and walked directly to it. I opened the drawer, peeled back the sheet and began drawing.

"It was awful, Uncle Tinh. Almost worse than the first time. I was almost sick again, but I forced myself to look at the boy as if he weren't really human. As if all the horrible things that had been done to him were merely *elements* of an elusive pattern.

"I concentrated on specific areas. First I sketched his face, then his torso. And then his arms and legs, hands and feet. I asked Joe to help me roll the victim over and repeated the process. Then I stepped away from the body and worked from my sketches, reassembling the pieces into a whole, trying to discover…"

Uncle Tinh's expression remained bland as his dark eyes studied me.

"And you found…?"

"A pattern so clear that I couldn't believe I hadn't seen it right away. And what I saw made me angry. Angrier, I think, than I've ever been in my life. I looked up, wanting to tell someone. Wanting someone to catch the fu—"

Uncle Tinh arched an eyebrow.

I bit back the obscenity as a sudden chill made me shudder and huddle back into my chair. Beauprix was right, though *that* was something I hadn't told him. Nothing in my work for Uncle Duran had prepared me for this.

Uncle Tinh frowned slightly. He stood, walked over to the liquor cabinet and poured two fingers of Glenfiddich into the bottom of a chunky tumbler. He recrossed the room and wordlessly handed me the glass.

"Thank you," I said as he settled back into his chair.

He nodded, lifted the wine bottle to refill his mostly full glass with more wine when something about the bottle seemed to demand his attention. After opening a drawer on a nearby side table, he found a pair of reading glasses and cleaned them thoroughly on the edge of his shirt before putting them on his nose. He turned the wine bottle slowly, examining its label.

I was grateful for the time he was giving me. I sat quietly sipping his expensive Scotch, letting it trickle its way down my throat and warm my belly. Then I returned the nearly empty tumbler to the table. At the slight sound, Uncle Tinh looked up, put the wine bottle aside and tucked his glasses back into the drawer.

"When I finally looked away from the body and drawing pad, I discovered that Beauprix was standing just inside the doorway, leaning against the wall near Joe's desk, watching me. I suspect he had been there for quite a while. When he saw that I was done, he crossed the room and took the drawing pad from me."

"And you told him what you saw."

I shook my head.

"Not then. When you called me in Washington, you said that three people had been killed. I asked Beauprix about them, asked what they had in common. Nothing, he said, except that they were all Vietnamese immigrants living in the same small community. And each of their bodies was dumped in New Orleans East, below I-10 where the Inner Harbor Canal meets the Intercoastal Waterway."

The area that Beauprix had described was sprawling, isolated and very industrial. Built to accommodate river-and ocean-going vessels and the cargo they carried, the canal and the waterway linked Lake Pontchartrain with the Mississippi River and the Gulf of Mexico beyond. Heavy industry and Port of New Orleans container terminals spotted the marginal land east of the canal and on either side of the waterway with busy, sprawling complexes. Every day, billions of dollars' worth of imports and exports were created, transferred, stored and transported.

"According to Beauprix," I continued, "bodies tend to turn up in that area with some regularity."

"And so?" Uncle Tinh said, sounding distressed.

"And so, the official view is that the killings are unrelated. They are an unfortunate coincidence in a city where it's not all that unusual for strangers of the same race living in the same neighborhood to end up dead. Not that Beauprix believes that. But he was working on instinct. The sketches— my observations—gave him something more substantial than his gut feeling."

I paused and, as I finished the Scotch remaining in my glass, I recalled how Beauprix had stopped speaking and simply stared at me when he'd turned over the last page in the drawing pad, the page that put all the pieces back together. What he had seen on the paper, or perhaps what he'd seen in my face, convinced him that his investigation needed me. Undoubtedly he was relieved to have his hunch confirmed by someone else. But, at that moment, he had looked at me as if I were something…alien.

That reaction was nothing new to me. Most of the people I'd worked with over the years had eventually been able to overlook my gender, my size and my appearance. But few were able to accept that which they didn't understand. And they didn't understand how observation, talent and memory could intertwine to produce insight. Witchcraft, a federal prosecutor had once judged it.

When I'd come to live in the U.S., I'd left behind the taunts that I was dust beneath the feet of true Vietnamese. No longer Vietnamese but not quite American, I struggled to find my place in a society where I was neither black nor Asian, but had Caucasian parents. It was my adopted uncles who taught me to value myself for who I was, to stand alone by choice. Thanks to both of them, I had grown into an adult who found it easy to ignore people's reactions to who I was and what I could do.

But when Beauprix had looked at me that way…

Why should I care what he thought of me?

Agitated, I stood, stepped out through one of the French doors onto the balcony. I braced my hands against the decorative wrought-iron balustrade and leaned forward, looking out over the convent grounds. On the wide brick promenade leading to the building's front door, the alabaster statues of three Ursuline nuns knelt in perpetual prayer. Deliver us from evil, I thought, thinking about the horrors that I'd seen that day and adding my silent petition to theirs.

Then I went back inside and told Uncle Tinh the rest of the story.

"Beauprix showed me photographs of the other victims taken on the scene and, later, at the morgue. He carries a set with him, admits he can't get their faces—their stories—out of his head. As he told me about the other victims, I sat beside him in the front seat of his car, studying the photos and sketching what I saw."

I tried to make my voice sound as cool and professional as Beauprix's had when he'd given me the information.

"The boy was the third victim. Multiple stab wounds. The official view is that the boy got mixed up with the wrong element. Drugs, maybe, though the investigating officers couldn't find anything in his background to suggest any kind of criminal activity. He was a college student, studying to be a graphic designer.

"Seven weeks ago, the only female victim was found beaten and strangled. Her name was Vo Bah Mi. She was fifty seven. Her ring had been removed from her finger." I shuddered at the memory of her hands. "Her husband didn't have an alibi, so he was taken into custody and charged with the murder.

"Beauprix thinks that Yu Kim Lee, thirty-two, was the first victim. He was found almost six months ago, bludgeoned to death. His extremities were crushed. There are no suspects."

As I spoke, I watched my uncle's horror grow, watched as it stretched his eyes and tightened his mouth.

"I'd already found the pattern in the third killing, so it didn't take much time to discover a similar pattern in the first two. Different methods, perhaps. But beneath the appearance of unrestrained violence, there was the same cold, calculating deliberation. The same focus on destroying their hands. And the same cruelty. Cruelty like I've never before seen, Uncle Tinh. It's the work of one person. I'd stake my reputation on it."

"May I see the sketches?" Uncle Tinh asked, and I heard the tremor that his business-like voice could not quite disguise. "Did you bring them with you?"

"They're in my briefcase. With my jacket, in the foyer. I'll get them."

As I began to rise, Uncle Tinh waved his hand in my direction.

"Stay where you are," he said. "Finish your drink."

He crossed the room to his desk, lifted the telephone that rested there and tapped two numbers into the keypad. From somewhere in the apartment, I heard faint ringing.

"Vin. My niece's briefcase is in the closet in the foyer. Bring it into the study, please."

He put the phone back in its cradle but, instead of returning to his chair, he perched on the edge of his desk. Vin came in, handed the glove-leather briefcase over to my uncle and scurried away.

"With your permission?" he said, and I nodded.

Uncle Tinh opened the briefcase, found the drawing pad, lifted the cardboard cover and began turning pages. A few pages in, and he shook his head, then looked at me.

"May I remove these?" he asked.

"Of course."

I watched the blood drain from my uncle's face as he began carefully tearing the pages from the pad and placing them, one by one, on the polished surface of his desk.

I didn't tell him that as awful as the drawings were, the reality was worse.

"The killer used his victims like an artist's canvas," I said. "He or she was creating images for a specific audience. Whether that audience is one person or many, I don't know. And whether the images were intended to horrify or satisfy or intimidate, I don't know. I guess that's what we—Beauprix and I—need to figure out."

By the time my uncle put down the last page, his mouth had tightened until the skin surrounding it was pinched and pale.

"Mon Dieu," he kept murmuring. *"Mon Dieu."*

Chapter 6

We went downstairs to the kitchen of Tinh's City Vu. Uncle Tinh went because it was his job, because he had a business to run and there was no reason not to run it. I accompanied him because I always visited his kitchen and I'd promised to try his new dessert. But mostly because I longed for an activity so wholesome and pleasant that it might, even for a short time, supplant the poisonous images I'd recorded on paper and would carry forever in my memory.

I was a step behind my uncle as he went through the back door into the busy kitchen. A grizzled older man with a pot belly spotted him, paused mid-motion as he slid a steaming rack of glassware from a dishwater, and called out a loud greeting.

"Hey, boss. Where y'at?" he said.

It was a warning, I thought, for the rest of the staff.

There were dozens of men and women working throughout the bustling maze of a kitchen, but certainly everyone within easy eyeshot of me and my uncle suddenly became more efficient. A group of young women stopped chattering in Spanish, glanced our way, then continued arranging a colorful assortment of baby greens into dozens of small salad bowls. A redheaded woman who I recognized from previous visits as a hostess and a black grill chef with a heavy Cajun accent were distracted from an argument that seemed more domestic than business. A tall, thin woman wielding a pastry bag paused briefly, flashed us a quick smile, then continued scolding two assistants who, like her, were dropping quarter-size blobs of dough onto large baking sheets.

Then, from an adjacent storage room, a boy with Asian features, large ears and a bad complexion came into the kitchen. He was, I guessed, no older than sixteen and dressed in baggy pants and a sleeveless black net shirt that showed off lean, muscular arms and a six-pack. His straight black hair was streaked with hot pink and brilliant blue, and his nose, lip and ears were pierced in a dozen places.

He had shadows under his eyes and the look of someone who was chronically tired, chronically stressed. The look, I thought, was familiar. And though he was far too young, I realized that his drawn, exhausted face brought to mind at least a dozen of the boys I'd played with when I'd lived in the refugee camp.

The boy balanced a fifty-pound burlap sack of onions on one of his shoulders. He was moving slowly beneath its burden when he turned into the narrow aisle between two stainless-steel counters and noticed Uncle Tinh and me. Abruptly he straightened his back and quickened his pace. Unfortunately the top of the sack wasn't completely sealed and his abrupt movements shifted its load. Dry red onions began tumbling to the floor. Startled, the boy took a half step forward to maintain his balance, put his foot down on one of the escaped onions and fell sprawling between the counters.

In the moment that it took the kitchen staff to recover from the sudden chaos, Uncle Tinh was on his knees at the teenager's side. As everyone looked on, he helped the boy to his feet and waited as the boy turned his head left, then right and flexed his arms and legs. Once he had proved himself uninjured, Uncle Tinh patted him on the shoulder and leaned in close.

"Di dau ma voi ma vang," he murmured quietly. *"Ma vap phai da, ma quang phai giay."*

I was probably the only other person in the kitchen who heard and understood what Uncle Tinh said. The old Vietnamese proverb cautioned against reckless haste. Loosely translated, it meant "hurry up slowly." The boy listened with eyes downcast and nodded.

"Then back to work, Tommy," Uncle Tinh said as he slapped the boy's back in a very un-Vietnamese-like gesture.

Vin, who had served us dinner upstairs, would have been terrified by such close interaction with his employer. But when Tommy lifted his head, his serious brown eyes, framed by long colorful bangs, looked directly at my uncle.

"Yes, sir," he said in English, in an accent that was pure New Orleans. "Thank you for your kindness."

Uncle Tinh watched as the boy began retrieving onions with the enthusiasm of a puppy chasing a roomful of balls. Briefly, a sad smile played across my uncle's lips, making me wonder if he envied the boy's youth. Or, perhaps, he was recalling how bittersweet youth could be. In any event, he gave himself a slight shake, stepped back beside me and addressed the entire kitchen.

"Everyone! Maybe you remember my niece, Lacie. She come from way up north to sample *Tropicale Vu.*"

The tall, thin pastry chef's head bobbed appreciatively as she shoved the first sheet full of pastry into a waiting oven, then took the next sheet from the waiting hands of one of her assistants. Uncle Tinh snatched a clean apron from a peg, a tall chef's hat from a shelf and a copper sauté pan from an overhead pot rack. Then he, too, went to work.

I found an empty stool in a relatively quiet corner, took my drawing pad from my briefcase and relaxed as I waited by filling a page with quick sketches of the kitchen staff. Then I turned the page and did a larger drawing of the boy, Tommy. Pimples, big ears, piercings and all. He had good bone structure, I thought, and nice eyes. Once his complexion cleared and he grew up a bit...

"Finis!" Uncle Tinh announced from across the kitchen, so I quickly put my drawing pad away. When I had more time, I promised myself, I would draw the teenager not as he was, but as he would be.

A short time later, Uncle Tinh and I sat together at a small round table just outside the kitchen door, and he watched eagerly as I sampled his creation. Colorful, delicate and bursting with flavor and texture, the dessert involved tiny pieces of tropical fruit encased in a crackling sugar glaze, ribbons of white chocolate, macadamia nuts and custard, and thin, round layers of buttery crust.

Like so many of Uncle Tinh's hallmark dishes, this one, too, was a dramatic and sophisticated blend of France, Vietnam and New Orleans. It was heavenly and would undoubtedly become a favorite among those who took good food for granted. I told Uncle Tinh just that.

As I finished off the last of the dessert, I listened as members of his staff came to my uncle for instruction and resolution of problems. Nothing about the conversations reflected anything but business as usual in a successful restaurant.

Then I returned our conversation to a far less savory business.

"So Beauprix told you about the murders and he asked you for help."

"Yes. But I was already considering calling you because of a...related...situation." Uncle Tinh shook his head. "If you were a stranger, I would have called sooner. But to ask such a favor of someone you care for—"

That thought was interrupted by Tommy, who approached the table confidently.

"Excuse me, sir," he said, his polite manner at odds with the rebelliousness his appearance suggested. "The pastry chef says the raspberries that were delivered earlier are unacceptable. The top layer looked fine, but beneath that the berries are spoiled."

"Tell her— No, I will tell her that we will no longer use that supplier. In the meantime, ask the cashier for some cash, drive quickly to the Market and obtain for us the quality we need. Can you do that, Tommy?"

Tommy nodded enthusiastically, then left on the errand.

"He is the first in his family born in America," Uncle Tinh said. "A hard worker in a land of opportunity. I think he will do well."

Then he waved his hand in the direction of the nearby hostess. She scurried to refill our coffee cups. Uncle Tinh waited until she was out of earshot before speaking again.

"I know you do dangerous work, Lacie. But I would not have called you if there were another option. No matter how competent you are now, my heart still sees the child you were. Perhaps that is why I am comforted that you have Anthony Beauprix as an ally. Working with another professional makes the situation safer. It made my decision to call you easier."

I was not surprised by Uncle Tinh's attitude, nor did I argue about whether or not I needed Beauprix. Though I often worked alone, I had never objected to having someone competent watching my back. And although I found his attitudes annoying, I had no doubt that Beauprix was competent.

"Tell me what you would have me do that the police cannot," I said.

He nodded.

"A man in my position hears rumors—and receives information—from many sources. I have already told Anthony what I am now telling you. A gang has taken over Little Vietnam, intimidating the merchants, as well as the residents. Many business owners now pay protection."

I told myself that if my uncle was himself the head of a criminal organization, he would have the resources to deal with this threat. But the moment of comfort I took from that thought might have been longer if I'd had less knowledge of immigrant gangs. It was too easy to remember that, less than a decade earlier, the well-entrenched criminal establishment in New York's Chinatown had been shaken to its roots by the invasion of a psychopathic gang called the Born to Kill.

"Protection only?" I asked, pushing Uncle Tinh for answers to questions he didn't know I had. "Or other activities? Like smuggling illegals? Or perhaps supplying them with documents?"

Uncle Tinh's tone was bland and, when his dark eyes met mine, his gaze was unwavering.

"Like all gangs, they engage in whatever is profitable. Certainly, counterfeiting documents and smuggling illegals are profitable. As are drugs, gambling and prostitution. Profitability also provides a ready motive for one murder. Or three. Or a dozen.

"These are violent, dangerous individuals, Lacie. Treat them with caution. With the information I have given him, even a white policeman might eventually be able to gather evidence against some of the *sai lows*—the foot soldiers. But to stop this gang from poisoning the Vietnamese community with their violence? To solve three murders and prevent others?"

Uncle Tinh put his coffee cup down, reached across the table and took each of my hands in one of his.

"To destroy the viper, one must have the skill and courage to cut off its head."

And that, it seemed, was my job.

Not too much later, I left Tinh's City Vu.
With an eye to the calories I'd just consumed, I decided to

walk back to the Intercontinental. It was late afternoon, a breeze stirred the damp air and the drizzle that had plagued the city on and off for days had stopped. But, wary of more autumn showers, I borrowed one of the big, black courtesy umbrellas emblazoned with the restaurant's logo that my uncle kept on hand for the restaurant's regular patrons. Then I stood beneath the canopy that sheltered the entrance of Tinh's City Vu from rain and sun and considered my route.

To my left, at the bottom of Ursulines Avenue, was the historic and very commercial French Market. Seven days a week, twenty-four hours a day, merchants sold everything from Creole tomatoes by the pound to fine jewelry by the carat. From the Market, I could wander along the wooden promenades and admire the commerce along the Mississippi.

The lure of sweet pralines, thick chicory-laced coffee and a view of river traffic navigating the crescent bend usually made the Market and the Moonwalk my inevitable choices. But I'd already had my fill of sweets, was too wired to need caffeine and was in no mood to stroll along the river. So I turned right, in the direction of the Royal Pharmacy, aiming to surround myself with the carefree, frenzied energy of Bourbon Street.

It was Friday and, like Uncle Tinh's place, the French Quarter's bars, restaurants and strip joints were gearing up for a busy night. Tourists and locals already filled the wide sidewalks, second-floor balconies and narrow streets of the Quarter. But an hour before dark, most were more interested in food and atmosphere than in getting plastered or watching topless dancers bump and grind.

The music, which was what I sought, was already beginning to flow from the clubs. Old tunes and new washed over Bourbon Street—jazz and Dixieland, rhythm and blues, soul and funk, Cajun and zydeco. I walked for blocks and took my time, letting the crowd pass unnoticed as I lingered in open doorways, inhaling the mixed odors of food, cigarettes and booze, and listening. Just listening.

On the streets of New Orleans, tradition and impulse, beauty and corruption, good and evil, coexisted and sometimes embraced. And the city felt more like home than any place I had ever been.

A rumble of thunder announced the downpour. Tourists clapped their palms over the tops of their alcohol-filled go-cups and ran for shelter. I opened my umbrella and stepped from the wide, brick sidewalk into the narrow brick-paved street to avoid the people congregating under overhangs and in doorways.

From beneath my portable shelter, I gauged my progress. It was nearly dusk. I had already walked past the double balconies and dormer windows of the Royal Sonesta Hotel and could no longer hear the piano and its accompanying male voice coming from inside the Desire Oyster Bar. Ahead of me, glowing through the rain and reflecting off the wet street, was the iron-work-framed, black-and-white sign of the Old Absinthe House. From there, I knew, it was just two blocks to Canal Street and then three more blocks to the Intercontinental.

Half a block past the Old Absinthe House and I was alone on the street. I stepped back onto the sidewalk, which was now cracked concrete rather than picturesque red brick. Even in good weather, tourists rarely bothered walking this far along Bourbon Street. There were few clubs, restaurants or bars to draw them. Despite that, the Quarter's characteristic smell of mildew, beer, vomit and urine wafted from the doorways, alleys and parking lots. But unlike the area frequented by tourists, here the litter of discarded go-cups was joined by the jagged green, brown and clear-glass remains of discarded liquor bottles and occasional used needles. It was a reminder of the area's potential for unsavory night life. Once the sun set, anyone walking alone invited trouble.

Despite the rain, enough daylight remained that I wasn't particularly concerned about my safety. But with no reason to linger, I walked briskly, my thoughts focused on a hot shower, soft towels and something warm from room service.

At the intersection of Bourbon and Iberville, I glance both ways, looking for traffic that wasn't there, then kept my eyes on the pavement as I stretched my legs to avoid potholes and the rush of dirty water through the gutters on either side of the street. I'd just stepped back onto the sidewalk and was walking past the boarded-up, vomit-stained entry to a crumbling brick building when I heard a distressed, muffled cry.

The sound came from behind me. I turned around, saw nothing but empty street and sidewalk, and stood, head tipped to one side, straining to hear beyond the sounds of the rain hitting my umbrella. I took another step in the direction of Bourbon and Iberville and heard the sound again. This time, more distinctly.

"Help!"

It was a male voice, stretched and urgent.

I hurried forward.

Suddenly a man lunged at me from around the corner of the building, reaching for me with grasping, gloved hands. But his timing was off and he had misjudged not only the distance separating us but his intended victim. His bad judgment gave me enough time to swing my open umbrella between us and thrust it, hard, at his face. When he stepped back to avoid the metal point at the umbrella's center, I abandoned it, spun on my heel and sprinted away.

I'd only had a glimpse of my pursuer, but that had been enough to terrify. He wore a black-hooded jacket and a mask, the kind that was available in nearly every tourist shop in the Quarter. Except for slitted eyeholes, it covered his entire face with glossy black feathers.

I ran as fast as I could up Bourbon Street, spurred on by the footsteps behind me. I hung on to my briefcase, mostly because it didn't occur to me to let it go, and my purse bounced against my body from the strap that hung from my shoulder.

I considered screaming, shouting for help, but couldn't spare the breath until I was closer to a place where my cries were likely to be heard. Impossible, too, to dig my cell phone from my purse without breaking my pace.

Between me and the lights and traffic on Canal Street was almost a full block of boarded-up businesses, vacant store-fronts and narrow, solidly locked entries to a handful of up-stairs apartments. I vaguely remembered that there was a Greek restaurant near the end of the block, but I wasn't cer-tain if it was still open. Even if it was out of business, there were always people waiting just across Canal at the "zero stop" for the St. Charles streetcar line.

My pursuer was no runner. I spared him only a single over-the-shoulder glance, realized that the distance between us was growing, and then kept my attention focused on the lights that marked the distant intersection. Only half a block, I told myself. I could make it easily. And then I would be safe.

As I passed the cavernous entrance to a long-defunct top-less bar, a second man stepped out directly in front of me, blocking the sidewalk. He, too, wore a feathered mask. It was crimson.

I swung my briefcase, hard, in his direction as I swerved around him, into the street and kept running.

He was fitter and faster than the first man. A few steps later he caught up with me. His heavy blow between my shoulder blades sent me to the ground. I landed in the gutter, ended up with my back against the curb. I tried to roll, but my long, loose hair betrayed me. My attacker stepped on it, trapping me.

Trying to protect myself from further blows, I curled my hands over my head and kept my forearms pressed tightly against my face. I lay there, gasping for breath, as cold water rushed around me, soaking my linen jacket and dress.

A rush of footsteps and harsh breathing announced the ar-rival of the other man. The man in the crimson mask leaned forward, grabbed my wrists and wrenched my hands away from my face. Then he straightened and stepped backward, freeing my hair as he pulled my arms over my head, lifting my upper body out of the gutter. I felt the rushing water tugging at the ends of my hair.

My captor was standing so that I couldn't reach him. But I fought anyway, trying to free my wrists from his unyielding grip. I bucked, kicked, twisted wildly, screamed at the top of my lungs. All the while, the man in the black mask remained on the sidewalk, his hands shoved deep into raincoat pockets, watching me struggle.

The man in the crimson mask dropped me back into the gutter so abruptly that my head and shoulders slammed flat against the pavement. Still holding my wrists, he jammed his foot into the intersection of my neck and shoulder and used it for leverage as, once again, he pulled my arms taut. This time, he gave my wrists a vicious twist.

Agony.

I was defeated. At least for the moment.

I stopped screaming. Stopped struggling. I forced myself to ignore the pain, to relax, to think, to plan. If they thought I'd been concussed or gone into shock, maybe they would let down their guard. Maybe they would release my arms. Maybe.

I went completely limp.

With shadowed, glinting eyes, my assailants peered down at me like carrion birds, the red-masked man from above my head and shoulders, the black-masked man from the elevation of the sidewalk to my left.

I made my face an expressionless mask of flesh, staring past them, focusing upward on the rain falling from a stone-gray New Orleans sky. It was a perspective problem, I told myself. How would I draw individual drops from this angle?

The carrion birds leaned in closer, their heads tilted, curious. The stretched tension on my arms relaxed, the vise on my wrists eased and the foot shifted on my neck.

I waited. In another moment the man who held my wrists would be overbalanced. Then I would use my weight against him, yank him forward, put him on a collision course with his colleague. Whether he released my wrists or hung on as he fell, I'd have an opening, an opportunity to scramble out of reach, a chance to get to my feet and run. I braced my spine and heels against the pavement, lifted my knees slightly, getting ready.

But the man in the black mask acted before I could.

His hands were still in his pockets when he lifted his right foot off the sidewalk and put it on my stomach, just beneath my ribs. He was a big man—not tall, but bulky. His foot spanned my body from side to side.

If he stepped on me with all his weight…

I remained still, holding my breath and tensing my abdominal muscles, hoping they would offer some measure of protection, knowing that they wouldn't.

The man in the black mask nodded at his accomplice, who tightened his grip on my wrists. Then the larger man pulled his hands from his pockets. He leaned in, putting more weight on my stomach.

I clenched my teeth, stared up into his black-feathered face, and imagined him smiling. I would not scream, I told myself. I would not give the sick bastard the satisfaction….

He raised his hands.

A click, a flash, and I was momentarily blinded by bright, white light.

A camera mechanism whirred.

Another flash. Then, suddenly, I was free.

And the carrion birds took off, running.

Chapter 7

The rain was steadily falling, the daylight rapidly failing and my attackers, not I, escaped to the intersection of Bourbon and Canal. I struggled up from the gutter in time to see them jog to the end of the block and around the corner.

My purse lay, undisturbed, on the sidewalk where I had dropped it and my briefcase was a yard or two beyond that. I staggered over to the purse. As I leaned forward to grab the thin leather strap, the throbbing in my head went from dull to acute, the world around me grew abruptly fuzzy and I made a frantic grab for a nearby light post. I caught it, hung on and lowered myself to the sidewalk.

I started to cry. No matter that I hated to cry and didn't want to cry, I couldn't stop my body's reaction to stress, pain and frustration. Hot tears streaked my cold cheeks and, into that exhausted, vulnerable moment came a devastating thought. If my attackers returned, I wouldn't be able to run away.

At some level I knew that my fear was irrational. Whatever they had set out to do, my attackers had done. And, goal met, they had gone, left of their own accord. But, like the tears, I couldn't control trauma-driven anxiety. The two men might have already doubled back. They could be nearby. Hiding. Waiting. Watching.

For the first time that evening—probably for the first time in my life—I panicked. After dark, the temperature had dropped ten degrees and I doubted it was much warmer than fifty. I was already shivering from the cold, but painful tremors now racked my body and I found myself gulping for air. My eyes darted up and down the street, searching the shadows. If I let down my guard, they would attack again. Fear twisted my stomach and bile rose in my throat as I waited, convinced that they would come back. Convinced that, this time, I would not survive.

Fortunately rational and irrational impulses coincided as I decided on my best course of action. I had to get help. Soon. With trembling hands, I snagged my purse and retrieved my cell phone. Easy enough and logical to call the police. Or Uncle Tinh. But instinct rather than logic prevailed. My hands continued to shake as I punched in the newest number on my speed dial.

Thank God, he answered.

"Beauprix, here."

"This is Lacie Reed," I said. "I need…your help. Please." The sob that I couldn't hold back carried over the phone.

"Where are you?" he asked.

"Bourbon Street, east of Iberville."

"I'm on my way. Are you hurt?"

"Yes," I said, my voice wavering. Then I reconsidered. "No," I corrected.

Beauprix's urgent voice became measured and ultra-calm.

"Lacie, are you bleeding?"

"No."

"Were you raped?"

"No. No. I'm fine."

He apparently didn't believe me.

"Is anything broken? Can you walk?"

"I'm okay. Really. Just some bruises. And my head hurts. I wanted to walk to Canal, but I got dizzy. So I sat down."

I looked around me, finally able to ignore the empty street and growing darkness. A burned-out neon sign surrounded by jagged, broken bulbs advertised a boarded-up strip joint.

"I'm a few yards west of a strip joint," I said. "Big Al's All Girl Review."

"Vice shut that place down last year. What the hell are you doing there?"

The effort I'd made to convince him that I was battered and bruised, not shot or stabbed, had gone a long way toward soothing my jangled nerves. And his drawled question, which sounded like an accusation, hit me like a splash of cold water to the face.

"Getting mugged," I snapped.

"Yeah. Okay," he said, sounding almost relieved. "I'm almost there. Five minutes, tops. You just keep on talking."

He made it sound like he was instructing a dim-witted child. He had called me "little girl," that morning, intending to offend, and I reminded myself that the man annoyed me. Annoyance felt a lot better than fear, so I encouraged the feeling.

Why, exactly, had I called him? I asked myself irritably. Police response time in New Orleans was sometimes slow, but I could have waited. Uncle Tinh would have overwhelmed me with his fussing, but I could have coped. Instead, I'd called the city's most chauvinistic cop.

"No need to tie up your line," I said shortly. "I'll redial if there's a problem." Then I disconnected.

While I waited, I worked hard on not feeling too pathetically grateful.

* * *

In a lobby streaming with refugees from the storm outside, Beauprix and I were an unremarkable sight. On Bourbon Street, he had wrapped his raincoat around me and run the heater in his car full-blast as we drove the few blocks to the Intercontinental. His arm was around my shoulders as we walked through the lobby and took the elevator up to the fourteenth floor. Though I was feeling enough improved that I was certain I could make it across the lobby unsupported, I was grateful for the additional warmth. I was no longer shaking from fear but from the beginnings of hypothermia.

"First, let's get you warm," Beauprix said once we were inside my room. "Then we'll talk."

He dropped my briefcase and my purse on the floor, then helped me out of the raincoat.

I kicked off my sodden shoes, took a few steps and lowered myself onto a chair that was just around the corner from the foyer.

With coat in hand, Beauprix disappeared from my line of sight as he leaned into the closet. He traded the coat for one of the hotel's extra blankets, gave it a quick shake to unfold it and wrapped it around my shoulders.

"You just sit for a minute."

He went into the bathroom and I heard the shower turned on full-blast. Then he pulled the bathroom door shut as he stepped back across the tiny foyer to the closet. My suitcase was there, lid unlocked and open, on the rack that the hotel provided. It never occurred to me that Beauprix would rummage through it. But moments later, when he stepped back into my line of sight, I discovered that he'd been doing just that. He was clutching a wad of my clothing in one of his hands. I identified my gray sweat pants, a baggy Northwestern University sweatshirt and a pair of pink underwear.

Oblivious to my growing irritation, he pushed open the bathroom door and held it wide as a cloud of steam escaped.

"Come on," he said, gesturing for me to step into the warm room ahead of him. "We need to get you out of those wet clothes."

I wasn't sure if he intended to help me undress. But he now seemed to think me incapable of doing anything for myself. Give a male chauvinist an inch, I thought irritably, and he'll take over your life.

I snatched my clothing from his hand.

"Thanks," I said. "I think I can handle it from here."

Then I firmly closed the door between us.

I worked the shampoo through my hair, using my fingers to discover and remove bits of the debris that the gutter had deposited in my long, kinky curls. Then I rinsed and shampooed again. Three shampoos later and I was convinced that the smell of the gutter was finally out of my hair.

After almost thirty minutes, I emerged from the bathroom, clean, dry, warmly dressed and completely exhausted. Beauprix had only tapped on the door once to ask if I was okay.

In my absence, he had opened the drapes. Wind-driven rain flowed down the wall of windows. The room was now lit by the twin lamps that flanked the queen-size bed. Room service had come and gone. A small writing desk, which was tucked into a corner between the bed and the windows, now supported a silver tray laden with a coffeepot, cream and sugar, a pair of porcelain cups and a plate piled high with cookies.

Beauprix was standing by the window, staring out into the darkness as he talked on his cell phone. In the window's reflection, I could see that he was frowning. He was wearing a dress shirt, which was open at the throat and rolled up to just below his elbows, in a shade of pale tangerine. His softly pleated slacks were black, as were his loafers. When he heard the bathroom door open, he looked in my direction and lifted an eyebrow and his chin in the direction of the bed. Then he turned his back on the room again.

Though my impulse was to sit in the room's overstuffed chair, just to prove I could, the promise of the soft, warm bed was too tempting. I tucked myself in between the quartet of cushy pillows, leaned my sore back and shoulders against the padded headboard and tucked my legs beneath the top sheet and a duvet-covered comforter.

"That's everything," Beauprix was saying. "Yeah, the witness is absolutely reliable. If she say's that's what she saw, that's what happened. Yeah, well, I trust her. I know, I know. And so does she. Just do whatever you can with it."

He flipped the compact phone closed, tucked it into his pocket and turned his attention to me. He didn't look happy.

"Bit of a problem selling the 'big bad bird attack' story?" I asked, trying to sound flippant, trying to *feel* flippant.

He didn't buy it.

"I'm sorry, Lacie," he said seriously.

And I couldn't tell if he was apologizing for the attack, the police department, or the fact that sometimes reality sucked. Maybe all of the above.

He lifted the carafe.

"I asked for decaf coffee," he said, "but if you'd prefer–"

"No. That's great," I said. "Lots of cream, no sugar."

He poured, added cream and handed me a cup. Then he moved the plateful of cookies to the edge of the table so that it was an easy reach from the bed.

I picked up a butter cookie and nibbled its fluted edge as he poured himself coffee, dragged the desk chair closer to the bed and sat down. He stretched his legs out in front of him and crossed them at the ankles, took a sip of coffee and regarded me over the top of his cup with serious, hazel eyes.

"I know it annoys the hell out of someone like you, but I was brought up believing that it was a man's job to protect a woman, to take care of her, to treat her right. Didn't matter whether that woman was family, friend, lover or stranger."

And suddenly I knew exactly what his earlier apology had

been for. He was sorry that he hadn't been there to take care of me. Which was silly. And sweet. And maddeningly male.

"By the way," he continued, "you look a hell of a lot better."

"Thanks," I said.

"My job," he retorted, then added a quick smile.

He took another few sips of his coffee, then put the cup aside.

"So, as you guessed, the investigating officer wasn't real happy with the information you gave me. Masks and hoods. Ordinary clothing. No odd gaits or mannerisms. One guy medium height and weight. The other slightly shorter and heavier, wearing dark-blue-on-white Nikes. Like you said when you described the SOBs to me, that about narrows the field to half the male population of New Orleans."

"Nothing like it has happened to anyone else?"

"No. It would have made more sense if you were robbed or raped or murdered—"

He hesitated, apparently hearing what he had just said. But I knew what he was getting at.

"I agree," I said. "This was too brutal for a prank, but too pointless to be much else. Except for the photo."

"Except for the photo," Beauprix repeated, half sighing. He uncrossed his ankles and shifted forward in his chair, his expression intense. "About a year ago, there was a case out west. A guy—a lawyer, I think—went around exposing himself to women, taking pictures of their shocked expressions. Kept the photos as souvenirs. Maybe there's a weird kind of sex thing going on here."

Or maybe, I thought, someone had followed me from Uncle Tinh's, deliberately targeting and threatening me, but not actually hurting me. Because of my relationship to Tinh Vu? I asked myself. But I couldn't think of how his enemies would know who I was or what the purpose was behind the attack.

I looked at Beauprix, who was pouring a warm-up into both of our cups, and wondered what he was thinking. Certainly if Uncle Tinh was connected to organized crime, Beauprix would know or suspect it. Perhaps that was the reason he'd come to Uncle Tinh. Perhaps he, too, was corrupt. But, although I hardly knew the man, I realized that it was difficult for me to imagine that Beauprix was anything but honest.

Beauprix felt my eyes, turned his head and flashed me a smile.

"It could have been just a random act of violence," I said.

Beauprix shrugged, then handed me my cup.

"Happens. A couple of guys come here from out of town, figure that there are no rules here in the Big Easy, mix booze and boredom with a disposition to violence…"

"Yes," I said, nodding. "It could have been that."

"Yeah," he said, not looking entirely convinced. "Maybe. Might also have been someone trying to scare you off."

"Only three people knew I was coming here. You. Uncle Tinh. Senator Duran Reed."

He grinned.

"That'd make me the most likely suspect and, I swear, I didn't do it."

I laughed, which I suspected was his intention.

"What about extortion?" he said more seriously. "Maybe someone wants money from one of your uncles."

As I considered the possibility, my carefully cultivated detachment failed me. Suddenly I was recalling the glittering eyes that stared down at me from a pair of feathered masks, recalling how helpless I had been. My stomach twisted and I shuddered.

"That would only make sense if they'd kidnapped me," I said. "Which would have been easy."

"But they didn't," Beauprix said firmly. "You're safe now, Lacie."

I felt better for the reminder, but I wasn't sure that I was comfortable with his quick perceptions.

I took a sip of coffee, watching as he spooned a little extra sugar into his own cup, and again asked myself about *his* relationship with Uncle Tinh.

"Would you like some food?" Beauprix asked. "I can call down to room service."

"No. No need."

I leaned forward slightly, thinking that I'd snag myself another cookie, and felt the muscles catch in my back and shoulders before I lifted my arm. So I hid my grimace with a smile, abandoned the task and settled back onto the pillows.

"Since you've already been through my suitcase, I don't suppose you'd mind rummaging through it again? There's some extra-strength ibuprofen in one of the pockets. Could you get me a couple?"

He did just that, then stood beside the bed, watching as I swallowed them with a sip of coffee.

Shifting back into overprotective male mode, I thought, noticing his expression. I raised my hand, palm out, to stop any anxious words.

"I'm not going to die of internal injuries. Promise. And I don't have a concussion. My headache is already gone. It's just that my back and neck are getting stiff. Not a big deal. Really."

Briefly, Beauprix continued to look down at me and I could read indecision on his handsome face. Whatever his thoughts, he apparently made up his mind.

"Turn over," he said.

"I beg your pardon?"

"If you didn't trust me, you wouldn't have called me tonight. So, Ms. Reed, if you'll roll on over, I'll rub your sore shoulders."

I didn't bother replying. Instead, I snuggled down under the blanket until it covered me to the waist and rolled over onto my stomach.

He sat on the edge of the bed, leaned in and put his hands on my shoulders. At first, he tried to massage my back through the bulk of my sweatshirt. After a minute, he made a noise in his throat that sounded like a growl.

"This doesn't work," he said.

He slid his hands under my sweatshirt and lifted it to my shoulders, exposing my back. At first, his touch was tentative, then more confident. His hands were warm and only slightly calloused, and he obviously knew what he was doing.

"The attack… Those two men… My God, Lacie, it was brutal. And, though I think you're putting a good face on it, terrifying. There's no doubt in my mind that you handled the situation then—and you're handling how you feel now—as well as anyone, man or woman, could."

As he spoke Beauprix's fingers moved along the muscles of my neck and shoulders, working outward from the spine, identifying knots and skillfully working them out. Silence stretched out into minutes and I tried not to think of anything but my muscles relaxing beneath his hands. No rough, brutal hands. No threatening feet. No carrion birds staring down at their prey.

"If I ever decide to quit the department," he said finally, "I think that I could make a damned good living as a masseuse."

"Mmm," I said, sighing in agreement.

"My daddy," he said by way of explanation, "had a stroke earlier this year. Left him partially paralyzed. That's why I moved back home. To make sure he has someone there… Not that I do all that much, mind you. He's got a fellow who comes in almost every day to help him out and a physical therapist visits once a week. The therapist—a black gal with a smart mouth and muscles that would make a pro wrestler jealous—keeps him doing his exercises right. She does massage therapy, too. Really seems to help him. So I learned enough to pitch-hit between appointments."

Beneath his touch, the ache through my neck and shoulders diminished. Efficient, caring and compassionate, I thought, considering some of Anthony Beauprix's more positive attributes. And it didn't hurt that he was easy on the eyes.

Underneath his probing hands, I lay relaxed, warm and unresisting. I'd had lovers in college and, less frequently, in the years I'd worked for Uncle Duran. Though Beauprix sat on the other side of the sheets and his hands strayed no farther than the space between my shoulder blades, I doubted that I'd ever been with a man whose foreplay was more potent.

"Do you do this sort of thing often?" Beauprix asked.

I started, wondering for a moment if his question had anything to do with a fantasy about a virtual stranger smoothing his oh-so-gentle hands over sensitive areas of my body. Then I turned my head, took a quick look at his face and realized that the question was professional interest.

Just as well.

"If, by 'this sort of thing,'" I said in the direction of the pillow, "you mean getting beaten up and dropped in a gutter, the answer is no."

As I spoke, Beauprix's hands had stopped moving. They lay passive against my body, heavy, warm and much too tempting. I stretched, shifting slightly from beneath his touch. Immediately, his hands fell away from me and he tugged my sweatshirt back into place. Then he moved back into his chair and poured himself another cup of coffee.

After I crawled up from the blankets and sat up against the pillows again, I rolled my shoulders and turned my head experimentally.

"Nice," I said, pleased by the results.

He touched two fingers to his forehead, moved them outward in an informal salute. Then his face grew more serious.

"From what Tinh said… This sort of thing…" Beauprix stopped speaking, reorganized his thoughts, tried again. "What I mean is, being attacked like this *isn't* business as usual for you, is it?"

At the suggestion, I pressed my lips shut, rolled my eyes.

"Uncle Tinh is proud of me, so he tends to overdramatize. I'm good at what I do, but I'm no Hollywood-style secret agent. My job is more a matter of keeping my eyes open and my mouth shut than getting my butt kicked."

He looked vaguely disappointed and, perhaps, a little relieved. Counterproductive, I thought, if he began underestimating me. Perhaps a little drama wasn't all bad.

"Though, I will admit," I said slowly, "there have been a few uncomfortable moments. Last month, I was in the desert, trapped in an abandoned trailer with several dozen illegals. I had my doubts, but we all lived."

Rosa, her infant daughter, and her husband were now living legally in New York City. A bonus from Uncle Duran for a job I'd done well. At my insistence, he'd pulled a few strings with the INS.

"And, a couple of years ago," I continued, "I leaped from a fire escape while trying to evade a couple of Chicago's finest, and I broke my arm."

Beauprix's eyes widened.

"Yup. Breaking and entering. There had been rumors of child labor in this sweatshop on Chicago's north side. Turns out they were using kids as young as nine to clean used transformers. Little fingers, it seems, do the best work. Under the best of conditions, it's an unpleasant job. But this place…"

I shook my head, remembering air that was thick with smoke and fumes, and nasty burns from soldering irons that went untreated.

"Anyway, I posed as a child, wore a hidden camera to work every day, made sketches of the men I couldn't get clear photos of, and built a solid case. But I wanted more. There was this woman who never saw those kids. Old family, old money, expensive lifestyle. She wasn't the type to get her hands dirty, ever. But she knew about the kids and profited by their labor. Didn't seem right. So I made a late-night visit to her office. I was on my way out, up on a flat rooftop, when the cops spotted me. I hid the camera and took off. Figured if I jumped across to the next building, I could use its fire escape to get to the ground. Unfortunately the fire escape wasn't in very good repair. I fell hard, they scraped me off the pavement and I spent a couple of days in Cook County's police infirmary before Uncle Duran fixed things."

Then I grinned at Beauprix, thinking the story would make him laugh. Instead, for the second time that day, he looked at me as if I were something alien. And it hurt.

Chapter 8

The Seventh District squad room reeked of stale coffee, rancid food and dirty sweat socks. The result, I diagnosed, of chronically long hours, mediocre housekeeping and too many male bodies occupying a small space. That morning, the malodorous background was diluted by the buttery scent of bakery-fresh *beignets* and someone's recent, heavy-handed application of aftershave. I was responsible for the *beignets*. I suspected that the heavy-set man with a toupee at the far end of the room was responsible for the Old Spice.

The area was furnished with a disorganized arrangement of battered metal desks, mismatched chairs, multiline desk phones and surprisingly new computer monitors and hard drives. Umbilical cords of coaxial cable, anchored mostly by strips of duct tape, ran from hard drive to monitor and then snaked upward and unsupported to the framework for the drop ceiling. From there, the wires disappeared beneath stained acoustical panels.

On every desk, adjacent to every computer, was some kind of stacked metal tray, shallow cardboard box or rectangular wire basket. Each held well-filled and obviously recycled file folders. The paperless society in action, I thought, recalling the better matched but similarly functional setup in my own office. Then I corrected myself. Like the setup in my former office.

Seven men occupied the space in the squad room. Four, including the guy with the toupee, were white. Three were black. In appearance, the detectives ran the gamut from fit to flabby, from early thirties to fifty-something, and from handsome to dissipated. The styles of their plainclothing ranged from the pages of *GQ* magazine to the resale bins at the Salvation Army.

All but one of the men were staring at me and pretending not to.

Anthony Beauprix was staring at his computer screen.

I couldn't imagine what the others found so fascinating. In deference to my aching body and a sunny, fifty-degree forecast for the New Orleans metro area, I had dressed for comfort. There was nothing remarkable about the worn blue jeans, raspberry-striped white cotton sweater and thick-soled black Skechers that I wore. And I doubted that lips colored with a bit of pale gloss, brown eyes touched with just a smudge of gold shadow and dark hair swept up into a thick twist had transformed me into an irresistible object of desire.

Beauprix's introduction had been casual.

"Y'all, this is Lacie."

He'd expanded on that by waving a couple of fingers in the direction of each desk and giving me a name. That prompted an assortment of waves, nods and "heys." No explanation of my presence was offered or requested, which, I suppose, left them to speculate about whether I was Beauprix's lover. In the males-only atmosphere of the Seventh District squad room, I couldn't imagine them thinking I was anything else.

I ignored the looks, sat beside Beauprix's desk in a chair that was upholstered in cracked leatherette, and watched the screen as his fingers pecked rapidly at the keyboard. We spoke quietly, our voices mixing with the ringing phones and the drone of other conversations in the squad room.

"Ah, this is what I wanted you to see," he said, pointing at a line. "Look here. Assaults." Another tap on the keyboard changed the screen image. "And here, under armed robbery." He pointed again, then scrolled down. "And here. Crimes against property."

Individually, the numbers were unremarkable. Taken together, they went beyond statistical probability. And now I understood what Beauprix had meant the day before when he'd described the crime rate in the area of the murders as odd.

"Technology in action," he continued, tapping the screen of his monitor for emphasis. "Crime is mapped by type and area, with stats updated weekly. The public can get the numbers through the city's Web site. Cops have access to better breakdowns, more details. If you crunch the numbers and graph the stats…"

Beauprix paused as, once again, his fingers flew over the keyboard and pulled up a graph. It was enough to pick out a dramatic plunge in reported crimes in early spring.

"Little Vietnam is maybe two miles square. And for months, except for spontaneous stuff like domestic violence, vandalism, a few minor drug busts, and some prostitution, there's been no crime. A hundred-plus businesses. Maybe nine thousand residents. And no crime."

"No *reported* crime," I murmured.

He nodded.

"Right. Which only makes sense if—as Tinh maintains— a gang has recently moved in and is putting the screws to the community."

As we were speaking, the guy in the toupee had made his way across the squad room to the water cooler. On his return trip, he lingered near Beauprix's desk, looking at the monitor. Apparently disagreeing with my unspoken reaction, the detective went from surreptitious listening to actively participating in our conversation. He took a few steps over to stand behind Beauprix's chair, bringing with him the strong smell of aftershave and the accents of backwater Louisiana.

"Anthony telling you about his theory? Our district commander, he thinks your friend here is... What was his exact word, Anthony? Oh, yeah. Obsessed. 'We ain't got enough crime in N'Orleans,' he say to Anthony. 'You ain't got enough work on your desk? Now you worrying about crime not happening?' You look like a smart girl, eh, Lacie? And you're one of them. Anthony don't believe Remy, but maybe he listen to you. I been telling him for weeks that your people don't make no trouble for cops."

No, no trouble at all, I thought sarcastically. At least, not for the past six months in Little Vietnam. And I wondered if Remy had ever heard of the Born To Kill gang. That group of Vietnamese thugs that had ripped through America's underworld in the 1990s, giving even established organized crime like the Chinese tongs and the Italian mafia something to fear.

But before I could say anything, Beauprix leaned back in his chair and flashed his colleague a smile that was all teeth and no humor.

"Don't you have something important to do? Somewhere else?"

Remy took the hint and sulked back to the other end of the squad room.

"There's no one better than Remy for grabbing onto an idea and chewing at it until he gets results," Beauprix said to me. Then he shrugged. "His blessing. Our curse."

I smiled, understanding.

"I worked with someone just like him a few years back. Different city, different accent, similar attitude." Then I asked him a question that, thanks to Uncle Tinh, I already knew the answer to. "Do you have someone inside the Little Vietnam neighborhood? A snitch? Someone undercover?"

He shook his head.

"If I'd had, it wouldn't have taken Tinh Vu to tell me about a new gang in town. Turns out the department's gang unit hasn't heard a whisper about them, either. Not surprising, I suppose. In places like Little Vietnam, if you're not on the inside, you don't get in. And if you *are* on the inside, you keep your mouth shut. And I'm not even talking criminals. I mean the majority, all those folks who are honest and hardworking and simply don't like cops. Not that they have a corner on *that* market. Hell, if they didn't want anything to do with cops before they immigrated, dealing with rednecks like Remy wouldn't do much to change their minds. So, bottom line is, even if someone in the department was willing to assign the personnel—and no one is—we don't have anyone who can go into Little Vietnam without raising all sorts of suspicions.

"You think the murders are tied to gang activity," I said, my tone making it a statement.

"It makes sense, doesn't it?" he said as he nodded. "That kind of brutality could silence an entire community, especially if they're not predisposed to working with the police."

"But the only way you're going to find out for sure is to have someone on the inside who's willing to talk."

"That's what I told Tinh over dinner at City Vu the night I asked him for advice. I don't think *he's* an insider, but he's well respected by the Vietnamese. I was hoping he might know someone, maybe make the right phone call, twist the right arms.... That's when he told me about you and I made that expensive—and damned stupid—bet."

It was then that I flashed Beauprix the same predatory smile he'd shown Remy.

"Then I'd better make sure you get your money's worth," I said.

He didn't say anything in return.

* * *

"Frankie and Johnnie's," Beauprix said immediately when I suggested lunch and asked him to choose a place. "Ever been there?"

I shook my head and he smiled.

"I think you'll like it."

He had picked me up at the hotel that morning, so we used his car to drive from the station. As we drove, I got the impression something was very much on his mind, but he didn't seem interested in talking about it and I didn't press him. Except for a few nods in the direction of landmarks I already knew, the only real dialog Beauprix had was with the drivers sharing the road with him. He cursed the snarled traffic under his breath, making occasional suggestions about particular drivers' skills and parentage, but he refrained from hitting his siren and moving the portable red flashing dome to his dashboard window. And, although he shook a cigarette out of the pack and placed it between his lips, he didn't light it.

I sat beside him, enjoying the show, unperturbed by the traffic. Though I kept my opinion to myself, I judged New Orleans's drivers and the eccentric, inefficient layout of its roadways to be no worse than D.C.'s. About thirty minutes later, we ended up at the Riverbend, on Tchoupitoulas at Arrabela Street, and Beauprix parked the car.

The atmosphere inside Frankie and Johnnie's was noisy, informal and hung with the smell of seafood and frying. As Beauprix and I waited for our food, his attention was briefly drawn to a ball game playing on the bar's TVs. The Cubs were winning and Beauprix nodded and laughed out loud at the disparaging comment that came from a knot of Tulane students. All around us, sitting at the crowded bar and tables, was a cross section of the city rarely seen by tourists—people in business attire, guys who parked their hard hats on the bar beside them, uniformed New Orleans Transit System workers, a pair of cops who Beauprix waved to as we came in and a scattering of family groupings.

The menu offered local food fried, boiled or simmered; it was supplemented by a specials board that included boiled crawfish, seafood chowder and turtle soup. Beauprix and I each ordered Dixie beer and a fried oyster po'-boy. Beauprix had his "dressed," New Orleans shorthand for tomato, lettuce and mayonnaise. I asked for mine plain.

As we waited for the food, we talked about Little Vietnam.

Beauprix had told me that he had been a regular visitor even before the murders. That was one of the reasons he'd noticed the odd crime stats and had made a connection between the murders that no one else had. Back in his rookie days, he said, he had walked a beat in Little Vietnam and still occasionally returned for the food and the shopping. He found the people to his liking—just like Tinh Vu, they were warm and hardworking. But unlike my uncle, the residents of Little Vietnam couldn't see a friend or an ally in the face of a white cop.

"No matter how hard I try to win their trust," Beauprix said, sounding frustrated, "they keep me at arm's length. Most everyone is polite and friendly, but when we talk, their smiles never reach their eyes. That attitude was inconvenient then. But now, damn it, it's costing people's lives."

It was then that I told Beauprix I intended to go undercover in the Vietnamese community.

He was less than enthusiastic.

"I don't see that you have an alternative," I said after we'd argued a bit.

Briefly our conversation was interrupted by the arrival of our food. My crusty French-bread sandwich was stacked high with oysters. I mixed horseradish, ketchup and hot sauce into a cocktail sauce and drizzled the oysters with it, then picked up the overstuffed sandwich with both hands, considered the best angle of attack, picked out an edge where an oyster was threatening escape, and took a big bite. The bread crunched and broke beneath my teeth, giving way to a moist, tender interior and a burst of juicy flavor. I chewed happily for a moment, then swallowed.

"You asked for help and now you have it," I said, still holding my sandwich in both hands.

For no particular reason, I noticed that the slate-colored shirt that Beauprix wore made his hazel eyes appear almost khaki green and that his dark hair had some gray in it. Then I recalled our near-silent ride across town.

"If there's something on your mind, let's hear it," I said.

Beauprix followed my lead, focusing on taking a few bites of his sandwich before answering me. But he managed to scowl as he chewed. Finally he put his sandwich down on its plate and proceeded to tell me why he didn't want me to do my job.

His overprotective male aspect was obviously in full ascendancy, I thought, and I didn't waste my time arguing with him. I just kept eating slowly, enjoying the delicious sandwich, letting the crunch of the bread in my mouth break up his words.

"…too dangerous…no back up…can't allow it…another way…against policy…irresponsible if I…"

Finally he ran out of steam. Or so I thought. I put my sandwich down, took a sip of cold beer and returned the bottle back onto the table. I was about to tell him what I thought when he started up again.

"Yesterday, at the morgue, you helped me, helped this case," Beauprix said. "You confirmed what I *felt*, gave me something more substantial than a hunch to go on. But there was nothing dangerous about you looking at that kid in the morgue. I should have stopped things right then."

He reached across the table and put his hand on top of mine.

"Lacie, you're smart and perceptive and you know your

stuff. And, hell, it doesn't hurt that you're pretty. I wouldn't mind spending more time with you. Professionally. Or personally. But there's no way I'm going to let you risk your life for me."

I stared at him, taken off guard by his touch, his admission, my body's reaction to it. But, unlike Anthony Beauprix, I wasn't about to let my emotions get in the way of my better judgment. Or doing the work I was committed to.

"I'm not doing this for you. Even with Uncle Tinh's information, how long will it take you to identify members of this gang? And gather enough evidence, enough witnesses, to bring charges against them?"

"I'll go to my superiors with the information I have. I'll keep at it, keep pushing them, talk to Tinh again. I'll find another way…."

"If Uncle Tinh is right—if this gang is also responsible for the three murders—how long do you think it's going to take before they kill again?"

He opened his mouth to argue, but I stopped him by pulling my hand from beneath his and pointing to his sandwich.

"Be a pity to waste that," I said.

His eyes searched my face, spending a moment apparently trying to read my thoughts and evidently not succeeding. Then he picked up his sandwich.

I waited until he had a mouthful of food before I spoke again.

"I'm going to do this," I said quietly. "You can help me. Or you can cut me loose. With no backup. No support. But I'm a civilian, I'm not breaking any laws and, bottom line, you can't stop me. Besides, the risk to me is minimal. I speak the language. I have the skills. I can look the part. Like it or not, Anthony, I have a perfect cover."

That was something Uncle Duran was fond of saying just before sending me on another undercover assignment.

"I know you can do this," the senator would say, usually

as he chewed the end of an expensive cigar. "For me, for your country, for these helpless people. But most of all, Lacie Reed, I want you to do this for yourself. You have the skill and the talent to do this job. Like it or not, your greatest gift is a perfect cover."

After his decision to give up smoking, Uncle Duran rarely lit his cigars, merely persisted in waving them around when he felt passionately about something. Not so Anthony Beauprix. By the time we stopped arguing, the cigarette pack was out of his pocket again and he smoked two in a row.

Later, Beauprix dropped me off on Magazine Street between Jackson and Napoleon. There, I spent the rest of the afternoon shopping, relaxing and making a point of not looking over my shoulder for men in feathered masks. A random act of terror, I kept telling myself. Although instinct kept telling me otherwise.

New Orleans's "street of shops" had everything I needed to buy for the next day's undertaking and many things I simply enjoyed looking at. I went into thrift stores, antique stores and dollar stores, and carried packages out of a few. A quick late-afternoon cup of coffee at PJ's and I was back in my room at the Intercontinental long before sunset.

Except for a quick trip to the front desk to retrieve an envelope sent over by Uncle Tinh, I didn't leave the hotel for the rest of the day. Then I gave myself the gift of self-indulgence. I took a leisurely bath, ordered a late dinner from room service, watched the local news and went to bed.

That night I slept deeply and dreamed that I was running through the narrow alleys of the French Quarter. As I ran, I glanced repeatedly over my shoulder. And though there was nothing behind me but darkness and empty streets, an overwhelming sense of dread spurred me forward. Thunder rumbled and crashed, and suddenly it was raining. But instead of droplets, black and red feathers fell from the lightning-ripped sky.

* * *

The next morning I showered, had a room-service breakfast and began packing. Except for a handful of toiletries and my hair dryer, I folded all of my clothing into the pair of suitcases I'd checked in with. After adding my briefcase and purse with most of their contents to the largest of the suitcases, I closed and locked each lid.

Then, for modesty's sake, I wrapped myself in the folds of one of the hotel's voluminous terry bathrobes and I phoned the front desk. I asked them to send a bellhop to my room. When he arrived a few minutes later, I sent him away with a generous tip, my baggage and instructions to store my belongings until I returned.

After locking the door behind the bellhop, I shed the robe, wrapped myself in a towel instead and went into the dressing room where the tools of transformation awaited me. I spent a few minutes considering my reflection, then picked up a pair of scissors.

Tommy, the boy at Uncle Tinh's restaurant, was my fashion inspiration.

I chopped off my hair, holding it out from my head in long, thick strands and sawing everything off to a three-inch length. Then I dipped into the bag of rubber bands and used them to gather my hair into uneven clumps all over my head. That done, I pulled on a pair of disposable gloves, readied my comb and a roll of cellophane wrap, and got artistic.

Within the hour I had towel-dried my hair, applied a hair product that looked and smelled like thick white glue, spent a few minutes with the hair dryer and tiny, metallic hair clips and stared in the mirror at the results. My head was now capped with poorly accomplished spikes of matte black, magenta and pink hair. Some slicked-down bits were anchored with the high-contrast silver clips.

Nasty, I thought, smiling at my reflection. But not nasty enough.

I smoothed on a thin layer of foundation in a shade that was just off enough to muddy my complexion, then laid on eyeliner and mascara with a heavy hand. Thin wire earrings hung with a few red beads and a cheap earcuff completed the look.

Then I stepped back from the mirror again. Better, I thought, and briefly considered having my nose or tongue pierced to enhance the look. Decided against it and, instead, applied lipstick in a color that did not exist in nature and slicked on nail polish in a shade of badly bruised.

As I waited for the polish to dry, I sat in the desk chair with my feet on the bed and considered my strategy. I needed a job. Something low level and unremarkable that offered lots of public contact. Then I would immerse myself in the environment and see what developed.

Thirty minutes later I bent my fingers over my palm, examined my nails, brushed a fingertip lightly across the palm of my hand to test the nail for tackiness and judged the whole lot to be dry. That done, I dragged several overstuffed plastic bags from the closet and dumped the contents into the middle of the bed.

My trip to the Salvation Army thrift shop had given me lots to choose from. I selected a pair of faded flared-legged jeans, pulled on a skimpy black tank top that was decorated with a pink rhinestone heart and pulled tight across my full breasts, threaded a wide macramé belt thorough the waist of the jeans and topped the whole outfit with a lightweight army-surplus jacket.

On the off chance that someone might actually catch a glimpse of them, I'd traded out my expensive underwear for the discount store's best black sleazy stuff. For comfort's sake, I'd kept two pairs of my own shoes—the black, round-toed and thick-soled Skechers and a pair of gray-on-gray New Balance cross-trainers. I spent a little time with sandpaper and the tips of the scissors making the Skechers look worn. The sneakers were a favorite pair and already looked worse for the wear.

I put the Skechers on, stepped in front of the full-length mirror mounted to the closet door and looked myself up and down. There's a fine line between a teenage girl trying to look grown-up and a hooker working on a Lolita look. I vamped in front of the mirror for several minutes, shot myself wide-eyed looks, sullen stares and shy glances, and decided I'd definitely stepped over the line into hooker. I considered the problem and then resolved the issue by scrubbing my face, going a bit easier on the eyeliner and mascara, and blotting my lipstick to a lighter shade. Finally, I put on another black tank top, a size larger than the original.

Good, I thought, looking at myself again. I was the kind of girl a sixteen-year-old boy like Tommy could fall in love with.

Except for the rhinestoned shirt, which I discarded in the wastebasket, I jammed my remaining wardrobe into a beaten-up Samsonite suitcase with a duct-taped handle. A thin leather belt took the place of its sprung locks. Tucked inside its lining was two hundred dollars' worth of twenties. Part of Uncle Tinh's delivery to me at the hotel. I added a pair of binoculars, a powerful little flashlight and my set of illegal picklocks to the suitcase.

The rest of the items from Uncle Tinh went into a beaten-up black nylon backpack that was waterproof, with adjustable, padded straps that could be comfortably slung over a shoulder. Into its zippered interior pocket, I tucked a slip of paper with an address on it and almost fifty dollars in cash, small bills and loose change. Finally, I added a new drawing pad, an assortment of pencils and a small pocket knife to sharpen them with.

Then I turned my attention to the denim purse I'd left out on the bed. It had frayed edges, metal studs and looked as though it had been attacked by a bottle of bleach. I bulked its soft sides up with items essential to a teenager: makeup, comb, styling gel, chewing gum and tampons. I carried no gun, no ID, no checkbook. Any of those risked blowing my cover.

For a moment, even though I had promised I would carry it with me, I considered leaving my cell phone behind. But even in the hands of a runaway teenager, a cell phone would be unremarkable. A risk only if it fell into the hands of someone who was already suspicious about me. Besides, it was easy to conceal and, if necessary, easy to discard. And it didn't fail to occur to me that a piece of technology smaller than the palm of my hand was the lifeline between who I was and who I intended to be.

Chapter 9

Weighed down by the blue suitcase and the black backpack, I left my hotel room and walked down the long, carpeted hallway to the elevator. As I passed by a couple just leaving their room, I noticed that the gray-haired woman reached back to the closed door, testing the room's security by giving the knob a quick tug. The house detective, who spotted me stepping out of the elevator, trailed me through the lobby. The cute blue-eyed doorman, who had held the door and smiled at me throughout my visit, now regarded me with the same narrow-eyed suspicion that the house dick had. He didn't offer to flag me a cab.

I hadn't, anyway, intended to take a cab where I was going. Instead, I walked to the bus stop on Canal Street, waited a few minutes for the No.66 Express to pull up, and paid the exact fare with quarters scrounged from the bottom of my purse. Lurching from the bus's movement away from the curb, I made my way to the nearest pair of empty seats, slid in next to the window and put my suitcase between me and the aisle.

For forty-five minutes, I watched the traffic and scenery beyond the window as the bus took me along I-10, past the levee that holds the waters of Lake Pontchartrain away from the lower-lying city center, and "over the high-rise," into New Orleans East. The area was a patchwork of marshes and canals, railroad yards and shipping berths, heavy industry, a variety of shops and business, and residential areas. Housing included everything from high-density to single-family to fishing resort, and the residents ran the economic gamut from ultra-wealthy to absolutely poor.

The bus crossed the bridge over the busy Inner Harbor Navigational Canal and then, for a time, the elevated roadway of I-10 passed over a no-man's land of heavy industry and forsaken marshland. The place where the bodies of three residents of Little Vietnam had been dumped.

In the distance I could see the towering quayside cranes swinging out to move containers from ship to shore and from shore to ship. The rectangular containers—some of them more than fifty feet in length—were stacked like building blocks on ships and barges for transport across oceans and along the Mississippi. On land, the containers moved across the North American continent loaded onto flatbeds to travel by rail or dropped onto wheels to travel the roadways as the trailer portion of a tractor-trailer rig.

I couldn't help but wonder if some of the containers I could see from my window hid desperate immigrants. It was a problem the INS was fighting at all the nation's large port cities. People risked death to come to America by ship, promising future earnings to pay as much as seventy thousand dollars in travel debts. Once in the U.S., many found themselves enslaved by those who had purchased the immigrants' debt-bondage contracts from the smugglers. A handful of forged documents were the prize—often unobtainable—for servitude in sweatshops and the sex industry. I couldn't believe my kindly Uncle Tinh could be involved in any aspect of this heartless business.

* * *

Just past Downman Road, where I-10 jogged northward toward Slidell, the No.66 left the interstate and continued east on Chef Menteur Highway. To the north was a narrow corridor of businesses and residences that followed the contours of Lake Pontchartrain. To the south, lightly populated marshland and Bayou Bienvenue.

At the midpoint was Little Vietnam.

Uncle Tinh's information after dinner on Friday had supplemented my scant knowledge of the neighborhood. Thanks to the resettlement efforts of the Catholic dioceses of Louisiana and the chronic vacancies in an apartment complex near Chef Menteur Highway, Vietnamese refugees had been added to the eclectic mix in New Orleans East in the mid-1970s. From that start, the neighborhood had grown into an island of Vietnamese language, tradition and culture.

The house where I would be living was off of Chef Menteur Highway, in a swampy, low-lying area too far from the bustling shops on Alcee Fortier Boulevard and the neatly kept residences on Saigon Drive to be considered desirable by almost anyone. Uncle Tinh had offered the place to me when I'd telephoned him from the hotel and outlined my course of action.

"Perhaps, *chère,* you can make good use of my associate's home," Uncle Tinh had said. "His renovation plans were, uh, interrupted when the state of Louisiana provided him with other accommodations. He gave me keys for safekeeping."

I'd thanked my uncle but told him I needed only the address, not the keys.

"Be careful, Lacie," was all that he said before he disconnected.

When I called Beauprix with the address, he, too, urged me to be careful. But only after arguing with me about my choice of neighborhood.

* * *

I stood on the cracked sidewalk with my suitcase at my feet and my backpack slung over one shoulder and looked past the weed-ridden yard to a structure obviously suffering from decades of neglect. A Greek revival cottage—two-story frame construction with a porch supported by twin pillars at the front.

The derelict building seemed perfect for my purposes. A teenage runaway would need a place to live and would be unlikely to have the resources to do anything but squat. But I didn't want to spend my nights fighting off high-demand pimps, desperate thieves or crack-addicted roommates. All this house needed was a bit of breaking and entering to make my residency seem authentic.

Unlike much of Little Vietnam, this area of New Orleans East had not benefited from prosperity, hard work, housing demand or urban renewal. For a couple of blocks in every direction, it looked like a war zone. Houses spotted the street, separated from each other by lots filled with the remains of collapsed structures and abandoned cars. A few of the less dilapidated structures might have been inhabited, but it was impossible to tell what lay behind the boarded-up windows.

Running down the center of the street was a wide median strip that New Orleans natives called neutral ground. In some areas of the city, it was a pleasant island planted with trees and flowers and spotted with benches. Here, the remains of a bench poked out from beneath a mound of vines, dead limbs lay on the bare, muddy earth beneath the parkway's few tall trees and drifts of garbage acted as a magnet for stray dogs. From where I stood, I could see—and hear—two scrawny brown mongrels fighting halfheartedly over something that looked like a dead rat.

I glanced up and down the street, looking for movement, wondering if anyone was watching me from behind some torn shade, ragged curtain or through the cracks of a boarded-up window. This didn't seem like the kind of block in which one wanted to appear helpless, out of place or abandoned on a front doorstep. And not because there were well-intentioned neighbors watching out for each other's welfare.

The front porch had a surprisingly intact waist-high decorative wrought-iron railing enclosing its sides. In the front, on either side of the entrance, half a dozen red clay pots were clipped to the interior of the iron railing. They were filled with soil and sprouted very large, very dead, plants. Between the tall oleander bushes, I could see that a sturdy-looking wooden lattice surrounded the space beneath the porch. But the half-dozen steps up to the porch sagged dangerously and about half the boards seemed to be missing from the section of floor between the steps and the front door.

I decided not to go in that way. Instead, I picked up my suitcase, went around the porch, tucking in close to the house as I walked along a packed-dirt driveway bounded by a thicket of overgrown oleanders and a six-foot tall kudzu-covered fence. The drive ended at a garage whose collapsing roof had trapped a derelict car inside, an overgrown yard and a back door with an overhang that sagged so badly that someone of average height would have had to duck to avoid hitting their head. I simply glanced upward and worried.

I dropped my suitcase and backpack beside the back door, spent a minute examining the lock and smiled happily when I discovered that this one was cheap and ill-considered. Hadn't the owner heard of double-bolt locks, I wondered, and celebrated that he hadn't. It made my job easier.

A few minutes searching among the pile of junk and construction rubble in the backyard yielded a hefty piece of iron pipe and a rusted wire coat hanger. Ignoring every skill I'd ever learned about breaking in and leaving no trace, I smashed in one of the eight-inch square, smoked-glass panels at the top of the back door. Tiptoeing to reach in through the broken window, I used the hanger to fish for the lock, snagged it and gave the hanger a tug. A satisfying click and I was able to turn the exterior knob and push the door inward.

I shut the door behind me, twisted the useless lock back into place and then turned and breathed out a slow, appreciative whistle. The beginnings of a ruddy sunset reflected brightly off the glossy black-and-white-tiled floor, white countertops and tall chrome-and-black kitchen stools. I stayed in the kitchen long enough to discover that the gas was on and the electricity—if the wall switch next to the back door was any indication—was off. There was hot water and a working oven and range. No phone, which didn't matter because I had my cell phone. The pantry, in the form of the cabinets and a brand-new matte-black refrigerator, was very bare.

Nice, I thought, and was briefly concerned. Anyone following me home would be hard-pressed to believe that this house was available to a squatter. Worry vanished as I stepped into the next room. Wall-to-wall drop cloths covered the floor and makeshift scaffolding divided the scarred walls at a point halfway up to the twelve-foot ceiling. The room smelled of damp plaster and mildew, and as I walked through ankle-deep tendrils of old wallpaper several enormous roaches scuttled noisily for cover. At the end of the room, I pushed through a doorway hung with overlapping translucent plastic sheets and then stopped short, convinced that a thoughtless misstep would be disastrous. An obstacle course of splintery lath, jagged chunks of plaster and broken two-by-fours bristling with nails lay before me.

With all my possessions in tow, I picked my way carefully through the debris to an open staircase to my left. The steps were uncarpeted and steep, and the absence of handrails made the climb treacherous. The fall wouldn't kill you. Maybe.

As I'd walked through the house, I'd noted the location of each door and window. Then I paused on the small second-floor landing, looked down over its unguarded edge to the rubble-covered floor below and considered what I had seen

In contrast to the flimsy lock on the back door, the windows on the first floor were all barred. Leaving the back door and front door as the only way in. Or out. But, though my imagination had offered the possibility of feather-masked men in every shadowy corner, there were no closets or human-size nooks where an attacker might hide. On the first floor, I was vulnerable to a surprise attack only when entering a room.

Renovation had not found its way upstairs. Blessedly, neither had demolition. The single door from the landing opened into a large bedroom hung with pale blue floral wallpaper that had been popular in the 1950s. An ancient gas heater made me grateful for the moderate October weather. The only light source besides the pair of guillotine windows that flanked the bed were dozens of candles. Melted and cooled wax had bound the varied sizes, shapes and colors into mounded sculptures on the tops of the mismatched dresser and nightstands. But the room was clean and nothing scuttled for cover as I crossed the bare wood floor to drop my suitcase in the center of the double bed.

I recrossed the room to investigate what I thought must be a closet despite the solidity of the door. At once, my imagination suggested that a masked man might lurk inside. Such thoughts were a reasonable reaction to trauma, I knew. I'd probably be fighting them for weeks to come. But that didn't keep me from being irritated with myself. Ignoring the slight increase in my heart rate, I yanked the door open.

And was greeted by birds. Dozens of them. Singing in the treetops beyond the house. Feeling a little foolish, I stepped through the doorway onto a long, narrow balcony. As I walked its length, my right shoulder brushed against the house's solid wood exterior and my left hip was just inches from a low wrought-iron railing crumbly with rust. Immediately below me was the driveway.

From the second-floor walkway, I could see past the kudzu-covered fence. Separated from me by a vacant lot was my nearest neighbor—a long, single-story shotgun double house supported by concrete blocks that lifted it above the damp earth. Trees—some whose trunks were five or six inches across—had grown, unchecked, from beneath it. Gaping holes replaced every window and the roof was collapsed in several places. I suspected the place was abandoned.

The balcony ended half a dozen yards from the bedroom at an ornate cypress door at the rear of the house. It had no exterior lock and opened into a large bathroom—an architectural afterthought oddly separated from the rest of the house and completely inaccessible from the first floor. Twilight crept in through a louvered, porthole-style window placed high on the wall overlooking the backyard. The weak light revealed facilities of 1920s vintage—a pedestal sink, a tall, narrow toilet and a claw-footed bathtub. The only modern innovation in the bathroom was a wholly inadequate aluminum hook-and-eye latch on the inside of the door. As I made use of the facilities, I wondered at the priorities of those renovating the house.

I returned to the bedroom, then checked all the drawers in the room. Except for a box of strike-on-anything stick matches, which was what I was looking for, they were empty. I spent a moment turning on my heel, examining every angle of the room. Once I was inside this room, I thought, I was safe. The thick cypress bedroom door with its heavy iron bolt and the solidly locked windows would discourage any unwanted guests. And when I slept, I could block the door out to the bathroom by jamming a chair beneath the knob.

Later, I promised myself, I would make a quick reconnoiter of the immediate neighborhood and "make groceries," including an extra flashlight and batteries, at the GNS Food Store back on Chef Menteur Highway. But right now, with time and daylight to spare, I took my sketch pad from the backpack, tucked it under an arm and unlocked one of the huge windows. Surprisingly, it moved easily in response to my gentle tug and rolled smoothly upward. I stepped through the opening onto a tiny vine-covered balcony that overlooked the street.

I sat cross-legged so that my presence was hidden by a leathery-leafed vine, settled my sketch pad comfortably against my knees and, from that vantage point, I watched the neighborhood around me. I listened to the traffic and occasional voices, heard the mournful whistle of trains from the nearby tracks, hummed along with a radio someone had turned on loud inside a distant house.

For a while I thought about the danger inherent in the task I was undertaking, carefully separating genuine danger from irrational fear. Would I be better off armed? I asked myself. I was a good shot and practiced frequently, so my competence was not at issue. Over the years I'd judged the danger of some assignments significant enough to carry a gun and risk exposing my identity.

I'd assured Beauprix that, if I maintained my cover, I would be in little personal danger while I was in Little Vietnam. In fact, if the attack on Bourbon Street was *not* random, disappearing into a new identity would take care of the threat. So until the situation warranted it, I would resist arming myself.

With that issue decided, I began to draw. At first, I drew to confront my fears. Quayside cranes looming like hungry predators. People trapped and dying among the containers stacked on the dock. Two men in feathered masks running along a darkened street.

As my mind drifted outward and my body began to relax, I moved beyond fear. I drew the face of the mixed-blood teenage girl I saw when I looked in the mirror. A shock of spiky hair angled over one of her dark eyes and she was sticking her tongue out at me. And I realized that, despite the punk look, she was very pretty.

Then I worked on a portrait of Anthony Beauprix as he'd looked in the moment he was staring down at the body of

Nguyen Tri. Before I began, I closed my eyes, recalling the sights and smells of the morgue, gradually focusing on his expression. It was not until I could see the slightest narrowing of his eyes, the set of his mouth and the tension that stretched and hardened his facial muscles that I began to draw. I struggled to capture his grief, determination and frustration, and the cold, clear anger that bound it together.

In the end, I turned the page, still dissatisfied by my work. There was something about the man, some complex emotional depth, that I'd seen and knew I hadn't captured. I'd revisit that drawing, I thought, until I got it right.

One last sketch, I thought, remembering that I'd promised myself that I'd draw the boy in the restaurant kitchen as a grown-up. Silly, but it was the kind of challenge that would take my mind off Beauprix's portrait.

I began with basic bone structure and built from there, projecting Tommy a few years into the future, leaving the tired eyes but building on the personality that could produce a winning grin.

I glanced up at the sky, gauging the fading daylight, then down at the drawing again. My pencil froze as my breath caught in my throat and I stared at the page, wondering if I'd just seen what I thought I had.

Family resemblance is a curious thing. Like a magician's trick. Now you see it, now you don't. Mannerism or genetic trait? Family feature or racial characteristic? A father's nose or wishful thinking? Illusion or reality?

Now you see it, now you don't.

For a moment I had seen it. Maybe. And maybe I now understood the sadness I'd seen in Tommy's eyes. I turned to a blank page, once again drawing Tommy's face. But this time I removed the personality that animated his features. Drew him silent and motionless, without wild hair, pimples or piercings. Then I recalled another face I'd drawn. I held that face in my mind and overlaid it on Tommy's.

By the time I was certain of what I had seen, the sun had set. I sat on the balcony in darkness, no longer able to see the pencil marks on the tablet. But I didn't need to. I'd already compared Tommy's boyish face, feature by feature, to a face distorted by violence and death. And now, there was little doubt in my mind. Tommy, whose last name I didn't know, was a close relative of Nguyen Tri, the boy I'd seen in the morgue. A cousin. Or a brother.

For all the information he'd given me, I wondered why Uncle Tinh hadn't told me that.

Much later that night, I phoned Beauprix. It was a call I'd agreed to make every night for as long as I worked undercover. We'd agreed upon that procedure over the remains of fried oyster po'-boys at Frankie and Johnnie's.

"Maybe when you work for Duran Reed, it isn't necessary," he'd said, though he'd sounded as if he doubted it. "But here? In New Orleans? With me? No. That's not how I do things. I'm not a big believer in solo acts. Or in unnecessary risk. Mostly, I don't like worrying about my friends. Or going to their funerals."

Friend, apparently, was a category I fell into. Though I wondered if he mothered his other friends so unmercifully, it cost me nothing besides a small scrap of my independence to do as he asked. And it was, to be honest, comforting to know that help—his help—was only a phone call away.

"I'm settled in," I said when he answered his phone. I confirmed my new address and told him enough about the house to amuse him, not enough to horrify him. "Tomorrow, I find a job."

We spent a few more minutes saying nothing in particular and then said good-night.

Chapter 10

On Monday morning the streets of Little Vietnam were already crowded with shoppers. I walked slowly down one block, then up another, reading store signs and shopping center marquis emblazoned with the flowing letters of my native tongue. Viet My Grocery. Thanh-Xuan Beauty Salon. Dr. Nguyen Nghiem, Dentist. Tran's Automotive. Bao Ngoc Jewelry.

I wore the outfit I'd chosen the day before. Jeans, tank top, torn and faded khaki jacket. Now, wrinkled from the bus ride, it matched exactly the image I was trying to project. With every step, with every sign I read, I let my adult personality drift away and encouraged a teenage girl to bloom within me.

I told myself that Vietnamese was the language I spoke at home. But I preferred to speak English because it was important to me to fit in, to be like every other American teenager. I wanted to belong. As I walked, I held my chin high. But I was careful not to make my stride confident. I was an inseure teenager pretending to be secure, a half-caste unsure of ny identity, a frightened runaway trying not to appear too oung, too poor or too desperate.

Uncle Tinh had given me a list of businesses that were rumored to have drawn the unwanted attention of an extortion acket. Though I continued to question his motivation for assing the information along, I had no doubt that his "rumors" were fact.

It would have been easier to get a job at one of the businesses on the strength of Uncle Tinh's recommendation. But nat would have required an explanation that, at the least, aised suspicions about who I was and why I might be there. And why someone such as Tinh Vu would make the suggeson.

"These people are afraid and that makes them cautious," Uncle Tinh had told me. "I know that the business leaders in ittle Vietnam respect me, but as for trust? Yes, they come to ne rather than the police but, in many ways, I am as much n outsider as you or Beauprix. My wealth, my business, my iends—all are tied into the French Quarter and the city, not ne Vietnamese community. But I assure you, *these* businesses are worthy of your attention."

Most of the places on his list were located along Alcee ortier, a few along Chef Menteur Highway. I memorized the ddresses, then made sure that the haphazard route appropriate to a teenager unfamiliar with the area would take me past ach location. I walked from shop to shop, reading any job otices—these, too, written in Vietnamese—that were displayed on bulletin boards, behind plate-glass windows or ped onto the backs of cash registers.

I needed a job I could get on my own merits. Rather, on ne merits of my teenage alter ego. Preferably one with significant public contact that didn't require skills that I didn't ave and couldn't quickly learn. My plan was to first apply or jobs that were advertised by the businesses on Uncle

Tinh's list. Failing that, I would go into those shops and try to cajole them into hiring me for some menial task like running errands or sweeping up. If that didn't work, I'd try to get work at an adjacent business.

I walked past a restaurant and a florist shop and, though the restaurant was on Uncle Tinh's list, neither store was advertising for help. Beyond them was a souvenir shop that was on the list. There was a Help Wanted sign in the window.

As I opened the door, the music of a Vietnamese pop vocal group surrounded me. I listened to the lyrics, bobbed my head in time to the rhythm as I wandered through the narrow aisles, looking at the merchandise. The tall shelves were stacked from ceiling to floor with items chosen to catch tourist's eye. Bins of painted silk fans. Tiny paper parasols used to decorate tropical drinks. Six-inch-long finger traps woven from flexible bamboo. Hollow red seeds containing tiny elephants carved from bits of bone. Dragon flags. Piggy banks. Lacquered boxes. And masks. Lots of masks. Hanging from hooks on a section of wall covered with pegboard. Among them were two styles of feathered masks. Black. Crimson. Twenty-nine dollars and ninety-five cents each.

The price of terror, I thought. But masks identical to these were hanging in shops all over New Orleans. They were cheap, vaguely exotic and probably sold by the thousands in the weeks preceding Halloween and Mardi Gras.

A long glass display case on one side of the store was filled with figurines carved from exotic woods, gold and silver jewelry, and a clutter of items that looked and were priced as if they were antique. The cash register was located at the far end of the case and was flanked by an abacus. A wizened Vietnamese man with thin gray hair and a scraggly moustache was dusting some of the items inside the case. When I approached, he put down his feather duster and smiled politely at me.

"May I help you?" he said in English.

"I would like to apply for the job," I replied in Vietnamese, just to let him know I spoke the language. I said the words loudly to be heard over the music. Then I continued in English. "I am a good worker."

The shop owner seemed to find that amusing.

Smiling broadly, as if at some private joke, he walked out from behind the counter and gestured for me to follow him. A door at the rear of the store opened into the warehouse. From where the old man and I stood, I saw that sturdy shelves reaching to the twenty-foot ceiling flanked the walls and held boxes of all shapes and sizes. Shrink-wrapped pallets, also stacked high with boxes, filled the open bay. A yellow fork-lift was parked halfway between the shop and the large over-head door at the rear of the warehouse.

"Job is carrying boxes, driving forklift, lots of lifting," the shop owner said in English. He patted my arm. As he delivered the sad news, he managed to suppress his chronic cheerfulness, adopting an expression that a funeral director would have envied.

"Job needs strong man, not tiny girl."

Briefly, bitterly, I wondered what it would be like not to be underestimated because of my size or gender. The answer that came to mind almost immediately twisted my lips into a grudging smile. Potentially fatal, I thought, given my line of work.

The shop owner saw my expression, looked relieved and flashed me a toothy grin. And it occurred to me that he'd been expecting me to cry.

"Baker across street need help," he offered cheerily as he slipped back behind the counter.

The bakery was on Uncle Tinh's list. I waited for a lull in traffic, then sprinted to the opposite side of the street. Past the wedding cake on display in the bakery's front window, I could see that a job notice was taped to the back of the cash register.

I went inside, pointed at the notice, and the young woman behind the counter called out for the baker. A squat, muscular man with salt-and-pepper hair and pockmarked cheeks immediately emerged from the back room, dusting his floury hands on his apron as he walked.

After the young woman explained that I wanted the job, he stared at me for an uncomfortable minute, then muttered something to the woman. She went scurrying into the back room as he came around the counter to stand in front of me. He was already scowling.

He doesn't like my hair, I thought. I'd already discovered that my spikes of black, magenta and pink drew occasional frowns of disapproval from strangers who passed me on the street.

But the color of my hair wasn't the issue.

"You say you're Vietnamese?"

He spat out the question in English and I replied more moderately in the same language.

"Vietnamese-American," I said, my accent appropriate to a girl born and raised in Louisiana. "But I speak English and Vietnamese. And I can work as many hours as you need me."

"Your father was a black man," he said. His tone made it an accusation. "An American GI."

What was true for Lacie Reed was not true for the girl with brightly colored hair.

"No," I said. "He wasn't a soldier."

But the baker was no longer listening. Though he was looking straight at me, his attention seemed to have turned inward. His dark eyes were unfocused and his mouth began to twist into a scowl. For a moment, I feared he would strike me.

His eyes snapped back onto my face.

"No job. Go away."

"But—"

"You heard me, daughter of a whore. No job. Get out, *bui doi*."

Impossible not to feel the pain of the childhood taunt. But that pain was Lacie's, so I allowed nothing but surprise to show on my face.

The baker grabbed me by an arm, pushed the door open, threw me out of the shop. The door slammed behind me.

Unbalanced, I fell forward. Lacie Reed would have rolled with the momentum and sprung back onto her feet, unscathed. But a teenage runaway was unlikely to have that skill. My fall was clumsy and disorganized. Unfortunately the impact was a little worse than I had anticipated. The rough concrete side-walk tore through the worn cotton of my jacket and scraped the skin off one of my elbows.

I got to my feet slowly, holding my elbow away from my jacket as I groped through my purse for a tissue. The pedes-trians walking along the sidewalk detoured around me, their steps quickening, their eyes averted. The sight of a stranger's blood now brought with it the specter of AIDS. And people, anyway, didn't like to get involved.

A man's voice speaking in Vietnamese immediately con-tradicted that conclusion.

"Do you need help, little sister?"

I turned to look into a male face that was fine-boned and almost pretty—smooth golden skin, almond eyes ringed by long lashes, a straight nose and full lips. He wore a tiny dia-mond stud in his right ear and was undeniably sexy in his white dress shirt and tight jeans. He was taller than I was by a good half foot, and I guessed that he was older than Lacie Reed by a decade; older than my current alter ego by two.

Just then, my searching fingers located a tissue and I spent a moment blotting my elbow and working tears into my eyes. When I could no longer see clearly, I looked back at the man, who promptly handed me a clean handkerchief.

"Here. Use this for your eyes," he said.

I took the hanky, quickly wiped my eyes and handed it back to him.

"Thank you," I said, managing to sound sullen.

Was he simply nice? I wondered. Or did he have an agenda? Like most big cities, New Orleans was a dangerous place for runaway adolescents. Here, a homeless girl was a magnet for pimps and pervs.

"Tell me what's wrong."

It was more command than request and even someone far more secure than a runaway teenager would have had trouble ignoring him. If this pretty boy was into victimizing little Asian girls, I thought, I would sure as hell put him on the cops' radar screen. So I kept talking to him.

"I asked for a job," I said in English, overlaying it with a home-girl accent and allowing my very real anger to work itself in between my sniffles. "The baker called me *bui doi.* Like that means something to me. He said my father was an American GI. As if! My dad died working on a oil rig when I was five. That senile old man. He's living in some other world."

The man lifted my chin with the tips of his fingers.

"You were born here."

I ignored the overly familiar gesture and answered him.

"Of course I was. Do I look like some refugee? Do I *sound* like one? People see slanted eyes, brown skin, they think foreigner. Stupid. I'm an American. Red, white and blue. Born in Baton Rouge."

His fingers dropped away from my chin.

"I've never seen you around here."

I concentrated on the pulse at the base of his Adam's apple as I outlined the past I'd fabricated for myself.

"My new stepfather's a stinkin' fisherman. I hate boats. I hate fish. And I hate him. He doesn't much like me, either. Except when my mother's not watching. Then the bastard tries to crawl into my bed. No way I'm going to go for that. So I hopped on a bus. Ended up here. Figure I'd have a better chance at getting a job...." I let my voice waver, then pumped it up with a burst of bravado. "I'm an artist. A good one. I was going to get a scholarship. For college. Everyone says I'm creative."

At that, the man's eyes traveled from my eyes to the multicolored mop I'd created and back.

"I can see that," he said, keeping a straight face.

"But leaving home pretty much screwed that," I said. "Maybe I'll get my GED. That's for later. For now, I need a job. To eat and stuff. Get it? I thought, maybe, the bakery. I can count change. And I'd be good at cake decorating. Then that stupid man…"

"Have you asked for a job there?"

He pointed to the opposite side of Alcee Fourtier Boulevard, in the direction of a glass-fronted restaurant I'd passed as I'd walked to the souvenir shop.

I shook my head.

"I went past it. No sign in the window."

"I know the owner. He needs a waitress."

Perfect, I thought, though I wondered why he was telling me about the job. I fell into step beside him and we jaywalked across the street, standing briefly in the middle, waiting for the traffic to clear. We paused again at the restaurant's entrance, this time because the stranger grabbed my arm.

"My name is Ngo. Vincent Ngo. What's yours?"

"Lai Sie Johnson," I said. "But my friends call me Squirt."

He grinned, released my arm and held the door open for me.

"Well, Squirt, I hope we can be friends."

Here it comes, I thought, wondering if this too handsome stranger would offer me a place to stay. Or, maybe, ask me to a party to meet some special friends. Or, perhaps, suggest a modeling gig because I had such exotic good looks. Runaway girls from bad home situations were particularly vulnerable to "genuine" suitors offering protection and love. From there, it was a fast descent into forced prostitution.

"I work down the street at the Refugee Center," he said, "trying to find people jobs."

I almost laughed. Not a pimp. A social worker. Who just happened to be teen-idol gorgeous. Not for the first time, I realized that over the years I'd been working for Uncle Duran I'd grown cynical and overly suspicious of any unexpected kindness.

I stood just inside the door as Vincent Ngo talked to the owner, a small man with a round face and a full head of snow-white hair. Ten minutes later I was the newest waitress at the Red Lotus Restaurant. Two-fifty an hour, plus tips. No proof of citizenship or social security number asked for or offered.

Chapter 11

The Red Lotus was a Vietnamese greasy spoon that served as many meals at its long, Formica counter as at its dozen tables. The food was decent, cheap, plentiful and definitely home cooking if you were raised Vietnamese. The blue-on-white teacups, bowls and plates were stained and chipped, and anyone who wanted to eat with utensils that were not stainless steel or disposable bamboo brought their own chopsticks. Except for occasional tourists, the customers spoke primarily Vietnamese.

The restaurant was a family affair. The owners, Mr. and Mrs. Yang, cooked, waited tables and kept the accounts. Mrs. Yang's elderly male cousin chopped the vegetables, washed the dishes and mopped the floors. The Yangs' twin teenage daughters worked as waitresses after school until 9:00 p.m. They also worked all day long on Saturday.

Twins, apparently, ran in the Yang family. I was the temporary replacement for a married daughter who, I was told, was the mother of a three-year-old and also very pregnant with twins. The eldest daughter, Mrs. Yang assured me, was a very hard worker. A judgment that Mrs. Yang was very well qualified to make.

The daughter's shift—now mine—was from seven in the morning until four in the afternoon on the weekdays. On Saturdays, I worked from 9:00 a.m. until the restaurant closed twelve hours later.

I remembered that Uncle Tinh, too, had worked long hours at his storefront in Evanston. Often, I would visit his restaurant after school and, if I didn't have homework, help with prep work for the evening's meals. I would sit on a stool at the cleared counter and chatter with my uncle as I helped snap tough stems from mountains of pea pods or folded hundreds of thin *hoanh thanh* wrappers around spicy bits of meat. Uncle Tinh always took Sundays off. When I was young, he and I went to church together, driving along the lakeshore into Chicago's near north side to attend one of the few Catholic churches in the city where Mass was said in Vietnamese.

The Red Lotus also closed on Sunday.

"The Lord's day," Mr. Yang told me. The Yangs, like many South Vietnamese, were devout Catholics.

Mrs. Yang, as was her custom, expanded on her husband's cryptic statement. When she spoke, she used pudgy, energetic hands—that matched her pudgy, energetic body—to illustrate her words.

"Sunday is day of rest. We go to church…"

She folded her hands in imitation of prayer.

"…clean house…"

A sweeping motion here.

"…buy groceries and visit grandchildren."

From her gestures, I understood that grocery bags were heavy and the grandchildren were very young.

"…and get ready for the next week," Mrs. Yang said finally.

Rest, I thought, had never sounded so exhausting.

* * *

It wasn't until midafternoon that I had time to think about anything besides waitressing. And that was thanks to the latest task that Mrs. Yang had assigned her new employee. As I washed the lunch counter with hot bleach water, I reviewed what I knew and what I didn't, and considered where I was going from here.

Three people had been brutally murdered in a city where brutal murders were not uncommon. But because I had seen the bodies, I had no doubt about what Beauprix had long suspected—the same person had committed all three murders. The murderer's rage was focused on the victims' hands and, based on the strength required to inflict the injuries I'd seen, odds were that the killer was male.

I finished the length of the counter and paused.

Why the hands? I asked myself. That, I didn't know.

"Lacie!"

Mrs. Yang's voice. Again.

As I turned toward her, I suppressed a sigh. And I made Squirt's expression wide-eyed and eager to please.

Mrs. Yang flipped her fingers at the bucket of wash water, then swept her hand in the direction of the tables that filled the main area of the restaurant. Finally she wiggled the first two fingers on her right hand in a gesture I'd already learned meant "move faster."

Careful not to slop water, I shifted the bucket to the nearest table. For the briefest of moments I thought about what my hands were going to look like by the time I left Little Vietnam. Then I plunged my hands and the rag back into the steaming water and wrung it out.

As I scrubbed the tabletop, my thoughts returned to the murders.

Beauprix and Uncle Tinh each pointed to Little Vietnam as the place where information about the murders—and possibly the murderer himself—could be found. Beauprix's suspicions had been triggered by the sudden drop in crime in Little Vietnam. Uncle Tinh reported that a criminal gang had invaded the small community. Contradictory information unless *reported* crime was down as a result of a gang tightening its control over the people in Little Vietnam.

I moved on to the next table.

Had the brutality of the murders been aimed at intimidating the entire community? I asked myself. Were the victims random, linked only by their residence in Little Vietnam? Or was there something they had in common that made them targets, something the police had missed? Something only an insider could know?

My job at the Red Lotus would quickly make me an insider. At the very least, I would be considered too young and too menial to be a threat to anyone.

I moved so that I was working within earshot of the only customers in the restaurant—a Caucasian couple dressed in business attire. He had paid the check and she had shaken her head when I offered to refill their teapot. Now, they were deep in conversation. I wiped the table nearest them, bent to wipe some imagined stickiness off one of the chairs and eavesdropped long enough to discover that they needed to be particularly careful because his wife was talking about divorce but had no proof…

I moved out of earshot.

Again and again, I plunged the rag into the bucket, gave it a quick twist to wring out the excess water and scrubbed another table. By the time the last one was done, Mrs. Yang was smiling her approval and I had a focus for my undercover work.

Just as I had in Mexico, I would identify the criminals and gather specific details about their activities, beginning with the extortion racket in Little Vietnam. If Uncle Tinh was correct, such an investigation would lead me to the reasons for the murders. And, perhaps, the murderer. But I didn't kid myself. I was not a cop. And now that I no longer worked for Uncle Duran, I had no authority, no credentials….

I steered my thoughts away from renewed uncertainty about my future, back to today's plan of action. I would provide Beauprix and the N.O.P.D. with the information they needed, but it would be up to them to break the gang's stranglehold on Little Vietnam and to bring a murderer to justice.

Except for the jungle of potted plants that flourished in the heat and light and partially blocked my view, the restaurant's broad plate-glass window was ideal for watching the busy sidewalk and street beyond the Red Lotus. Between taking orders, picking up plates and bowls full of food from the serving window that linked the kitchen to the dining area, delivering food to the customers and cleaning up, I kept my eyes on the window. I watched the traffic passing by—pedestrian and vehicular.

Certain vehicles quickly became familiar. Some passed by early in the morning every morning—people on their way to work, kids getting dropped off at school, folks who stopped at the bakery across the street for pastries and coffee. Cars and delivery vans belonging to shop owners and employees parked in many of the metered spaces along the busy street. Other vehicles became familiar simply because they drove by often throughout the day. I memorized makes and models and—whenever I could—license plates, creating a list of cars and schedules that grew longer with every day that passed.

I also drew people with an eye, once again, to those who were regular customers or frequently walked past. Because of the restaurant's busy schedule, I held each day's faces in my memory and moved them to paper at night. Using the candles in the bedroom, I sat in the center of the surprisingly comfortable bed and drew quick studies of customers or passersby who had caught my eye.

Some of the sketches I made were the basis for more thoughtful portraits. I drew the Yangs, including the twins and the elderly cousin. Family, I thought, united by love and blood and ambition.

I created a portrait of the baker, who pretended not to see me when I served him his food; his eyes were sad and I wondered about his experiences during the war. I drew the nervous fish vendor, who seemed to know that her clothing reeked of the seafood she handled; she never lingered at the restaurant to eat but scurried away with her daily carryout order clutched in bony hands. And I sketched the face of a woman of about fifty whose hair hung raggedly over most of her face; she never spoke and her eyes were focused on some faraway scene. Shell shock, Mrs. Yang explained, and we never charged her for meals.

Each day, the hours at work passed quickly. Before I knew it, it was late afternoon and the Yangs' two younger daughters would be coming in through the front door. The pair made a point of responding to my daily greeting with silence and matching frowns of disapproval. Then they would tip identical noses upward, stalk past me to tuck book-filled backpacks beneath the counter and march into the kitchen. I would always continue waiting on customers as the twins greeted their parents and the elderly cousin, pulled their glossy dark hair back into thick braids and slipped on big white aprons over blue Catholic school uniforms. Finally, they would emerge from the kitchen, scowl at me, and that was my signal to go home.

On Wednesday, my third day of work at the Red Lotus, I was once again washing down the counters and tables. It was late afternoon and, at the moment, there were no customers in the restaurant. So I was hurrying to complete the task before anyone came in.

Mr. Yang was on his stool behind the cash register, counting dollar bills and facing them all in the same direction. The important job of counting the receipts was his exclusively.

I looked up from washing one of the tables when he called my name.

"Finish. Then we talk," he said.

My first thought was that he intended to fire me. Though I'd been scolded once or twice about daydreaming as I stared out the window, I was generally a hard worker and couldn't imagine why I deserved firing. But I could think of no other reason that Mr. Yang would want to converse with me.

I had discovered that he was as abrupt as Mrs. Yang was gregarious, rarely speaking more than a few words to me in the space of a day. Communications between us were generally limited to a pointed finger or a nod in the direction of a task. As was appropriate for a male of Mr. Yang's generation, he spoke to his wife or to the elderly cousin if he needed to tell me something more complex. It was left to them to pass on his comments, which is why I knew he'd noticed that I liked to look out the window.

A few minutes later I'd finished cleaning and stood behind the counter just a few feet from Mr. Yang. I waited politely as he ran a quick total on a hand-size calculator. Beside the cash register was the money he was counting.

Mr. Yang hit the total button on the calculator, made a noise in his throat that I interpreted as approval, and put a number in the final line of the deposit slip. He put the slip on top of the bundle of cash and rubber-banded it all together. Then he swung his stool a half turn and handed the money to me.

My eyes widened with genuine surprise.

"You take today's deposit to the bank," he said.

As he described the location of the bank, I worried about my cover. Was there a problem with the persona of Squirt, I asked myself, that Mr. Yang had been able to look past my bright hair, odd clothing and age to see someone he could trust? The bank might only be a block away, but the loss of the lunchtime receipts to a dishonest employee would devastate the little restaurant. Maybe, I thought, Mr. Yang simply understood teenage girls.

"More responsibility for good employee," he was saying. "Maybe, next month, a raise."

I sincerely hoped that I wouldn't be here that long, but I nodded my head, unsure of what else to say.

"Little Vietnam is very safe," Mr. Yang continued. "Very protected. But do not be careless."

Unlikely that Mr. Yang would tell me who, exactly, protected Little Vietnam. But I asked him anyway.

"Protected?"

I'd caught him off guard.

He hesitated, his eyes darting around the room, landing anywhere but on my face as he worked to come up with a good answer. After a moment he pointed at a lighted niche mounted on the opposite wall, overlooking the dining area. In it was the Infant of Prague, a baby-faced statue of a standing Christ child. No more than eighteen inches tall, the statue's porcelain body was dressed in lace-trimmed red satin. A heart and a cross hung from jeweled chains around its neck and a gold crown topped its golden curls. A globe of the world was in its left hand; the right was lifted in a blessing.

I had knelt many times in front of similar statues in Catholic churches in Saigon and Illinois. Each time, I lit one of the dozens of votive candles that were arrayed at the statue's feet. And always I prayed that my real father would find me.

Inside the Red Lotus, there was no candle to light, no childish petition to make and no faith to be devastated.

"Jesus protects," Mr. Yang intoned.

But I doubted he provided the kind of practical, on-the-streets protection Mr. Yang had mentioned. That was usually achieved by handing over a percentage of profits.

I raised an eyebrow, looked disbelieving. But Mr. Yang was apparently done answering questions. He swung his stool around, took a copy of the weekly Vietnamese language newspaper out from a shelf beneath the cash register and spread it out on the counter.

"Thoi gio la vang," he said without looking up. Then he repeated the old proverb in English. Just in case, I suspected,

someone of my generation might not understand. "Time is money."

His attention remained on his paper as I tucked the deposit deep into my apron pocket, waved to the elderly cousin as I stepped briefly into the kitchen to grab my jacket from a peg in the utility closet, backtracked through the dining area and headed down the street.

As promised, the short walk to the bank was uneventful.

During my first week in Little Vietnam, I spent my evenings becoming familiar with the neighborhood. I walked and shopped along Alcee Fortier Boulevard, Dwyer Road and Chef Menteur Highway. I mingled with tourists and residents, looked in shop windows and wandered through stores. I bought groceries, treated myself to ice cream and Vietnamese pastries, thumbed through racks of clothing and bought the kinds of inexpensive items that would catch a teenage girl's eye. I wanted those who lived and worked in Little Vietnam to become familiar with my presence, to see me as someone who belonged in the neighborhood, too.

Then I strolled along streets like Saigon Drive, Henri, Cannes and Lourdes. In old New Orleans neighborhoods bordering the Mississippi River, statues of the Virgin Mary were traditionally faced toward the levees with hands outstretched, symbolically holding back the floods. But in Little Vietnam, religious statues dotted manicured front lawns and were surrounded by flower gardens. Children played in fenced yards and snatches of conversation drifted from patios and porches and open windows. I strolled along the streets like the teenager I was supposed to be—a girl apparently going to or from a friend's house.

My intent each night was to observe the environment in which I had placed myself. Patience was essential to understanding the community's normal patterns. Persistence was key to revealing anything that deviated from those patterns.

Instinct and luck would, I prayed, put me in the right place at the right time.

Each night after I returned home and settled in for the night, I phoned Beauprix to check in. One night, I chatted with him as I drew the butcher, who I'd seen for the first time that day. Beauprix didn't seem to be in any hurry to hang up, so I told him about the man I was drawing.

"He looks like a storybook villain," I said. "He's a giant by Vietnamese standards. Well over six feet tall and large. Not fat, just big. He has scars on his face, a crooked nose and un-even teeth. When I first saw him, he reminded me of the leg-endary Raksasa, who carries away maidens."

"Best be careful, little girl," Beauprix said. "Else he'll eat you."

I laughed at the suggestion and, much to my surprise, found that I was more touched than offended by being called "little girl."

"Only if I'm covered in crushed hot peppers, which he shakes in a thick layer on all his food. Besides, he's in love with the owner of the florist shop next door. She's as pretty as he is ugly, which sounds like another fairy tale, doesn't it? Today, when she was having lunch, he brought in a basket-ful of newborn kittens for her to see. She likes him, too."

I drew the butcher with one of the kittens cuddled against his cheek and, on the same page, started a sketch of the lady who owned the florist shop. She had glossy hair, a bow mouth and sculpted eyebrows that winged out over chocolate-brown eyes.

After we stopped talking and just before I blew out the can-dles and slept, I drew Anthony Beauprix. Partly because on sev-eral occasions I'd noticed him walking or driving past the Red Lotus. But mostly, I admitted to myself, because I liked the man and because there was nothing more isolating than work-ing undercover. And I warned myself that my feelings were based on nothing more than a little lust and a lot of loneliness.

* * *

By my fourth day of work at the Red Lotus, I was certain that something odd was going on around me. There was a palpable tension in the business community. I saw it not only among the Red Lotus's customers, but observed it on my evening walks. Those who owned or operated businesses along Alcee Fourtier seemed particularly fearful. They were quick to startle and I noticed their eyes darting toward windows and doorways when they spoke to each other. Spontaneous laughter was often cut short, as if humor was somehow unacceptable. A failing economy might have explained the atmosphere, but business was booming in the little community. Unfortunately, my perceptions didn't solve or prove anything. Undoubtedly, Beauprix's coworker, Remy, would quickly judge me delusional.

That afternoon, I saw Tommy again.

In a lull between customers, Mr. Yang had set me to cleaning the inside of the plate-glass window. When the young man walked past, I was balanced on a chair, holding a bottle of cleaner in one hand and a wad of newspaper in the other. I was, at that moment, attempting not to add droplets of my own blood to the tiny red flowers of the Crown of Thorns. The plant—Mrs. Yang's favorite—had overflowed the bulbous ceramic pot on the ledge and climbed up a corner of the window almost to the ceiling.

I saw distinctive pink-and-blue-streaked hair through a screen of barbed, woody branches and ammonia-streaked plate glass and recognized Tommy even before he paused. He did a classic double take and turned an acne-reddened face in my direction.

As we scrutinized each other through the window, I noticed the same careworn face and tired eyes that I had in Uncle Tinh's kitchen. But since I'd seen him last, he'd added a piercing above his right eye. Now two small silver balls, connected by a slim silver post that slid beneath his skin, framed his dark eyebrow, top and bottom.

After a moment's staring, he backtracked to the door.

For a moment I feared that somehow he'd seen through my disguise. If he came in asking why Tinh Vu's visiting niece was working in a place like the Red Lotus, I would be hard pressed to provide a reasonable answer.

He pulled the door open, setting off the jingling bell that alerted the staff to customers, and leaned into the restaurant, his feet still outside on the sidewalk. Mr. Yang looked up briefly from a Vietnamese-language magazine, then ignored the youngster to go back to his reading.

I had worn a short black skirt and a tight double-knit red top to work that day, and Tommy's eyes made the trip from trim ankles to outrageous hair before settling back on my face. Judging from his expression, I decided the only thing he'd recognized was the potential for a kindred spirit to be lurking beneath the ragged cap of black, magenta and pink hair. The quick smile I shot him as I continued rubbing the window with my damp wad of newspaper was inspired mostly by relief.

"Um," he said by way of introduction. He cleared his throat, then added in English, "You're new."

"Uh-huh."

He looked better rested than when I'd last seen him, but there was still a pinched look to his face. As if, despite the rebellious teenager that his bright hair and body piercings suggested, he had matured well beyond his years.

"My name's Tommy," he said.

"They call me Squirt."

"Squirt," he repeated, nodding. "Cool. Well, I've gotta go to work. 'Bye."

"'Bye," I said.

He backed out of the doorway and took off down the street at a jog. I went back to washing the window, but not before I noticed that the elderly cousin had watched our exchange through the small window into the kitchen where I dropped off the customers' orders and picked up prepared dishes. It had taken very little time to discover that he and Mrs. Yang competed to know as much as possible about other people's business. Their willingness to gossip with a harmless girl was an asset that could quickly turn into a liability. Given the tension that seemed to permeate Little Vietnam, I suspected the Yangs would fire me if ever they began questioning my curiosity.

When I finally returned my cleaning supplies to the utility closet in the kitchen, the elderly cousin was busily chopping onions. I stood by his elbow, watching, as I asked the kind of question a teenage girl would ask.

"That kid with the cool hair... Do you know him?" I said casually.

The rhythm of his chopping remained unchanged as he nodded.

"Tommy Nguyen. Very nice boy. He is Mr. Yang nephew."

And I suspected that Mr. Yang's nephew was also the third victim's younger brother. Nguyen Tri's name was arranged in the traditional manner—family name first, then the individual's name. But Tommy Nguyen was all about being nontraditional.

I recalled Tommy's care-worn expression. Was he just a boy in mourning? I wondered. Or did he know why his brother was killed?

"Does Tommy live around here?" I asked the elderly cousin.

He nodded again.

"Kim Drive."

Then the bell above the front door jingled, Mrs. Yang called my name and I ran to wait on new customers.

I called Beauprix as soon as I left work and immediately heard the stress in his voice.

"Is everything okay?" I asked.

"Everything's fine," he said, but from the speed and tone of his reply, I knew it was automatic.

"Okay," I said neutrally.

His deep sigh carried over the phones.

"Oh, hell, Lacie. Nothing's fine at the moment. I just took a fourteen-year-old child into custody for killing her baby. Social services placed them with a relative who apparently left town weeks ago. The girl figured she could handle things on her own and she did. Right up until last night. Then the baby got sick. An ear infection from the sound of it. Baby screamed and cried into the night. Neighbors banged on the walls and finally one threatened to call the cops if she didn't keep it quiet. So the girl pressed a pillow against its face."

Nothing I could say would improve that situation, so I just let him talk. After describing the absolute futility of his job and swearing that it was long past time to quit, Beauprix went on to eventually convince himself that maybe it was all worthwhile.

"Thanks for the advice," he said finally, though I'd done little more than listen and make encouraging noises. "So, how are things going for you?"

I gave him a quick recap, quickly turning to the subject of Tommy Nguyen.

"There's a boy of about sixteen who works in the kitchen at Uncle Tinh's restaurant and lives in Little Vietnam. I think he's the younger brother of the last murder victim, Nguyen Tri. Do you know about him?"

"No, never heard of him. But I didn't interview the family. If there was nothing suspicious about this kid... Tommy... He wouldn't have been mentioned in the reports I saw. Though you'd think that Tinh would have mentioned him." Then a shrug that I couldn't see touched his voice. "Maybe he thought I already knew."

Maybe, I thought. But that didn't explain why he hadn't told me.

It was an indication of how distracted Beauprix still was that, when I asked for Nguyen Tri's address, he didn't ask me why.

Chapter 12

After showering in the house's odd, detached bathroom, I selected a wardrobe appropriate for visiting the house on Kim Drive. This would likely turn into a social call, I told myself, so I dug through the clothes I'd picked up from Goodwill and bought during a wardrobe-enhancing stop at the Salvation Army's resale shop on Chef Menteur Highway. I was looking for an outfit that would impress a teenage boy.

In under a week Squirt's fashion sense, as well as her personality had become second nature. Tonight, I put on a little extra makeup and spiked my hair into stiff points, dressed in trendy jeans and a tie-died top that was tight and cropped. A quick look in the candle-lit mirror and I knew something was missing. Bling-bling, I thought, reminding myself of the current slang for glitzy bangles. I added a strand of red beads, a matching bracelet and dangly earrings. Then I looked in the mirror again, judged Squirt's look to be complete, and frowned at my reflection.

"Sucks to be you," I said in Squirt's best backwater accent, at once acknowledging and dismissing my longing to dress like an adult again.

Before I left the bedroom, I slid my picklocks into my purse. Just in case. Then I made my way through the house to the back door with the broken pane, which I'd replaced with cardboard. I let myself out, popped the cardboard out to reach in and secure the lock, then stuck the cardboard back in place. Silly to think that system would keep out even the most casual intruder, but it did secure the back door against wind and rain.

I never went out through the front door. I was supposed to be squatting, and squatters are notoriously shy. Besides, I didn't have a key. But mostly, I didn't want to be bitten by one of the dogs that lived, very literally, in my own front yard. I'd told Beauprix about the dogs. Warned him, actually. And, in the unlikely event he should ever need to get inside, I described the safest route into the house.

During the day, the dogs were unthreatening. When the weather was clear, I'd seen them sunning themselves in the middle of the street, getting up only to dodge the few cars that cruised down the block. They were a motley pack of strays, medium-size mixed-breed brown and completely unremarkable. Except for a squat one-eyed male with short, reddish-brown fur and a missing rear leg. His attitude marked him as pack leader. His remaining legs were bowed, his right ear was torn and his left was missing, and his tail was docked. When I'd first seen him, I'd recalled an old joke, snickered to myself, and named him Lucky.

Mostly, I was lucky he hadn't yet attacked me.

At night, Lucky and his pack claimed my front porch and the lattice-enclosed area beneath it as their own. The missing boards had provided them access to what was apparently a comfortable den. Every time I passed the porch, I would see reflections of canine eyes staring out from between the arrow-straight branches of the oleander bushes or glimpse furry forms skulking into the shadows at the far corner of the porch.

I'd realized the dogs were full-time residents when I'd come too close to the porch as I returned from a quick look inside the shotgun house next door. I had discovered that it was unoccupied and my own front porch was not. Lucky had growled at me from the other side of the porch's wrought-iron railing, his single eye shining eerily in the shadows. The growl, deep in his throat, was only a few feet away from me and was definitely a warning to stay away.

"You win," I'd said, keeping my voice firm and calm. "The porch is yours. But take one move in my direction and I'll…"

I'd let my voice trail off because the tone was more important than the threat and I didn't, at that moment, have a tactic for dealing with him if he came up and over the railing at me. The self-defense I'd learned, thanks to one of Uncle Duran's many contacts, had focused on using psychological advantage and hitting vulnerable areas hard and fast. As I crossed the driveway to the opposite side, staying close to the fence until I'd reached the backyard, I considered how that advice might be used to advantage against a canine, rather than human, adversary. That yielded no strategy I considered very effective.

So I'd settled on bribery.

Undoubtedly, the elderly cousin and Mrs. Yang felt they were feeding a starving teenager with the stale pork-filled buns they bagged up for me to take home every night. But, in fact, the buns were used to enforce an uneasy truce. And bribery seemed to be working. The one-eyed leader of the dog pack no longer growled at me when I approached the porch to lob steamed buns over the decorative iron railing. He'd actually started wagging his tail when I approached.

But still, I remained cautious. Tonight, as usual, I used only the back door and walked quietly along the far side of the driveway until I reached the sidewalk. There was movement on the porch and I resisted the urge to look back over my shoulder. But from the sounds of nails clicking on the sidewalk, I knew that one of the dogs—probably Lucky—was following me. Fortunately, away from his territory, he'd shown no tendency toward aggression. By the time I rounded the corner, I was fairly certain he'd returned to the porch. I stretched my legs and added a confident bounce to my walk as I headed toward Kim Drive.

The Nguyens lived at the end of the block in a neatly kept two-story that was set back from the street. Between them and the community garden next door was a lush growth of banana trees. It was from there, as I pretended to admire the flowers and vegetables in a nearby plot, that I watched the house. The light was on over the front porch, but there were no cars in the carport.

The blinds on the front windows were open and the rooms inside were lit. From my vantage point, I could see into several rooms. After fifteen minutes, no one had moved inside. No one home, I diagnosed. I looked at my watch and guessed that the family was out for dinner. Or shopping. Or some school activity.

I wandered along the edge of the garden, then along the marshy path that ran behind the Nguyens' backyard. It was obviously a family home, with a tire swing hanging from a big oak tree, a basketball hoop mounted on a pole adjacent to a wide slab of patio and a pink-detailed girl's bike leaning up against the house. Inside a small attached screened porch, I saw a weight bench and a punching bag and recalled how muscular Tommy was. I suspected this was why.

Just above the flat roof of the screened porch was an open window. Good, I thought, nodding when I saw it. It would provide my escape route if the Nguyens came home while I was inside. I went back around to the front of the house but, this time, I walked up the sidewalk to the front door. I had intended to ring the doorbell to ask Tommy if he wanted to hang out for a while. And talk. But an empty house would yield some quick information.

Though I was fairly certain no one was home, I rang the doorbell anyway. I rang it several times, just in case some-one was bathing. Or sleeping. Easier to apologize for ob-noxious behavior than to explain my uninvited presence inside someone's front door. When I was satisfied that no one would answer the door, I slipped the ring of picklocks from my purse and applied one of the thin metal rods to good pur-pose. It wasn't a difficult lock and, though I hadn't practiced lately, it took me only a minute to open the door.

Inside the house and beyond the front foyer, generations of framed family photos were displayed on a wall in the liv-ing room. The oldest, which was black-and-white and faded, showed an elderly woman wearing an *ao dai*—a two-paneled overdress layered over silky slacks—and a man of similar age wearing loose black trousers and a shirt. They stood in the courtyard of a house that reminded me of Grandma Qwan's. Another photo showed a group of young soldiers smiling happily from the open bed of a heavy truck. A jungle was in the background. From more recent photos, I picked out the current Nguyen family group. A mother. A conspicuously absent father. One daughter, obviously the youngest. And two sons. One of the boys was Tommy, the other undoubt-edly his older brother, Tri.

I slipped through the first floor of the house, opening books, reading messages on the corkboard in the kitchen, thumbing through the address book beside the phone. The number for Tinh's City Vu was there, which was no surprise since Tommy worked at the restaurant. But scrawled beneath that was the number for Uncle Tinh's private line and I had no ready explanation for that.

In the mother's bedroom I looked through the closet, pulled out every drawer and checked behind every picture and under every piece of furniture. From the lack of anything masculine in the room, I suspected that her husband was long gone.

I searched all the rooms on the first floor for something hidden, something out of the ordinary. Listening constantly for the sound of a car on the driveway or footsteps on the front stoop, I worked as quickly as I could. And I found nothing. So I went upstairs.

There were three bedrooms, one for each child.

The younger sister's was filled with clothes and books, toys and trinkets, barrettes and chaos. I spent only a few minutes there, handling every stuffed animal and doll to be sure that nothing was hidden inside one. A diary offered little insight into the family, exposing only abysmal spelling and her unrequited love for a boy named Smitty. Only the day before, Smitty had eaten lunch just three seats away from her. But at the same table.

Despite the seriousness of my situation, that made me smile.

Across the hall, another closed door was labeled with bright yellow warning signs emblazoned Tommy and Restricted Area. Inside, the room was a study in contrasts. Silver jewelry and an array of acne medication and hair care products were carefully laid out on the dresser. Books and magazines overflowing from a pair of bookcases were an eclectic mix that included science-fiction, car mechanics and poetry, though the majority were devoted to cooking and math. An intact PlayStation, a dismantled PC and a layer of dust covered the surface of his desk. What looked like homework in progress was spread across his neatly made bed. The space in between his mattress and box spring hid a smutty novel. I checked the pockets of the clothes that hung in his closet and encountered about ten dollars' worth of loose change.

Tommy was an interesting boy, I thought, but I knew that

already. Nothing in his room suggested that he was anything besides what he seemed to be.

When I opened the door at the end of the hall into Tri's room, I discovered a memorial frozen in time, a testament to the love of a family still in mourning. Too easy to believe that Tri might return at any moment to take up his life, to finish the jigsaw puzzle laid out on the floor beside the bed, to put his feet in the athletic shoes lined up in front of his dresser, to wear the jeans and sweatshirts folded into his drawers. I searched his room carefully, located his checkbook and a file full of bank statements and discovered that he didn't balance his checkbook regularly and didn't have a lot to balance. A series of framed pictures suggested that he'd loved the same girl since high school.

Tri's computer, an expensive model with a large screen, was password protected. But the software boxes, users' manuals and books on his shelves yielded their own information and justified the quality of his PC. He had been a full-time college student and was interested in architecture and art. I riffled through the portfolio I found tucked beneath his bed, examined the finished pieces he'd mounted on his walls, looked at the half-finished drawing on his drafting table. He was precise, intuitive and had a good eye.

I took a final look around the room. A college kid, living at home, apparently not into drugs or alcohol. An artist, like me. So what had made him a victim? Nothing I saw suggested an answer.

Noise from downstairs, then voices in the foyer, increased my heartrate and brought a quick halt to my examination of the upstairs bathroom. I rushed back to Tri's room, opened the door quickly and closed it softly behind me, and went out the window. I crossed the rooftop, laid flat and slid over the edge, hung by my fingertips and dropped to the soft ground.

I left the Nguyen's home frustrated.

* * *

Late that night, I called Beauprix again.

I didn't intend to tell him about breaking into the Nguyens' house. I hadn't gained any significant information and, besides, it was better not to unnecessarily challenge his good-cop sensibilities. In fact, there was nothing I had to tell him. Not really.

After returning from Kim Drive, I had locked myself into the bedroom and was now sitting on the edge of the bed, my back propped with pillows, my feet stuck in a big pan I placed on the floor beside the bed.

"I made five dollars in tips today," I said after we'd talked for a few minutes. "And I spent it on epsom salts and candy. Even as we speak, I'm soaking my feet and eating M&M's Peanut."

Beauprix's deep chuckle carried across the connection.

"I like the blue ones best."

"I'll save 'em for you," I said.

"You can trade them for a foot rub."

I couldn't help it. Suddenly, I was imagining his strong hands on the soles of my feet, smoothing over my ankles, his fingers working along the taut muscles of my calves, then slowly upward.... I shook my head, told myself I was being foolish, said a quick goodbye and disconnected.

That night, I ate several packages of M&M's, blues included.

Chapter 13

On Friday morning I added glittering pink gel to my black, magenta and pink spikes of hair. When I arrived at the Red Lotus at 7:00 a.m., the Yangs and the elderly cousin smiled warmly at me as I tied my white apron on over a purple shirt and acid-washed black jeans and went immediately to work.

At just a few minutes before ten, a dozen Vietnamese men came streaming into the restaurant and took seats at the large round table in the corner. I rushed to take a tray from underneath the counter and began stacking it with a pair of teapots and a teacup for each place at the table. That was part of my job, and I was a determinedly hardworking employee.

But Mrs. Yang had surprised me by taking the tray from my hands and walking it over to the table herself. Usually she only helped with the customers if I became overwhelmed. But the other tables in the restaurant were empty and no one sat at the counter. Mrs. Yang waited on this table anyway, and the elderly cousin busied himself in the kitchen preparing food that was not on the regular menu. *Vit nau mang*—stewed duck with vegetables—filled the restaurant with the sweet licorice smell of star anise and the earthy smell of black mushrooms.

After just a week in Little Vietnam, I recognized all of the men who seated themselves around the table. They were all business owners and their ranks included the cheerful owner of the souvenir shop, the giant of a butcher and the angry baker. As a group, the age, manners and dress of the men marked them as "old country," immigrants all. The butcher, who I guessed to be around fifty, seemed to be the youngest man at the table; certainly the oldest was the souvenir shop owner who was at least seventy. About half of the men wore traditionally styled shirts with straight hems untucked over dark trousers.

Though they greeted each other cordially, and a few seemed to be friends, the formality of their interactions indicated that this was a meeting rather than a social event. By 10:05 a.m., all the seats around the table were taken, except for one. The men waited, sipping hot tea. Then white-haired Mr. Yang walked over to the table and seated himself. He tipped his head in the direction of the souvenir shop owner and the meeting began.

As the group talked, Mrs. Yang had rushed repeatedly from kitchen to table and back, snapping directions and waving her hands at me—directing me to prepare another plate of fresh cilantro or to fill more tiny bowls with fermented fish sauce— *nuoc mam*—or with the pungent dark red oil from crushed peppers. She finally relaxed when each of the men pulled ornately carved and silver tipped ivory chopsticks from their sleeves and deep pockets and began eating. Only then did she whisper an explanation to me.

According to Mrs. Yang, there were two businessmen's associations in Little Vietnam. Both groups met weekly at the Red Lotus on Fridays. This one, the Little Vietnam Benevolent Society, met in the morning; the Young Vietnamese Busiessmen's Association gathered late in the afternoon. Though he cautioned me to treat the men from both organizations with maximum respect, she clearly favored the group her husband headed.

A few minutes into the meal and Mr. Yang gestured for his wife to come over to the table. The conversation that took place then involved the heads of those around the table periodically turning in my direction. The souvenir shop owner made a point of smiling at me, the baker scowled and the others managed looks ranging from idly curious to vaguely disapproving.

When Mrs. Yang spoke to me next, she asked, *"Parlez-vous Français?"*

Lacie Reed spoke French and half a dozen other languages. Squirt did not.

I looked up at Mrs. Yang blankly and said, "Huh?"

"I said, do you speak French?"

"Uh, no. Sorry."

Mrs. Yang patted my arm.

"Not a problem."

Then she nodded in Mr. Yang's direction and told me that I now had the honor of watching to see if the gentlemen needed anything.

Earlier, the conversations I'd overheard at the table were in Vietnamese and occasionally in English. Now the men were speaking exclusively in French. But though they believed I couldn't understand the language, the members of the Benevolent Society appeared to be extremely cautious men. I was discouraged from lingering within earshot. On the few occasions that a quick wave of the hand, snapping of fingers or a raised eyebrow brought me to the table, I could catch only snippets of conversation. Most of them irrelevant.

Before they left, each man passed Mr. Yang a red envelope, one traditionally used to give a gift of money. The men's body language supported my theory that this was a ritual, the contributions voluntary. As they relinquished their envelopes, most of the men looked passive, a few seemed resigned. No one seemed angry. Dues, perhaps. Or a donation. Certainly nothing about this suggested protection money.

As the membership of the Little Vietnam Benevolent Society trailed out of the restaurant, Mr. Yang went over to the cash register and put the red envelopes in the drawer.

The lunchtime crowd began arriving. In between taking orders, I considered the significance of the single bit of information I'd overheard during the meeting. Some important shipment would soon be arriving at the Port of New Orleans and would then, within a day, be moved up north to Chicago.

Beginning the first day he'd helped me get a job, I saw Vincent Ngo every afternoon after the lunchtime rush was over. He'd sit at the counter, sip hot tea and eat a bowl of *pho* or the lunch special, then leave thirty minutes later. Though my first day as a waitress and my evening reconnoiter through the neighborhood had left me footsore and weary, I'd taken a few minutes to draw him, easily recreating his smiling, handsome face. As I'd finished shading in around his eyes, it occurred to me that Vincent was younger than he looked. Probably not much older than thirty.

Vincent enjoyed talking and had quickly discovered that I didn't mind listening. Though I learned from Mrs. Yang that he'd never been a regular customer, apparently he was now. So I poured him tea, served him lunch and tried to be a good audience. It was an occupation I quickly discovered Mr. Yang disapproved of. While Vincent was in the restaurant, Mr. Yang found any excuse he could—short of being rude to a paying customer—to keep me busy elsewhere. I quickly became a master at arranging my work in ways that enabled me to pay attention to whatever Vincent had to say.

Occasionally the weekly Vietnamese language newspaper provided Vincent some tidbit worth remarking on. Usually though, he would point out some news item in the daily *Times-Picayune* that was delivered to the Red Lotus for its customers to read. As with everyone I'd talked to and every conversation I'd eavesdropped on, Vincent never spoke about the three murder victims who had lived in the small community. If there was gossip or speculation about their fate, I never heard it. And, although a direct question or some broad hinting might elicit some information, Squirt was a stranger who had arrived in Little Vietnam *after* the murders had taken place. Her curiosity would raise suspicion, and suspicion was exactly what I didn't want.

Today, I had very little time to chat with Vincent.

The members of the Young Vietnamese Businessmen's Association had come into the restaurant shortly after he had and seated themselves at the big table in the corner. There were eight of them, the oldest about forty, the youngest not yet thirty. With their Western manners, conservative haircuts and expensive clothing, any one of them could have eaten, unremarked, in most of the city's restaurants. But their numbers and attitude at the Red Lotus suggested that this was exactly the gang that Uncle Tinh had been talking about.

Thought Vincent looked as though he would fit into the group, he remained at his usual place at the counter when they came in. He made a point of keeping his back to them.

"They're punks," he muttered to me when I'd taken a moment to refill his teacup. "I don't know why you cater to them."

"They're customers," I replied, surprised by his resentment. And I thought that it was possible he was jealous.

Mrs. Yang seemed to feel no obligation to cater to the Young Businessmen. In fact, when they came into the restaurant, she had busied herself with the hazardous task of trimming dead branches from the Crown of Thorns in the window. Once, I caught her glancing in the direction of the men gathered at the large table. Clearly she didn't like them. Mr. Yang remained behind the counter, near the cash register. When he looked at the men sitting at the round table, his face was stiff and expressionless.

Which left me running my feet off.

Besides the members of the Businessmen's Association, there were a dozen other customers, including Vincent, scattered at tables throughout the dining area. All were Vietnamese from the immediate neighborhood. Fortunately the Young Businessmen selected simple dishes from the regular menu and the elderly cousin hurried to fill their order. Though they spoke English and Vietnamese and didn't seem to guard their conversation when I came to the table, I had little time to eavesdrop.

At the end of the meal Mr. Yang sent me into the kitchen while Mrs. Yang continued to work on her plants. As I walked through the doorway, the elderly cousin nodded to someone over my shoulder—I assumed it was Mr. Yang—then told me to keep an eye on some egg rolls that were in the fryer. He walked into the restaurant and began slowly scraping and stacking the dirty dishes that I'd deposited in the bin beside the counter.

Odd, I thought. That was usually my job.

I quickly discovered that if I tiptoed, I could still see the big, round table where the Businessmen's Association was meeting through the serving window. I stood with a set of long bamboo tongs in my hand, my attention torn between the egg rolls and the dining area.

Mr. Yang approached the table and passed two items to one of the Young Businessmen. The first was a rubber-banded stack of red envelopes—the very ones he'd collected from the Benevolent Society that morning. The other was a thick, brown business-size envelope.

The Young Businessman passed the rubber-banded bundle to one of his associates who nodded as he tucked it into his breast pocket. Then, ignoring the other customers in the restaurant, he made a great show of opening the brown envelope and carefully counting the stack of money it contained.

I didn't know why the red envelopes were handed over but this, obviously, was protection money. A bribe that Mr. Yang paid for the privilege of running a business in Little Vietnam. Friday, apparently, was collection day.

Mr. Yang was standing passively beside the table, watching the count.

"Short," the Young Businessman said, loudly and in Vietnamese.

Mr. Yang looked startled.

I couldn't hear his murmured reply, but the Young Businessman's snapped retort carried easily into the kitchen.

"*I* say what's enough. This is not. You are one hundred dollars short."

There was no reaction from the customers throughout the restaurant. Vincent and the others seemed suddenly to have gone deaf. And blind. Public extortion was, apparently, an unremarkable occurrence in Little Vietnam.

Mr. Yang's fists curled as anger touched his face.

"You are dishonorable men!" he said, and his voice trembled.

The Young Businessman who'd done the counting didn't react. But the men on either side of him slipped their hands beneath their suit jackets.

Besides the men at the table, everyone else in the restaurant—including Mrs. Yang and the elderly cousin—seemed to be holding their breaths, afraid to move. I didn't blame them.

I wanted to shout at Mr. Yang, to grab his shoulders and shake him, to tell him not to be stupid. This is not worth your life, not worth devastating your family. Suddenly, I realized how much I'd begun to care about Mr. Yang and his family.

There was nothing about Mr. Yang's expression that suggested he was going to back down. And something about the other man's expression suggested he was looking for an excuse for violence. He was almost smiling.

How could I distract them, give them something more to think about than money? As my mind raced, looking for a solution, the untended eggrolls began burning in the wok in front of me.

There wasn't time to create the carefully controlled fire I'd set at Beauprix's home. For a heartbeat, I balanced the possible risk to the Red Lotus against the very real threat to Mr. Yang's life. That made the decision easy.

I used the bamboo tongs to give the wok a shove, sending hot oil slopping onto the gas burner. Flames whooshed almost to the ceiling. Inside the wok, the egg rolls fueled the burning oil and smoke poured from the stovetop.

"Fire!"

I screamed the word. In Vietnamese or English, it didn't matter. My tone and the flames behind me reinforced my message as I ran into the dining area.

Confrontation forgotten, the Yangs and the elderly cousin raced toward the kitchen, snatching up fire extinguishers and a nearby container of salt, intent on saving their business.

I stood in the doorway between the kitchen and the dining area, monitoring the activity in both rooms. There wasn't much to see in the dining area. All the customers, including the Young Businessmen, had fled the restaurant. The Yangs were apparently expert firefighters and, within a few minutes, had doused the flames.

Then, because I was supposed to be a teenage girl and needed to react like one, I started crying. My eyes were just irritated enough by the smoke that it was easy.

"Sorry," I kept repeating in English. "Sorry."

Mrs. Yang put down the empty salt container she held and walked over to stand in front of me. I noticed that she was not much taller than I was.

"The fire," she said, keeping her dark eyes fixed on my face. "On purpose?"

There was no point in telling a lie I didn't have to.

"Mr. Yang was in trouble."

She nodded, then wrapped her arms around me in an un-characteristic display of affection. I'd never seen her hug her daughters or her husband in public.

"Yes, bad trouble," she said. "But you are good girl."

Then she patted me briefly on the cheek and gave me a gentle push in the direction of the kitchen.

"Everyone clean up. So we can cook."

By the time the kitchen was cleaned up, my workday was almost at an end. I waited impatiently for the twins to arrive so that I could go home. I wanted to phone Beauprix and tell him what I'd witnessed. And I wanted to draw each of the men as soon as possible, knowing that it would require all my skills to make them appear as individuals.

Undoubtedly, I'd discovered the body of the viper. Now I needed to collect evidence, to build a case against them. And to begin searching for the head.

At exactly 4:00 p.m., one of the twins called. I answered the phone, endured a snotty comment, then passed the phone to Mr. Yang. Amazing, I thought, that such pleasant people could have such miserable children. A few minutes later, Mr. Yang hung up the phone and turned to me to deliver the bad news. The twins, it seemed, would be late. And he needed me to continue working. Please.

I could understand why he hadn't insisted the girls come into work when they didn't want to. Certainly I wouldn't have wanted to deal with their temperaments after the trau-mas of the day. And I wondered if he feared, as I did, that one of the Young Businessmen would be back before the restau-rant closed. To collect.

So I stayed.

Mrs. Yang, apparently anticipating the same problem I

had, tucked a hundred dollars in twenties beneath the tray in the cash drawer.

"If they come back," she said to her husband, "you pay. Understand?"

He didn't argue with her.

Chapter 14

Half an hour later, Tommy's arrival offered a welcome distraction from an onerous task. He came into the store, whistling cheerfully, and swung the door open and closed twice so that the bell jangled uncontrollably. Mr. Yang was stacking teacups and plastic drinking cups at the far end of the counter—usually a job reserved for one of the twins—and paused long enough to scowl at the boy.

"Hey, Uncle Yang," he said, obviously aware that he was annoying the man. "You're looking real busy."

I was at the table nearest the kitchen door.

Tommy looked around the nearly empty restaurant, spotted me and grinned.

"Hey, Squirt! Where y'at?"

In front of me were many, many pounds of raw shrimp. No right-minded teenager would appreciate the task of cleaning them all. But that was the job Mr. Yang had assigned to his "very good, responsible" employee. To distinguish me, I supposed, from his less responsible twin daughters.

"Doing okay, I guess," I said, sighing dramatically.

Tommy crossed the restaurant and stood looking at me across the mountain of shrimp. I picked up another one, snapped its head back and peeled off its legs and shell, then deveined it and dropped it onto the large platter at my right elbow. A lot of shrimp was required for crispy rice with shrimp and there was, by far, more raw shrimp on the table than there were cleaned shrimp on the plate.

Tommy ran a hand through his pink-and-blue-streaked hair and whistled despite the ring that looped around his lower lip.

"You've got a job and a half there," he said.

I sighed again.

"The twins," I said darkly as I picked up another shrimp, "have to study. So they'll be just late enough that this job will be done before they come to work."

Tommy laughed.

"I guess that they remembered that tonight's special is *xoi man*. Good to eat, but a bitch to fix."

"You've got that right."

Tommy detoured to the kitchen, washed his hands and returned with another large platter. He sat down opposite me and used the edge of his hand to split the pile of shrimp approximately in two.

"Bet I can finish before you do," he said, lifting a single shrimp by its feelers and waving it in front of me.

I'd wanted an opportunity to talk to him alone and this seemed like a good opportunity to arrange one. Talking to Beauprix could wait.

"Last one done buys dinner," I said.

I grabbed a greenish-brown, thumb-size crustacean body from my pile, slipped an index finger between its two rows of brittle, jointed legs and popped the pale meat from the shell. And the race was on.

Tommy peeled shrimp with the speed and ease of someone who had done it most of his life. Which, given his family, he probably had. But Squirt, too, was a master of the task. It was a skill that Tommy and the Yangs would expect from a girl whose stepfather was a fisherman. In fact, it was a skill learned by a girl whose adopted uncle was a restaurateur.

The twins sauntered in before we finished. I spared them a glance and received pure Vitriol in return. Tommy was a hunk so, no matter that he was their cousin, they clearly didn't appreciate an interloper, especially someone like Squirt. Identical frowns twisted identical faces as they tied identical white aprons over identical high-school uniforms. As I concentrated on the next piece of shrimp, I wished them identical zits on their identically tipped-up little noses.

Then a group of almost two dozen well-dressed women unexpectedly invaded the little restaurant. Mr. Yang and the elderly cousin rushed to arrange several small, square tables into a long, rectangular one. Once seated, several of the women loudly demanded tea and chopsticks even as the twins rushed to provide them. The women's accents placed them in a number of towns, none of them New Orleans, and their petulant voices promised impossible-to-please customers who would inevitably leave a lousy tip.

I couldn't think of a more appropriate punishment for the twins.

Tommy's hands continued moving with a precision born of long hours of practice. As another limp, naked piece of shrimp joined the pile on his platter, he lifted his head slightly to assess my progress. His mound of remaining shrimp was slightly larger than the one in front of me. He grimaced, used the back of his right wrist to rub his itchy nose.

"I think you've got me beat," he said, bending over his work again.

I made sure that my fingers stumbled as they peeled the next few shrimp.

A few more minutes passed.

"Done," he announced, looking up. Then he grinned. Two shrimp still remained in front of me.

"Phooey!" I said good naturedly as I congratulated myself on losing.

Tommy slid the pile of discarded shells into a large stock pot; they would be boiled into a broth that would flavor tomorrow's soup. He took the pot into the kitchen, then returned to pick up one of the mounded platters and showed off by balancing it at shoulder level on the palm and outstretched fingers of one hand.

I followed with my patter held carefully in both hands, hoping that I wouldn't suddenly find myself showered with falling shrimp. As Tommy helped the elderly cousin move the shrimp from platter to a large tray, I rinsed a bleach rag in hot water and returned to the dining area to wipe the table.

One of the women seated at the long table at the very front of the restaurant complained loudly that she could smell bleach. Mannerisms and genetics combined seamlessly as both twins shot me quick glares. I waved and ducked back into the kitchen with my rag in hand.

The elderly cousin was already coating the shrimp with salt and cornstarch. Soon, they—and strips of pork tenderloin—would be fried one portion at a time, mixed in a pungent sauce laden with black mushrooms and poured over deep-fried crispy rice. Delicious, if you didn't already feel a very personal connection with every other piece of shrimp.

Tommy seemed to read my mind.

"Come on, Squirt," he said enthusiastically. "You owe me dinner."

He grabbed my hand and began pulling me behind him in the direction of the back door. From the corner of my eye, I saw the elderly cousin laugh and Mrs. Yang hide a smile behind her plump hand.

As Tommy dropped my hand and held the door to the alley open, he named a truck stop that was a few blocks away on Chef Menteur. As we walked into the alley, he started ticking off items on the proposed menu, investing the words with enough drama to make it clear that Shakespeare's *Macbeth* would be an easy role for him.

"Cheeseburger. Your choice of pickles, catsup, mustard, onions. Lettuce and tomato, if you must. French fries—real thin, crispy ones, my darling Squirt. And a shake. Your choice of flavors."

My mouth began watering.

"We can take my car," he offered.

I shook my head. I knew that the place he'd mentioned was only a few blocks away.

"Let's walk. And enjoy air that doesn't smell of shrimp."

We sat opposite each other on the booth at the front of the diner and watched cars and trucks whiz by on Chef Menteur Highway as we made small talk and waited for our food.

I told him I wanted to be an artist. To be famous.

"But I don't think Squirt's much of a name for an artist," I told him. "But it's a nickname. My real name's Lai Sie." I said it the way Uncle Tinh did. Lie See. And it sounded as Vietnamese as it was. "My dad was Vietnamese. He died a while back."

Then Tommy told me what I already knew, a bit of gossip that the elderly cousin and Mrs. Yang had shared after he'd come into the restaurant to introduce himself.

"My dad ran off years ago. Just after my kid sister was born."

"Did your mom remarry?"

Tommy shook his head.

"You're lucky, then," I said. "Mine remarried and changed our last name to Johnson. The name sucks, just like my step-father. I hate him. I'm thinking of going back to my real last name. Nguyen. Lai Sie Nguyen. It sounds pretty good, don't you think? I mean, it's the kind of name an artist could have."

Tommy took the bait as I had hoped he would.

"Hey, that's too cool," he said. "*My* last name's Nguyen. It'd be a *great* artist's name."

"I figured your name was Yang, like your uncle's," I said. He shook his head.

"Our families are related by marriage. An in-law married to an in-law kind of thing. That's why the Yang twins are always hinting around about me taking them out. Because we're not really cousins. But before I'd go out with either of them, I'd date my kid sister. And there's *no way* I would do that. She's a spoiled brat. A classic Vietnamese-American princess. Give her a few years, she'll make the bitchy twins look like amateurs."

And *that* was the opening I'd been steering him toward.

"I know what you mean," I said. "I have an older brother and two younger half brothers. My older brother's okay, but Jimmy and Luke…" Instead of finishing the sentence, I shuddered. "So it's just you and your sister?"

I tried not to hold my breath. Would he lie? I wondered.

"I had an older brother, too. He was killed last month."

"Jeez, I'm sorry," I said, and then pushed a little harder. "Some kind of car accident, I suppose…"

I reached out, clumsily, to pat his hand. And I *was* sorry. Not that it stopped me from probing an obviously fresh wound. I watched the spark disappear from Tommy's eyes and he seemed to age as the sadness returned to his expression.

Squirt reacted as she was supposed to.

"Hey, I didn't mean—" I said, deliberately stumbling over my words. "I mean, it's none of my business—I mean, you must think that I'm just like—"

I tried to pull my hand back, but he caught it, held on to it.

"It's okay. We're friends, Squirt. So I don't mind telling you."

I deserved the pang of guilt and pure self-loathing that I felt.

"My brother was murdered," he said.

"My God! Why?"

I was watching his face carefully, moved my fingers so they pressed ever so slightly across the pulse on his wrist. I saw a flicker, a movement, the slightest shift in posture that betrayed his willingness to share a confidence. And my every instinct told me that he knew something about his brother's death.

At that moment the waitress arrived with our food.

Tommy pulled his hand away from mine, segued the movement into taking a very full plate from the waitress, and the moment of weakness, his moment of temptation, passed.

"I don't want you to think that Tri was some kind of crook or something," he said once the waitress left. "He was like you. He wanted to be an artist. He was always trying to help people. Especially people just arriving in this country. That's what got him ki—"

He picked up the glass of Dr Pepper he'd ordered and drowned the impulse to share a confidence in a couple of big gulps.

"It's just, well, sometimes bad things happen to people who only deserve the best," he said, firmly closing the door on the subject of his family.

Then he lifted up one of the French fries, which were hot and crispy brown, and started telling me about a potato dish that was the specialty of the restaurant he worked in. Within moments, his enthusiasm for life seemed to return and he proceeded to tell me everything I already knew about the kitchen and food at Tinh's City Vu.

I was, as always, a good audience. I listened carefully, futilely, for any useful information. Then, near the end of our meal, he lowered his voice and spoke conspiratorially.

"Do you know what I really want to do?"

I arched an eyebrow.

"What?"

"I want to be a chef. Not just a cook like my Uncle Yang or the cousin. A real chef. Like my boss, Mr. Tinh. He's my friend, too. I want to train in Paris, learn how to create, um masterpieces like he does. For now, all I can do is read abou it. And sometimes watch Mr. Tinh work. But someday, when I've saved enough money…"

I would mention the boy's ambition to my uncle when had an opportunity, I decided. I owed Tommy that much. As he spoke, I tried to remember if I had ever been so young. And knew that I never had. Post-war Vietnam, the desperate jour ney by boat and the refugee camp had taken that from me Then I recalled the way that Tommy had looked earlier, when he'd thought about his brother, when he'd pulled his hand away from mine. And I realized that he, too, had left child hood behind. For the past few minutes he had simply been revisiting it.

When the check arrived, Tommy went to pay the bill and I objected.

"You won the contest," I said. "So it's my treat."

We argued for a minute, then compromised by paying fo our own meals. Just outside the truck stop entrance, we stood for a few more minutes and I turned down Tommy's offer to walk me home. The highway noises made it difficult to hear so we leaned in close to each other as we talked.

"I had a great time," Tommy said finally. "A really grea time."

Then he bent forward and landed a wet kiss full on my lips

That night, I told Beauprix about the money I'd seer changing hands—the red envelopes from the Benevolent So ciety and the extortion payment. I mentioned that the argu ment about the extra one hundred dollars had been interrupte and the Young Businessmen had left without it, but I didn't tell Beauprix what the interruption was. No point in making him think I was a pyromaniac.

"The two payments are odd," he said. "And I agree with you. One was definitely protection money. But I can't imagine what the other was for."

Though I knew he couldn't see me, I shook my head.

"I don't know. Maybe they're middlemen in some transaction."

"That's as good an explanation as any, I suppose. Do you think these guys are our murderers?"

"Certainly, they're cocky enough to kill," I said. "And they have the community so intimidated that they weren't worrying about witnesses. Maybe it took a few murders to reach that point."

He must have heard the hesitation in my voice.

"But?" he prompted.

"They have a motive for murder, but why attack and mutilate each of the victims' hands?" I said. "Besides, the Nguyen family doesn't own a business in Little Vietnam. Tommy told me his mother works at a coffee warehouse. Why would they pay—or not pay—protection?"

Then I told Beauprix what Tommy had said about his brother. And implied that the information I had about Tri's artistic abilities also came from that source.

"Maybe it's because of the kind of work I do," I said, "but Tommy's comment about his brother's desire to help people just arriving in this country and the technical ability Nguyen Tri obviously had suggests the possibility that he was counterfeiting breeder documents."

Beauprix wasn't familiar with the term, so I explained to him how desperate undocumented immigrants were for proof of citizenship or permanent residency in the United States. And how unscrupulous employers and criminal organizations could force illegal immigrants into virtual slavery by withholding documents and threatening to turn the immigrants over to the INS.

I didn't tell him about Uncle Duran's accusations or about finding Uncle Tinh's unlisted number written in the Nguyens' phone book. I told myself that I didn't want Uncle Duran's suspicions to taint Beauprix's perspective as it had mine. That I wasn't trying to protect Uncle Tinh from suspicion for the sake of preserving a childhood relationship. Then I admitted that I wasn't very good at lying to myself.

There was silence on my phone as Beauprix considered what I'd told him.

"It's a stretch," he said finally. "But you may be on to something. Any idea why Nguyen Tri was killed?"

I had no answer for that, but I had another question.

"Do you recall what the other two victims did for a living?"

Though I knew Beauprix was at home, he replied as if the files were open in front of him. Confirming my belief that he'd looked over those three files so often he'd memorized their contents.

"The woman, Vo Bah Mi, worked at the courthouse," he said slowly. "In records."

"That would give her access to death certificates—dead people tend not to notice when someone else begins walking around using their vital information. What about Yu Kim Lee?"

"A printer," he said, and he couldn't keep the excitement from his voice.

For a time we talked uninhibitedly about ideas and possibilities, celebrating the knowledge that my time undercover was already paying off, allowing ourselves to feel optimistic. We were on to something and we both knew it.

When Beauprix said good-night, he was already yawning.

I said goodbye and felt the usual stab of loneliness when he disconnected.

Before I went to sleep that night, I spent some time considering the number scrawled in the Nguyens' phone book and I prayed that Uncle Tinh would not turn out to be a point of connection between three victims.

Chapter 15

I heard about the hijacking before I got to work on Saturday morning.

Every morning before the Red Lotus opened, I stopped at the bakery down the street, one that was rival to the place where I hadn't gotten a job. I was usually one of the first customers of the day. As I sat at one of the little tables and dipped pieces of warm French bread into chicory-laced coffee, I watched the story unfold on the little TV behind the counter.

Late Friday night, a fully loaded semi-truck had been hijacked just after leaving the Jourdan Road Terminal. And the truck hadn't merely been hijacked, an unremarkable occurrence in one of the world's largest port cities. There'd been a shoot-out.

The Jourdan Road Terminal was located near the intersection of the Inner Harbor Navigational Canal and the Intracoastal Waterway. It overlooked the Turning Basin, an expansive area of deep water ideal for maneuvering the massive container ships. Though it was several miles away in a heavily industrial area, it was still "over the high rise" in East New Orleans. Thus, the news item was of more immediate interest to the people in Little Vietnam than any of the day's happenings in the city.

According to the report I watched on the television, the trucker had been cruising north on Jourdan Road bound for the entrance to I-10 when the road was blocked by a stalled car. When he stopped his rig, several men wielding sawed-off shotguns jumped out of hiding.

The trucker was enthusiastic about sharing his moment of fame.

"Those fellas pulled me out of the cab, made me lay face-down on the shoulder of the road. All of 'em had ski masks on, but they sounded like foreigners. Asians, maybe. Or Arabs. But that wasn't the worst of it. One of them's already up in my rig when this other car comes squealing up. Four, maybe five guys pile out, hit the ditch on the other side of the road.

"They start blasting away at each other like they was somewhere in Iraq. What with bullets flying this way and that, I keep my head down. Then, 'bout the time I hear police sirens, a car start burnin'. It belonged to the second bunch of guys, I think."

I went to work and, within minutes, the morning paper and a procession of customers who spoke excitedly about the event filled in the remaining details.

By the time the police arrived, the combatants had scattered, leaving the driver alone and uninjured on the shoulder of the road. And the truck was gone. The police said the car that had burned was stolen and the fire that destroyed it was caused by some kind of incendiary device.

Within an hour of the hijacking, the police found the rig abandoned. The locks on its steel doors had been pried open, but the cargo was still inside the trailer. According to the police, the driver, a representative of the shipping company, and everyone who came into the Red Lotus, this was definitely odd.

I suspected that I wasn't the only one who wondered why cargo *hadn't* been listed on the manifest. I could think of only two possibilities—drugs or humans.

As I'd expected, working all day with the twins was a trying experience. Most workdays at the Red Lotus, I made a point of thinking and acting like the teenage girl I was supposed to be. But on Saturday, I made an exception for the twins. They oozed cheerful camaraderie in my direction whenever anyone was looking. But when I was the only one within earshot, I was treated to their extensive, if not particularly creative, vocabulary of obscenities and slurs. They apparently didn't know the term *bui doi*. But American slang had given them plenty of alternatives.

Squirt was tempted to knock them silly. Lacie Reed ignored them.

Vincent came in around 2:00 p.m., looking particularly sexy in a black turtleneck and slim black jeans. His appearance was not lost on the twins, who paused in their work to watch him cross the restaurant.

"Did you hear about the hijacking?" I asked when he settled into his usual seat at the counter. "Everyone's talking about it."

Vincent shrugged dismissively.

"Gang stuff," he said. "I have something more important I want to tell you about."

I cast an eye in Mr. Yang's direction. As usual, he didn't look happy that I was talking with Vincent. But he was even more unhappy when one of his daughters abandoned her customers and rushed to pour Vincent tea. Mr. Yang chased her back to work, loudly scolding her for being lazy.

Vincent ignored them. The adult in me couldn't suppress a smile.

"I'm writing a book," Vincent said after I took his order.

Over the past week I'd discovered that Vincent had been raised in New York City, was well-educated and widely read, and had interesting perspectives on social and political issues that Lacie Reed considered important. As I watched him interact with the residents of Little Vietnam, I wasn't surprised that his social activism and "northern" sensibilities kept him from fitting in. He might be respected, I thought, but he certainly wasn't understood. During our much-interrupted conversations over the lunch counter, I often regretted that I couldn't react to his ideas in the context of my own beliefs and experiences. Instead, I privately admired his patience as he explained concepts to the bright but uneducated teenager I was supposed to be.

I stayed in character as I reacted to his announcement.

"Wow. A real author. What's your book about? Finding jobs for people?"

He shook his head.

"No. About being Vietnamese in America."

"Is that so different from being anything else in America?"

"Of course it is," he said. "We didn't come here as ignorant, starving peasants. In our country, we were well-educated and affluent. We were used to having the good things in life."

To placate Mr. Yang who was still scowling, I neatened the area beneath the counter as I listened to Vincent talk. His voice was passionate and angry, but there was something about his delivery that made me suspect that this was an often-repeated complaint. I didn't contradict him by remarking that his description fit only a fraction of Vietnamese immigrants.

"Even in America, not all of us have that," I said as I opened another package of paper placemats emblazoned with the characters of the Chinese horoscope and added them on top of a dwindling stack.

For a moment the hard lines of his face softened.

"No, not all, Squirt. But many were raised to expect that success—wealth, power, position—would be ours as a matter of right. In Vietnam, it would have been."

"And here?" I said, wondering but not asking about his background. Certainly *he* was no bi-racial child of the vanquished enemy. Maybe he'd been born to some high-ranking Vietnamese bureaucrat. Or businessman. Or an officer in the South Vietnamese army.

Instead of answering me, Vincent held out his empty teacup, tapping it with his finger in the style of someone with high social status.

I hurried to refill it, as any intimidated child would.

Vincent took a careful sip of the hot liquid, then looked at me over the rim of the cup. His expression was hard and dangerous.

"Here, in America, there can be success. But only for those who are smart enough to find it. And strong enough to keep it."

I stood very still, almost holding my breath, maintaining a reaction appropriate to Squirt—awe mixed with admiration and more than a little fear.

"I am strong. And smart," I volunteered.

At that, like the sunrise after a long and terrifying night, Vincent's smile came out. Then he ordered the special, which on Wednesday was *bap cai don thit*—meat rolls in cabbage leaves.

I smiled back, made a point of letting Squirt's body relax. But when I left to attend one of the other customers, it was not difficult for my adult mind to imagine his eyes staring at my back. No matter that he seemed to genuinely care about Squirt, my every instinct told me not to trust him.

My twelve-hour workday finally ended.

I went into the utility closet in the kitchen, this time not only retrieving my jacket, but unplugging my cell phone. That perk was compliments of Mrs. Yang. I'd asked her permission and offered to pay for the trickle of power my cell phone charger needed. When questioned, I told her the truth—there was no electricity where I lived. She'd asked nothing more, simply pointed to the outlet low on the closet wall.

The restaurant had been closed for several minutes. Mr. Yang had his business checkbook out on the counter and was organizing invoices that needed to be paid. His Saturday, I thought wearily as I made my way through the dining area, was going to be even longer than mine.

As I reached for the handle of the front door, Mr. Yang cleared his throat. This, I'd learned during my first hours at the Red Lotus, was his signal for anyone within earshot to pay attention. Mrs. Yang, the elderly cousin and the twins were in the kitchen sharing a meal. Which meant that Mr. Yang wanted to talk with me.

I turned my head.

He lifted his dark eyes from his paperwork and looked squarely at me.

"Vincent Ngo is not a good man."

"Why?" I asked.

Mr. Yang shook his head, apparently having no intention of expanding on his cryptic message. Then he flicked his fingers to encourage my progress out the door.

One of the perks of working late at the Red Lotus was an after-hours meal that was free. And good. But by dinnertime, I'd known I couldn't face the prospect of spending any more time than was absolutely necessary. So the elderly cousin, who I think suspected that the twins were being less than pleasant, had fixed me the Vietnamese equivalent of a po'boy—*banh mi*. He had stacked crumbled shrimp cake, cucumber slices, cilantro and shredded green chilies between the split halves of a long French loaf and cut it into sections so that I could easily eat my sandwich between waiting on customers.

So, although I was footsore and weary when I approached my house, my stomach was comfortably full. And I still had enough energy for my nightly commune with Lucky.

His missing eye seemed not to affect his ability to grab morsels midair and it was an indication of how entertainment-deprived I was that I found his skill fascinating. So I spent a few minutes each evening breaking up pork-filled steamed buns and tossing him pieces as I carried on a one-sided conversation.

"I'm staying in tonight," I told Lucky that night. "My feet are sore. Does that ever happen to you? I suppose, though, with only three legs, you're twenty-five percent less likely to have blisters."

On the other side of the porch railing, Lucky wagged the stump of his tail, apparently approving my nonsense math. I tossed him another bit, deliberately throwing it so that it would land close to the railing.

He hesitated, too fearful to step out of the shadows to pick it up.

"Come on," I said. "You can do it. No one's going to hurt you."

Finally, when the temptation was too much, he stepped forward quickly. For a moment he fixed his single eye on me and lifted his lips to expose a lot of teeth. Then he snatched up the morsel and retreated.

"Clearly you have issues with trust," I said, lobbing the last piece well into the porch area. "But don't we all."

I walked down the driveway to the back door and let myself inside.

By now the house was familiar territory. I no longer needed my flashlight to navigate after dark. Even the open staircase wasn't a problem—nine steps up and the tenth put my foot on the landing. Another six steps and I was standing in front of the bedroom door.

I usually carried the flashlight anyway, placing it on the ounter nearest the back door so that it was readily at hand hen I returned home. And I always carried it upstairs with e when I retired for the night. Mostly, I used it when I ossed the living room. The beam of light sent the house's ches-long roaches scuttling for cover.

Once on the steps, the roaches were more scarce and a mis-ep rarely produced a crunch underfoot. But I never leaned gainst the loose wallpaper as I went up the stairs. Instead, d learned to stay at the center of each step, away from the nprotected edge on my right and the wallpaper that moved eneath my hand on the left.

I made my way upstairs to the bedroom, eager for a long th and the softness of my bed. After a week's practice, I was expert at pretending that the thick-shelled, antennaed nas-es despised the cleanliness of my bedroom and the isolation the bathroom. Only once had reality contradicted my fan-sy. On Wednesday, I'd stepped from the shower, reached for towel and received a painful, pinschered bite for my efforts. hat hadn't stopped me from showering, but now I never abbed too quickly for anything.

When I called Beauprix that night, I was leaning against y pillows and thinking seriously about sleep. I was too ed, really, to focus on drawing. But as soon as I hit his num-r on my speed dial, I had, from habit, picked up my sketch d and pencil from the nightstand.

As we conversed, I doodled.

I asked him about the hijacking.

He, too, had been intrigued by the abandoned cargo.

"Any idea what was taken?

"No. But it sure wasn't drugs. I had Remy check with one his buddies in vice. He said that the drug dog showed no terest in the truck's interior. Or its exterior, for that matter."

Which left a human cargo as a likely shipment, I thought. nd then I asked myself if my recent experience as part of

such a shipment might be influencing my judgment. So
didn't mention my suspicions to Beauprix. But talking abou
the hijacking reminded me of something I'd heard the day be
fore and had forgotten to tell him.

"Friday morning, during the Benevolent Society's mee
ing, I overheard them talking about a shipment they wer
expecting to arrive. It was headed up north."

I drew a frowning Vietnamese elder riding a dragon, usin
a chopstick for a crop.

"Is it relevant, do you think?" he said. "After all, they'r
businessmen and New Orleans is a port city."

His tone solicited feedback rather than making a judg
ment. So I told him of their shift to speaking French once the
were assured Squirt didn't understand that language.

"They were secretive, which makes me suspect that ther
was something about the shipment that was out of the ord
nary."

"It'd sure help to know what, if anything, went missin
from that truck," he said.

And I agreed.

Then I told him about Vincent Ngo.

"It was weird, Anthony. Everyone I met was talking abou
that hijacking. Speculating about the cargo like we are. O
sympathizing with the driver. Or, at the very least, talkin
about the crime rate in New Orleans and what was the cit
coming to. Then Vincent came in and simply shrugged off th
news. But it was late afternoon when I talked to him. Mayb
he was just tired of hearing about it. But that wasn't real
what I found disturbing."

I described Vincent's anger about being a Vietnames
immigrant.

"Maybe it's nothing," I said. "Maybe I'm looking too har
reading too much into it. I get the impression he's workin
hard to impress Squirt. He wouldn't be the first guy to fall f
a streetwise kid who's ten, twelve years his junior. Anywa

there's definitely something about him that doesn't feel right. And I'm not the only one who feels that way."

Then I told him about Mr. Yang's warning.

Without focusing on details or style, I drew Vincent and Mr. Yang, put a wok piled full with dollar bills, coins and gift envelopes between them. And added a flame beneath it.

"Though I can't for the life of me figure out how it's all connected," I continued.

I must have sounded apologetic.

"But your gut tells you there's some link between them," Beauprix said.

"Yeah."

As we'd spoken, my pencil had moved on, leaving my conscious mind behind. After a few more minutes of conversation, I happened to focus on my drawing pad and saw that I'd begun obliterating Vincent's face with a feathered mask. I shook my head, certain that Vincent had nothing to do with the attack. Not only didn't it make sense, but I was good at recognizing body types. There was no way Vincent had been one of the men who'd attacked me. What the drawing meant was that my conscious mind apparently agreed with my subconscious. And both agreed with Mr. Yang. Vincent Ngo was not a man to be trusted.

"…instincts," Beauprix was saying, and I realized that I'd stopped listening to him.

"Sorry," I said. "Bad connection. I lost you there for a moment. Would you mind repeating that?"

"What I was saying is that if you feel there's something going on there," he said, "then it's worth checking into."

The vote of confidence coming from Beauprix felt better than it should have. You're falling for a voice on the phone, I scolded myself. Never mind that the voice was deep and gentle and encouraging.

I looked around the bedroom. More interesting to look at than the insipid floral prints that the home's owner seemed to favor, I'd gotten into the habit of tearing finished work from my pad and taping it to the walls. I used the drawings as an immediate reference, periodically rearranging and retaping them, grouping them by relevance. I updated portraits by taping new ones over the old. One person: one portrait.

Except for Anthony Beauprix.

His face looked at me from several drawings. Smiling. Laughing. Solemn. Angry. And I'd drawn his hands. They were square and strong, with blunt fingers and manicured nails. If I shut my eyes, I remembered more about him than a mere photographic memory should have provided. The slightly spicy smell of his cologne, the confidence of his touch, the passion in his voice...

My God, I thought, suddenly understanding what should have been obvious. No matter that my taste in men had always run toward smooth-skinned Asians who looked good in tight jeans. Or that I figured I carried enough psychic baggage of my own that I deliberately avoided emotional involvement with anyone in law enforcement. Or that I preferred to date Washington professionals—cool, ambitious men who treated women not only as equals but as competitors. Despite all of that, I showed every sign of being in love with an overprotective, chauvinistic, white Southern cop.

Lacie Reed, I told myself, you have lost your mind. Face it, you're reaching out to him just because he's available. Because you're tired of pretending to be a teenage girl. With him, you don't have to be on guard, don't have to pretend that you're someone you're not. Undoubtedly, that's what's stressing you out and making you emotionally vulnerable. Emotionally stupid.

Never mind that, for all the times I'd spent not just weeks, but months alone undercover, I'd never before felt inclined to fall in love.

Chapter 16

On Sunday, I went to early Mass at the neighborhood's Catholic church and spent some time lingering on a residential block I hadn't visited before. Then I took advantage of my time off from the Red Lotus and watched one of the busier streets in Little Vietnam.

Little Vietnam was its own small town. Though major purchases and special occasions might be spent in New Orleans proper or, more likely, across a less trafficked bridge to Slidell, most of the people who lived and worked in the little community also shopped, banked and went to school here. And ate and gossiped and prayed here. The odds were good that anyone I'd seen at the Red Lotus I would, sooner or later, see driving or walking on one of the major routes through the community.

I multitasked by doing a week's worth of dirty clothing at the coin op laundry while watching traffic move along Dwyer Drive. Later, because the weather was beautiful, I sat on a bench in a small park on Saigon Drive. I dipped a carry-out order of *bahn khoa*—a rice-flour crepe stuffed with shrimp, chicken, sprouts and onion—into peanut sauce, sipped an iced tea and watched the traffic there, too.

When I returned home at dusk, I congratulated myself on a successful day. I had managed to match two faces I'd seen at the Red Lotus—two members of the Young Vietnamese Businessmen's Association—to specific cars and license plate numbers.

Sunday evening, I rested.

On Monday, I went back to work at the Red Lotus. That day, I added more blisters to my feet and a few handfuls of loose change and dollar bills to the jar I kept in my bedroom. And I was able to surreptitiously bag one of Vincent's teacups and tuck it in my jacket pockets. I would pass it on to Beauprix. It would, I was sure, yield a nice set of prints. But, before I called him, I was intent on adding several more teacups to the collection.

That night, despite my exhaustion, I couldn't sleep. Mostly because I was lonely. Talking with Beauprix had helped, but our relationship lay in an odd limbo between professional and personal. And I couldn't, anyway, tell him the details that had torn my sense of family apart.

My adoptive parents had retired to Europe. To live and work in the vineyards of Spain. It was their dream. They had loved me, raised me, taught me that there were people in the world I could trust. But, for the past five years, they'd been little more than quick e-mail messages, occasional letters and a phone call at Christmas.

I hadn't really missed them because I had my uncles. Both of them. And my work. Before this was over, I asked myself, would I have lost not only my job but the friendship of both of my adopted uncles? Not that I had a choice. Helping Uncle Tinh had been the right thing to do. The only thing to do.

I rolled over in my bed, spent a few minutes torturing my pillow into a more comfortable lump and stared at the ceiling as my thoughts turned to the Yangs. Usually, when I considered the Vietnamese part of my dual heritage, I couldn't help but think of myself as *bui doi,* as someone who would never belong. But my time at the Red Lotus, working with Mr. and Mrs. Yang and the elderly cousin had somehow changed my perspective. Like so many of the people I'd encountered in Little Vietnam, I was *Viet Kieu.* Vietnamese in the land of golden landscapes. That was the last thing on my mind when I drifted to sleep.

On Tuesday, my apron pockets were full of change and more customers were leaving than arriving by the time Vincent came in. When I served his meal, only he and two other customers remained. I poured him more tea, then walked down to the far end of the counter where the two businessmen were finishing up their lunch. After asking if I could get them anything more, I left them each a check, then gathered up the scatter of dirty dishes and carried them to the kitchen. The cousin was there, standing with his back bent, his arms elbow-deep in sudsy water.

"A busy day," the elderly man remarked in Vietnamese as he took the dishes from me. "Good for business."

"Hard on the feet," I said.

He gave me a soapy wave.

"And on the hands."

I laughed as, through the kitchen door, I caught a glimpse of an entering customer out of the corner of my eye. A tourist, I thought immediately. A Caucasian with dark hair. He was dressed in faded blue jeans and a yellow sports shirt. I stepped back into the restaurant area just in time to see him take a seat at the table near the door with his back to me.

What the hell was he doing here?

Mr. Yang was sitting on a tall stool in front of the cash register reading his paper. Responding to the bell, he jerked his head in the direction of the new customer without once looking up.

I filled a teapot with oolong tea and carried it, a clean teacup and paper napkin-wrapped utensils to the table. Beauprix's attention seemed to be on the battered menu.

If I had known you were çoming, I could have slipped you Vincent's teacup, I thought. As it was…

He looked up as I began to set the table and there was nothing in his face or manner that implied recognition.

"Good afternoon, sir. Would you like to order?" I asked in English and made a point of popping the gum I was in the habit of chewing openmouthed.

He gave his head a little half shake and smiled politely.

"Yes, miss. The *mein ga,* please."

He gave me his order in passable Vietnamese.

No doubt my shocked disbelief showed on my face. I was glad that I had positioned myself beside Beauprix's chair so that my back, too, was to Vincent and Mr. Yang.

I shook my head, replied in Vietnamese, wondering how fluent he actually was.

"There's not much left, sir. Part of it spilled earlier today."

"Mot mieng khi doi bang doi khi no," Beauprix said. It was an old Vietnamese proverb: a bite when hungry is worth a bowl when full.

As my eyes widened, Beauprix's smile broadened.

Smart-ass, I thought as I glared down at him.

"I hope you still believe that when you reach the end of a very meager bowl," I said, keeping my voice pleasant.

I returned to the kitchen, reached for one of the large bowls that were stacked on the shelf above the stove, filled it with a generous portion of noodles. Resisting the urge to spike the meal with oil infused with hot peppers, I added what remained of the chicken soup to the bowl and put it on a small tray. Beside it, I placed tiny, separate dishes of green onion, chopped celery and chopped hot peppers. I smiled at Vincent as I walked past him on my way to unload the tray at Beauprix's table.

"Enjoy your meal, sir."

I returned to the counter, began washing its Formica surface with a bleach-soaked rag and tried to pretend Beauprix was just another customer.

"He speaks our language well," Vincent remarked. "I wonder where he learned it? He's too young, I think, to have been a soldier in Vietnam."

"Doesn't matter," I said pettishly, "as long as he pays his bill and leaves a decent tip."

Vincent left the restaurant before Beauprix did, which was just as well. Because, along with the tip, Beauprix left a packet of M&M's Peanut. I opened it, poured the candy out in my hand, and laughed. I didn't know how he'd managed it, but inside the characteristic yellow wrapper, all of the M&M's were blue. There were enough of them, I supposed, to trade for a foot rub.

I called him that night.

"You didn't tell you spoke Vietnamese," I said.

"You didn't ask."

Then made his reply sound less flippant by offering an explanation.

"When I was a kid, our housekeeper was Vietnamese. And my daddy… Did I tell you he was a diplomat? Well, he speaks Vietnamese, too. I picked it up listening to the two of them. When I joined the force, that rusty language skill landed me on a beat in Little Vietnam."

Before I hung up, I thanked him for the candy.

On Wednesday, two members of the Young Vietnamese Businessmen's Association came into the restaurant. The man who'd challenged the amount of the protection payment was not with them, but I recognized one of the men as the driver of a red Toyota I'd seen on Dwyer Drive on Sunday.

As soon as they'd taken a seat at one of the smaller tables, Mrs. Yang marched over to the cash register, pushed her unresisting husband aside and took out the hundred dollars she'd tucked into the cash drawer on Friday. I watched as, without a word, she handed it to the Toyota's owner. He took it without comment, then went back to talking with his associate.

I interrupted the men long enough to take their lunch requests and, not too much later, I delivered their food to their table. One order of rice-flour crepes stuffed with shrimp, chicken, sprouts and onions. A plateful of steamed buns split and overflowing with hard-cooked egg and red sausage. Though I wanted to linger nearby to eavesdrop and to snag their dirty teacups for fingerprints, the restaurant was too busy at lunchtime that day for me to do, either.

When they'd come into the Red Lotus, I'd suspected from their small number and informal attitude that their intention was not to collect money but to eat lunch free. They confirmed that near the end of their meal by tearing up the check I gave them and letting the pieces flutter to the floor.

On Wednesday—as on all the other days I'd worked at the restaurant—one of my jobs in the afternoon was to empty the thirty-gallon plastic barrel that was tucked underneath one corner of the restaurant's serving counter. Throughout the day, when Mrs. Yang or I cleared the tables, it was the repository for used paper napkins and placemats, the wrappers from fortune cookies and disposable chopsticks, and the scrapings from dirty plates. By midafternoon, it was usually half filled.

On my first day of work, Mrs. Yang had judged me too small to do the heavy job. But I had insisted, thinking that it would be good to impress the Yangs with my industry and knowing that a wealth of information often landed in the trash. During his breaks, the elderly cousin sat on a rickety chair outside the back door, smoked a cigarette and read martial arts comic books. Earlier, when I'd had to ask him a question, I'd noticed a pile of cinder blocks stacked nearby, against the restaurant's exterior wall.

To prove myself capable of taking out the garbage, I'd spent a few minutes in the alley restacking the cinder blocks nearer the steel Dumpster, then dragged the plastic barrel through the kitchen and lugged it into the alley. With Mrs. Yang and the elderly cousin looking on, I'd hauled the barrel up the makeshift steps, lifted it until its lip was balanced on the edge of the Dumpster, and tipped out the contents. Mrs. Yang had nodded, the elderly cousin had smiled, and the task of taking out the garbage was mine.

I still held to the same technique I'd demonstrated that first day. Except that when no one was looking—and after that first day, no one ever was—I tipped the garbage out slowly, one clumpy layer at a time. I brought the barrel back onto the step several times in the process, sifting carefully through each newly exposed layer, watching for anything of interest.

That was how, on Wednesday afternoon, I noticed that someone had drawn on one of the restaurant's placemats. I picked the piece of paper from the garbage, smoothed it out against the side of the Dumpster, and discovered that it was torn. I held a ragged half, with part of a rectangular drawing ending at its torn edge.

The drawing was done in blue ink with several lines of red paralleling the blue. Some of the red lines had arrow-tip wedges at one end. And one of those lines looped completely around a wedge-shaped blue rectangle. It was certainly a map, I thought. Directions to someone's house? A bus route? Or something more significant? I needed the rest of the map to find out.

Over the weeks, I'd dug many such scraps from the garbage, brushed away the clotted remains of food and discovered nothing more significant than stick figures or geometric doodles or numbers that had meaning only to the person who'd written them. Though there was every possibility that this one would be the same, I used a discarded chopstick to push through noodles and rice and limp vegetables until I found another piece of paper with similar ink markings.

I matched the halves of the placemat and recognized the crudely drawn map for what it was—a diagram of the area's streets, distinctive because of the catch basin and the odd, segmented residential areas created by the canals. I'd already noticed the regularity with which some vehicles drove past the Red Lotus several times each day. One of those vehicles was a red Toyota.

As I dumped the rest of the garbage into the bin, I thought about which tables I had bused and which ones Mrs. Yang had cleared. And I remembered that several customers had come in as the freeloading Young Businessmen had gotten up to leave. By the time I'd returned to their table, Mrs. Yang had already cleared it, denying me my teacups. But now I had a map.

That week I had moved my nighttime activities beyond the bright lights of Little Vietnam's business district and the safety of its residential streets. Deliberately, I searched out places that were alien to most of the honest, hardworking citizens of Little Vietnam. Places where predators and corruptors could operate with impunity. Important, I thought, to familiarize myself with all the areas in the community.

Each night, I moved through the darkness with the sensibilities of a cat burglar, knowing that if some suspicious cop frisked me and found my picklocks, Beauprix would likely have some bailing out to do. My activities centered on the industrial area south of the railroad tracks that paralleled Chef Menteur Highway. There, booming industries and abandoned factories were tied together by tall-grassed marshes, poorly lit roads and railroad sidings. A variety of tall fences were designed to make things challenging for the human denizens of the area.

I hadn't found the fences to be much of an impediment. Even when they were chain-link topped by barbed wire. As I walked along fenced perimeters, I found places where heavy rain had eroded the soil beneath the fence and aggressive grasses had crumbled the pavement adjacent to it. Generally, though, I climbed rather than burrowed. Around most of the factory yards I entered, Louisiana's climate and human nature gave me that option. Thick woody vines softened the sharpest barbed wire and overhanging tree branches defeated the tallest fences. Occasionally, I found places where a section of fence had already been cut or the fence had simply sagged away from its support. But easiest of all, I was able to walk onto the grounds of one active warehouse complex because someone had neglected to lock a closed gate.

On Wednesday night I also began searching for a building with a panoramic view, focusing my explorations on the tallest buildings in the area.

I'd never been afraid of heights and—thanks to one of Uncle Duran's contacts and a towering, retrofitted grain elevator in Oklahoma—I had quickly learned to free-climb. Easy enough, now, for me to cling to near-vertical surfaces with fingers and toes or to support my body's weight by wedging it into any shallow depression or outcropping that nature—or structure—allowed. But I was also more than happy to climb onto a fire escape or cling to the rusty rungs of escape ladders.

Once up on a rooftop of a factory building, I played my flashlight through skylights and clambered down onto ledges to look into upper-story windows. Windows in a few of the buildings had been left open and I slid in through them. I dug through accessible paper files, read documents left on desks and in drawers, looked at shipping labels affixed to bales and boxes, and surveyed documents on computers that were not password protected.

I saw nothing else remarkable. Except for the perfect vantage point, which I located at 2:00 a.m. on Thursday morning.

All day Thursday, I worked at the Red Lotus. All night Thursday, I spent up on the rooftop, using my binoculars to watch the streets below me, searching for lights on in vacant buildings and activity on loading docks that were supposed to be closed. I saw surreptitious drug deals, scabrous prostitutes plying their trade, stray dogs, weary shift workers walking home from the bus stops and homeless alcoholics who lived down by the tracks. Mostly, though, I watched for certain traffic patterns along the streets of Little Vietnam. The crude map I'd rescued from the garbage made my job relatively easy.

I called Beauprix very early on Friday morning. His voice sounded sleepy, and as I apologized for waking him, I couldn't help but imagining him in bed. Stretching languorously. Naked in the midst of silky tan and cream bedding. Muscles rippling beneath his smooth, olive skin. And above him, the gilt-framed painting of the *U.S.S. Constitution*, its large cannon pounding away….

I told myself I needed to get a life.

"Can you meet me tonight?" I asked, working to keep my voice absolutely steady.

He yawned, agreed, and told me once to slow down as he scribbled notes on the location of the factory building and the route he'd need to follow to join me on the rooftop. There were iron rungs set into the mortar on the east side of the building. From there, he needed to go up and over a gently pitched corrugated rooftop, up a short ladder to an adjacent flat roof, then to the next building across the top of an enclosed pedestrian walkway.

Beauprix didn't object to the route. He objected to my being in that neighborhood. Day or night. And he didn't approve of my trespassing on private property. Dangerous and illegal. As for crawling up the sides of buildings and crossing rooftops…

"I know you're doing what you think is right, but can't you try to be a little safer about it all?" he asked me over the phone.

That's when I laughed.

And he got angry.

We argued about his right to tell me how to do my job. He thought he had the right. I assured him he didn't.

Shortly after that, we ended our conversation.

I was so agitated by thoughts of Beauprix—some irritated, most irritatingly not—that I couldn't get back to sleep. So I went to work early, thinking that I could catch the elderly cousin as he did the restaurant's early morning prep work. I'd ask a few oblique questions to see if he had any interesting gossip that he was willing to share.

The first light of dawn illuminated my walk to work. Birds sang, dogs barked, traffic was at a minimum. Peaceful. Until I heard the sound of smashing glass. I was less than half a block from the restaurant and I saw the car squeal away. A light-colored sedan. But I was too far away and the light was too weak for me to pick out any other details.

Then I heard the elderly cousin's angry shout.

I sprinted the remaining distance to the Red Lotus. By that time, the elderly cousin had moved onto the sidewalk. The angry baker from across the street and the pretty florist from next door had apparently heard the noise and came running, too. We all arrived at about the same time and stood beside the elderly cousin, surveying the damage.

Someone had thrown a brick through the restaurant's plate-glass window. It had plowed through the towering, woody tendrils of the Crown of Thorns, leaving a few thick, ragged stems growing from the big clay pot. On the floor inside the restaurant was a scattered mess of thorny branches, tiny blood-red leaves and shards of glass the size of kitchen knives. And feathers. Crimson and black feathers. Torn from the pair of masks that someone had secured to the brick with duct tape.

As I stood looking at the disaster with the cousin, the baker and the florist, my stomach twisted and I began trembling.

Undoubtedly the Yangs would assume the broken window was payback for paying protection money short and late. But I knew better.

The carrion birds had found me. But how?

On the night of the first attack, only three people knew that Lacie Reed was in New Orleans. Uncle Duran. Uncle Tinh. And Anthony Beauprix.

Only two knew that Lacie Reed and Squirt were the same person.

Uncle Tinh.

Anthony Beauprix.

It made no sense for either of those men to terrorize me.

But if not them, then who?

The elderly cousin looked at me and his tight-lipped expression became a frown. He misinterpreted whatever he saw in my face, reached out and patted my shoulder.

"Don't worry, Squirt," he said. "We clean it up. You'll see. Good as new by tomorrow."

Of course, the police were not called.

By the time the Benevolent Society came in for their weekly meeting, the restaurant was clean and plywood covered the window. As on the previous Friday, the meeting was conducted in French. But today, no red envelopes were passed. And Mrs. Yang was too busy administering first aid to her shattered plant to wait on them. So the job fell to me.

One of the men said something disparaging about me in

French, something guaranteed to redden the face of a teen-age girl. I didn't react. But, even with that assurance that I couldn't understand them, the men still spoke as if they might be overheard.

Mr. Yang announced that the shipment was in good condition, but was now in storage. Documentation had been delayed by a week, perhaps a few days more. So the shipment's northward journey would be postponed.

That caused a furor, with the butcher finally demanding to know if there would be additional costs. Weekly payments to the thieves had already put his business at risk. And now this had happened. Mr. Yang had assured them that everything would go smoothly. And it hadn't. He, for one, could pay no more.

The others around the table looked at Mr. Yang.

"I proposed this venture," he said. "I will bear any additional expenses."

Everyone nodded, though few eyes traveled in the direction of Mr. Yang's face. Over the next few minutes, the others trailed out of the Red Lotus, leaving Mr. Yang alone. For a time, he sat unmoving, staring unfocused at the Infant of Prague in its niche on the wall. Then he propped his elbows on the table and covered his face with his hands.

As I watched Mr. Yang, I thought about who the members of the Benevolent Society were, who they might once have been. Their postures and attitudes suggested military men. Certainly, they were the right age to have fought in the war. But more than that, I suspected they had fought side-by-side. They struck me as old soldiers and longtime comrades, as men whose bond went deeper than business or friendship.

Mr. Yang stood, went over to the cash register. As he did at about this time every day, he checked to be sure we had enough change for the afternoon. I went into the kitchen to fetch more clean teacups.

What shipment awaited documentation? As I stacked teacups by the counter in anticipation of the lunch crowd, I thought about the incident near the Jourdan Road terminal and found it easy to imagine the membership of the Benevolent Society pulling off an ambush, building and using incendiaries, successfully hijacking a truck. And its secret cargo.

Any lingering thoughts I had of the stupidly violent carrion birds were banished by the real horror I now confronted. If my suspicions were correct, the immigrants who made up the Benevolent Society were more than simply innocent victims of an invading gang. They were, themselves, criminals.

Protection payments had to be pushing their businesses to the brink of bankruptcy. Could decent men be so intent on saving the lives that they'd built for themselves and their families that they could justify the unthinkable? Could men who were themselves immigrants exploit, then destroy, the dreams of other immigrants?

My experience told me that it had happened before. My instincts told me that it was happening now. And my heart—

I shook my head, banishing my heart from the equation. My job—the job that I had dedicated myself to—was stopping the exploitation of immigrants and bringing their exploiters to justice. No matter who the exploiters were. No matter how much I cared about them.

Later, the Young Businessmen came in.

"Redecorating?" one of them asked Mr. Yang sarcastically.

Though Mr. Yang undoubtedly thought that they had thrown the brick, he didn't react. I suspected he had other things on his mind.

The Young Businessmen ate their lunch, counted the money in the envelope Mr. Yang handed over, and left without creating a disturbance.

I rushed to clear the table, placed their teacups carefully aside and later bagged them and tucked them into my pocket.

* * *

I spent the rest of the day taking orders, serving food, picking up dirty plates, tucking quarters into my apron pocket and thinking. I knew that finding a shipment of contraband, even human contraband, would be virtually impossible in a city the size of New Orleans. Even if they were hidden within the radius of Little Vietnam, a directionless search was unlikely to yield results. There were too many places where people could be locked in and kept alive for eventual shipment. But if I could locate the source of the delayed documents, I might be able to follow the documents to the shipment. If I could find out when the documents would be delivered, I could follow whoever picked them up to the shipment. And liberate the cargo before it left New Orleans.

Chapter 17

On Friday when I got home from work, I kicked off my shoes, crawled into bed and slept because I had to.

I dreamed that a flock of crows was chasing me through the narrow, deserted streets of the French Quarter. Striking at me, over and over, until their beaks were tipped in blood. Terrified, desperate, I looked for shelter, for escape. And found a trailer abandoned, its door partly open, in the middle of the road. I dove inside as the birds blackened the sky, gathering for a final attack. But now I was sure I could save myself. The overhead door was just within my reach. I reached upward, intent on pulling it closed. And discovered that my hands had been completely pecked away.

I woke up, gasping.

It was just before midnight, two hours before I was to meet Beauprix.

I got dressed anyway. I put on black jeans, a sweater with deep, buttoned pockets and lightweight boots that tied up above my ankles and had slip-proof soles. I tucked my phone and flashlight into my pockets and then spent a few minutes loosening the straps on my purse so that I could strap it over my shoulders.

That done, I filled my purse with a couple of candy bars, a bottle of water, my binoculars, the wrapped teacups and the papers I wanted to give Beauprix. Then I rigged the straps so the backpack rode comfortably between my shoulders and pulled on a dark, camouflage-colored poncho. I'd bought it and the boots at a surplus store that had been a quick bus ride down Chef Menteur Highway. The poncho was made of some kind of heavy plastic material, reeked of chemicals and hung well past my knees.

A cold rain made the night miserable, but the poncho's hood kept water from soaking my hair and trickling down my back and the nasty weather cut down on the number of people who might notice me.

I had time to spare before I was to meet Beauprix. No point in wasting it.

For a while I watched the traffic that crossed the bridge spanning both one-way lanes of Dwyer Road. That activity yielded the license number of another car belonging to a Young Businessman. The map, license numbers and fingerprints might give Beauprix enough evidence that he could push the N.O.P.D. into supporting him. But even as I considered that, I realized that without a complaint filed by Mr. Yang, the whole thing could be dismissed as mere speculation. As nothing more than overactive imagination. But I would not give up. And neither, I knew, would Anthony Beauprix. And *he* would believe me.

I left Dwyer Road for the no-man's land of the canal and catch basin that separated Chef Menteur Highway from Little Vietnam. Just like the police, I assumed that anyone I saw hanging around at that hour was probably up to no good. Little that I saw contradicted that belief.

A lime green Dodge Neon with at least twenty thousand

dollars' worth of custom mods and a young white male behind the wheel cruised down Dwyer and parked. For the next
quarter hour, traffic on the street increased as cars cruised past
the Neon, slowed, then stopped just long enough for drugs and
cash to exchange hands.

Near the fence surrounding the catch basin, several kids
hung out beneath a makeshift canopy of raincoats and tree
branches. They were so preoccupied that I walked within a few
yards of them, close enough to hear them giggling and to listen to snatches of dialog. By its odor, I guessed they were
smoking a Swisher Sweet. Based on their conversation, I knew
that homegrown weed had replaced the cigar's tobacco interior.

But I was no vice cop, and I doubted, anyway, that what
I'd seen had anything to do with the murders. Except that
murder, apparently, hadn't put much of a crimp in this type
of business-as-usual activity.

As my meeting time with Beauprix approached, I made my
way south of Chef Menteur Highway into the marshy edges
of the bayou, where train tracks, empty lots and industry con-
verged. Carefully avoiding the glare of security lights, I
watched the marsh grass and water-filled ditches warily for
any snakes and gators that hadn't gotten the message that the
wildlife refuge was a mile down the road. Back on higher
ground, I knocked the mud off my boots as I walked along
the tracks, skirted the edges of parking lots, and moved in the
deep shadows between buildings.

I followed the now-familiar route onto the flat rooftop of
a coffee warehouse facility. The complex was a block square,
made up of several structures that butted up to each other or
were attached by enclosed walkways. The roofline was irreg-
ular, but the building that faced north was one of the tallest
for miles. Its view of the streetscape was unmatched.

There was nothing about the flat-roofed warehouse that offered shelter from the rain. That, I'd expected. But I hadn't

expected Beauprix to be late. I glanced at my watch, realized that another five minutes had passed. It was 1:45 a.m. Which made him fifteen minutes late. No big deal, except that he struck me as a man who was rarely late for appointments.

By two, I was beginning to wonder if I'd inadvertently placed him in jeopardy. He was so powerfully built, so obviously fit, that I hadn't considered that he would have a problem meeting me on the roof. Despite the rain puddling on its flat surface, I'd crossed the twenty-five-foot length of the pedestrian walkway without a thought to the paved, barbed-wire enclosed freight yard three stories below. The tarred roof of the walkway was at least six feet wide, but maybe he wasn't as sure-footed as I was. And that was assuming he would have no problem climbing the vertical ladder that went two stories up the side of a building.

I wondered if Beauprix was too proud, too stubborn, to tell me that he couldn't do what I'd asked of him. But, for all his chauvinistic tendencies, he didn't seem to be the foolishly macho type. I dug beneath my dripping poncho, took the cell phone from my pocket and punched his number on speed dial. After a couple of rings, my call rolled over to voice mail. And it occurred to me that this was the first time I'd called him that he hadn't answered.

"This is Lacie," I said. "Call me, please."

And I hoped that I'd managed to keep my concern from tainting those few simple words.

Then I went back to watching the street through my binoculars, ignoring my watch to keep my eyes on the traffic. The pattern that I wanted Beauprix to see was holding true for tonight. The vehicles I'd spotted seemed to follow overlapping, carefully timed and obviously well-planned routes. Though I could see only a section of the main business area and swatch of residential streets, I didn't doubt that there were several more cars and small trucks engaged in the late-night activity.

Undoubtedly, the Young Businessmen ran an organized patrol on the streets of Little Vietnam every night. And, I suspected, a similarly organized patrol during the day. And that, I thought, as I picked out another of their cars and used my binoculars to follow it until it disappeared from sight, explained the lack of crime in Little Vietnam. Young Businessmen on patrol. Businessmen who were armed and dangerous and extorting the area's residents. And maybe providing counterfeit documents. Was that, I wondered, what the red envelopes from the Benevolent Society were purchasing? Or was there—as Uncle Duran had suggested—a supplier who was better known to me?

I glanced at my watch again. Thirty minutes late had become forty-five. And it was too easy now to imagine that somehow Beauprix had slipped and fallen on his way across the rooftops. Unlikely that anyone else would be around at this time of night. And the gusty wind would make it difficult for me to hear his cries. Assuming he was conscious.

Unconsciousness, I supposed, would make him incapable of using a phone. Or answering it.

Five minutes later and anxiety overcame my very real belief that he had simply forgotten our appointment and I was simply being irrational. So I backtracked all the way to the top of the tallest escape ladder, taking time along the way to check the ground below every potential hazard. Not surprisingly, I didn't find his bruised and broken body.

Even as I felt relieved, I cursed the man for making me worry. Cursed myself for worrying. Undoubtedly, if I were this late and my absence unexplained, he would be frantic. Undoubtedly, that was exactly how I was feeling.

I left the roof at 3:00 a.m. As I began making my way along the railroad tracks, heading toward the street, I saw Beauprix. He was hurrying along the tracks in my direction, following the route I had described to him, occasionally looking up but mostly watching the crossrails to avoid a misstep. The next time he looked up, he saw me.

He was hatless. And coatless. In the pouring-down rain.

"I'm sorry I'm late," he said when we were close enough not to have to shout. He waved his arm in the direction of the building I'd come from. "Go on back. I'll follow you."

Even if I thought his disheveled state was normal, there was nothing normal about the tension I heard in his voice. Another murder was my first thought. But he would have phoned.

And then he was standing in front of me.

I stepped in close, pushing back my hood and looking up into his face. Even through the darkness, I could see that something was terribly wrong. But before I could ask, he spoke.

"You said there was something on the roof you wanted to show me," he said, almost brusquely, looking toward the rooftop. "Best not waste any more time."

I stayed where I was and raindrops dripped from his face onto mine.

"What's wrong?" I asked.

He flinched, his hazel eyes flicking away from my face, then back again.

His body language was transparent. Whatever was wrong hurt like hell. And he wasn't ready to talk about it.

"I tried to call," he offered, "but my cell phone didn't work inside the hospital. I went to the desk, asked to use theirs, but the doctor came in just then."

Though I feared the reason for his presence at the hospital and wanted a coherent explanation *now,* I didn't interrupt him. His voice was still over-controlled and oozed tension. But as he edged closer to the source of his distress, his delivery became increasingly agitated.

"And then I had to get away from all of them. Not for long. Just for an hour or two. Just enough time to *think.* So I got in my car and started driving. Anywhere. Nowhere. And, after a couple of minutes, I remembered that you were waiting. And I was late. And I apolo—"

I put my fingers gently over his mouth to stop the tumble of words.

"Anthony," I said quietly, "please tell me what happened."

I shifted my hands to cup them both around his wet cheeks. Felt his muscles working beneath my fingertips as he clenched his jaw, fighting to control his runaway emotions. And I waited.

"My father had another stroke," he said finally.

Then he choked and swallowed hard, clenched his teeth and briefly pressed his eyes shut. This time, when he spoke again, his accent was pure Louisiana and his voice was thick with unshed tears.

"My daddy died tonight," he said simply.

And there in the rain, in the middle of the night, standing on the railroad tracks behind a coffee warehouse, I wrapped my arms around Anthony Beauprix and held him as he wept.

I climbed back to my lookout point with Beauprix on my heels.

While we still stood on the railroad tracks, at the point that Beauprix had straightened and stepped back from my embrace, I'd suggested that he come back to the house with me. I offered the same remedy that he'd offered me back in my room at the Intercontinental—a hot shower, decaf coffee, cookies to soothe *his* nerves, someone to watch over him as he rested.

He thanked me, said no and, instead, demanded that we climb onto the warehouse roof. As planned.

When we reached the top, I suggested that we share my rain poncho.

"No. I'm okay," he said, then he moved his chin in the direction we'd just come from. "I owe you an apology for what happened back there. I was just…tired. There was a problem at work and then, when I finally got home… Well, it's just that I haven't slept for more than a few hours in the past couple of days."

Obviously he was not okay. He was soaked and shivering, beyond exhaustion, physically and emotionally. And, though I was sure he'd never admit it, he was probably in shock.

I stripped off my poncho and dropped it at his feet.

"What the hell—"

"You can put it on. Or you can share it with me. Or we can both sit like fools in the driving rain. You choose."

He opened his mouth to object.

"Don't bother, Beauprix," I said. "This is one you're not going to win."

And so we knelt, side by side, beneath the poncho we'd draped over our shoulders. And, eventually, I felt him stop shivering as his cold body relaxed against the warmth of mine.

Odd to be tucked in next to a man who was now all business, who only a few minutes earlier had held on to me as though he were drowning. And I hadn't minded that he'd chosen me to hang on to. But, on the rooftop, it seemed as if those few moments of intensity had driven a wedge between us.

"What do you have?" he asked.

I kept my tone as neutral as his and told him everything I knew, everything I suspected about the Young Businessmen. I gave him the bundle with the teacups, the map, the license numbers. Then I told him what I suspected the members of the Benevolent Society had done.

I offered Beauprix the binoculars and we remained in near silence for the next half hour as he watched the patrol route. Focusing on the business at hand, I supposed, so that the immediate past would slide away. For just a little while.

Finally he put the binoculars aside and looked at me. And even in the darkness, I could see that his tears were still too near the surface.

"We need evidence," he said, struggling to keep his voice from cracking too badly. "Or a witness. But I can't… I'm sorry. But not right now… In a day or two. But until then…"

"We have time," I said. "At least a week."

"Lacie, ask your uncle for help. Tell him what you suspect. Maybe he can convince someone at city hall."

This was not the time to explain why I couldn't do that.

"Don't worry," I said, lightly touching his cheek. "For the time being, leave this to me."

"Check in with me every night. That hasn't changed. Promise me."

So I promised.

Chapter 18

On Saturday, I worked all day and stole the extra key to the Red Lotus's front door from its corner in the cash drawer. Late that night, I returned to the restaurant, let myself in and used my lock-picking skills on the metal file cabinet in the utility room. I sat in the middle of the floor for hours, looking over Mr. Yang's books.

Though he'd kept no record of the payments he was making to the Young Businessmen, in the past year the restaurant's reported income had been steadily declining. And, as I suspected, it was on the brink of failure. A motive, I thought. But I still needed to prove there'd been a crime.

Sunday, I followed the Yangs through their day. I watched them at church. I watched them at home. I watched them do nothing.

On Monday, Squirt called in sick.

"Female problems," I said, and wasn't pushed for details.

I walked to a bus stop where I was sure I wouldn't be recognized and took a bus back into the center of the city, paying the extra twenty-five cents for a transfer. I watched as the bus cruised past the massive Louisiana Superdome and got off at the next stop with a crowd of other passengers, a few of them with babies and toddlers in tow.

The entrance to the New Orleans Center was on Poydras Avenue near Sugarbowl Drive, and we all headed that way. Once inside the big glass doors, the other passengers were quickly lost to the mall's sixty upscale shops and mobs of mostly well-dressed female shoppers. Beneath the center's soaring marble atrium, I shopped under the watchful eyes of suspicious salesclerks.

I felt out of place and, no doubt, created considerable interest among security personnel throughout the mall. I ignored them all, continued with my business, and made a point of paying for merchandise at the nearest counter and keeping receipts for every purchase. Then I carried my packages with me into the mall's very nice public rest room.

A sign—Women—was all that kept a pair of male security officers in dun-brown uniforms from following me inside. They lingered near the door, and I passed them as I walked out of the rest room and headed in the direction of the mall's main entrance. As I hailed a taxi, I imagined them finally closing down the washroom and discovering that the mixed-race teenager with multicolored hair, wearing low-slung jeans and a skimpy top, had somehow escaped them.

I slid into the back seat.

The driver didn't bother to turn around, but slowly pulled away from the curb as his eyes examined me through the rearview mirror.

The woman he saw wasn't the type to stiff a cabdriver.

I was dressed in a black, two-piece linen suit. The skirt was fashionably, but not unacceptably, short. Dark hose over shapely legs and high heels made me look taller than I was.

Beneath the soft, feminine tailoring of the jacket, I wore a mocha-colored silk top with a straight, simple neckline. It matched a silky wrap-style hat that completely covered my hair. A gentle application of makeup emphasized my high cheekbones, slanted eyes and full lips. And the only jewelry I wore was a pair of thin gold hoops in my ears. Squirt—or, at least, the clothes that made her—now rode beside me in a Lord & Taylor shopping bag.

"Where to, ma'am?" the cabbie asked.

I reminded myself of who I was and spoke in Lacie Reed's voice—a voice that was solidly midwestern and hadn't, for many years, carried the accents of Vietnam.

"I have a funeral to attend at St. Louis Cemetery Number Two," I said, opening an expensive leather clutch purse. "Can you take me there?"

I was no stranger to the customs of New Orleans. I made it clear I knew exactly how far away the cemetery was, we negotiated a price for him to stay and wait for me until the funeral was over, and I paid half in cash up front. The cabbie flipped off his meter and drove.

Old New Orleans families are buried in old New Orleans cemeteries, and the Beauprixs had been around long enough to have taught the pirate Jean Lafitte some tricks of the trade. They also were probably among the first families to build an above-ground family crypt in St. Louis Cemetery No. 2.

That was back in 1823, when a yellow fever epidemic overwhelmed the original St. Louis Cemetery. The city fathers, perhaps wiser in the way of contagion than they'd been when Cemetery No. 1 was opened, located No. 2 in another swamp, this one a full third of a mile from the inhabited French Quarter.

Thanks to modern drainage, the contagious dead were no longer a problem. Thanks to a deteriorating inner city and the no-man's land created beneath the elevated interstate roadway, the criminal living were. Most guidebooks warned tourists away from solitary visits to Cemetery No.2, even in the middle of the day.

It was the middle of the day, but the funeral of Charles Beauprix was not a solitary affair. The taxi dropped me just outside the Bienville Street gate, where more than a hundred people were already gathering for the procession. The driver went to park the cab around the corner on north Claiborne Street. Or, perhaps, to pick up another fare while I attended the funeral. I only hoped that the unpaid half of our bargain was enough temptation to bring him back.

I stood at the fringes of the crowd, among those who were there not out of grief, but out of respect.

Anthony, his brother, and his sister stood near the hearse, shaking hands and hugging those whose tears marked them as close family and dear friends. Occasionally, Anthony would turn to greet another well-wisher or to speak with the Catholic priest who stood close by or to move his hand from his sister's hand to his brother's arm. Then I would get a good look at his face.

My lost parents had been mourned slowly, their absence a chronic sadness that eroded away, year after year, until nothing was left of it but an empty place where love and memory were supposed to be. But here in the cemetery and, days earlier, when I'd held Beauprix as he'd wept, I could see that his grief had an immediacy, a razor-edged sharpness. Time would pass, I thought, but Charles Beauprix would always be loved. And I envied his son his memories.

The procession formed, slowly unwinding like a snake and flowing into one of the wide aisleways. This was no unrestrained New Orleans jazz funeral replete with musicians and dancers celebrating a soul's return to God. It was a solemn, quiet affair where the faithful struggled not to resent their loss.

The cemetery's clamshell roads had long ago been covered over by smooth, pale concrete. It reflected the sun, bringing heat to an otherwise cool autumn day, as the line of mourners—led by the priest and the small, lonely knot of Charles Beauprix's remaining family—fell into place behind the slow-moving black hearse.

I was one of the last to leave the tall, wrought-iron gates of the Bienville Street entrance. So I was one of the few who saw a limousine pull up and a chauffeur jump out to open the car door. I paused, recognizing the chauffeur, waiting for the limousine's passenger.

Uncle Tinh.

He smiled when he saw me, waved, and his characteristically energetic step carried him quickly to my side. He had clothed his slim body in a well-tailored dark suit, white shirt and dark tie. His clean-shaven head was bare, but dress shoes had replaced his usual sandals.

I was glad to see him. His home was to have been my first stop after the funeral. There were now too many lives at stake to leave important questions unasked.

He gave me a brief hug, and we lingered for a moment, speaking quietly.

"Ah, Lacie. I didn't expect to see you here."

"I wasn't going to come, but…"

I shrugged, unable to explain to Uncle Tinh what I couldn't fully explain to myself. But he seemed to understand.

"As for myself, I thought the same," he said. "But in the end, it was an easy enough thing to do for a friend."

Together we hurried to catch up with the end of the procession. Then my adopted uncle threaded his arm through mine and we walked together in silence.

The broad cement aisleway along which we were led was lined on both sides with ornate tombs, most of them little more than the height of a tall metalwork doorway and a gently peaked roof. The older crypts were whitewashed bricks or granite, the newer made from white marble. The crosses, urns and angels that topped the crypts stood starkly against the slate-colored New Orleans sky. Flowers and candles decorated the doorways and the single steps up to the tombs, and occasionally I spied the glint of an *immortelle*—a wreath created from tiny beads of black glass.

The procession crossed Priest's Aisle, then began to slow. And stopped. The mourners pressed in closer, once again a crowd rather than a procession. But this time there was no murmur of conversation. Everyone's attention was on the priest and the eldest son. One spoke of earthly life and immortality; the other, more briefly, of love and family. Uncle Tinh put his arm around my shoulders, his touch somehow comforting a sadness I hadn't, until then, realized I felt.

Finally the body of Charles Beauprix was placed on a flat stone shelf inside the crypt. Local law required that he be interred for at least a year and a day—time enough for the heat within the crypt to turn his corpse to ashes. Then, according to local custom, his remains would be pushed past the back edge of the shelf, into the ash pit below the crypt. There, death united the mortal remains of families and generations.

The procession moved back to the gate.

Once again, I hung back at the edge of the crowd. This time, with Uncle Tinh by my side. The Beauprix family began loading into the car that had carried them to the cemetery. Anthony had his arms around his sister, who was pressed in close to him, crying. As he helped her into the car he turned his head and, by chance, saw me watching him. He managed a smile, took a step away from the car in my direction. Then his sister leaned out, caught his hand in hers, and I saw her speak urgently to him. He nodded at her, took a moment to smile again in my direction, then ducked to follow her into the car.

I watched the car pull away. When I looked away from it, I noticed that Uncle Tinh's dark eyes were on my face.

"This Beauprix fellow is a good man," he said.

I nodded.

"Yes, Uncle Tinh. Anthony is a very good man."

I paid the waiting cabbie and sent him off without his passenger.

Then I walked back to the limo.

A young, muscular man with dark Asian features sat in the front passenger seat. A bodyguard, I thought. Though I'd never before known my uncle to use one.

"Trouble?" I asked, lifting my chin in the direction of the bodyguard as Uncle Tinh's driver held open the door to the back seat.

I slipped inside first.

Uncle Tinh spared the man in the front seat a quick glance before shrugging.

"A ward against trouble," he said. And he didn't offer to explain what that trouble was.

A thick plate of opaque glass between the front seat and passenger compartment kept conversations private from the men in the front seat, and the dark tint on the limousine's windows shielded us from curious eyes as we drove through the streets of New Orleans to Uncle Tinh's business and home on Ursuline Street.

"Have dinner with me," he suggested as we got under way.

I doubted he would want my company by the time our conversation was done. But I didn't want to offend him unnecessarily.

"Thank you, but not tonight," I said, shaking my head. "I'm tired, it's getting late, and I still have to change my clothes and return to Little Vietnam."

"Change?" Uncle Tinh asked.

"Change. An outfit to match my hair."

I pulled off the wrap that had covered my head.

Uncle Tinh laughed merrily, lines crinkling the smooth skin by his eyes.

"I had heard about your disguise from Beauprix. But *mon Dieu!* The reality! The boy in my kitchen, Tommy Nguyen. I think he would be in love."

I was not in the mood for laughter. But I was glad that Uncle Tinh had brought up the boy's name.

"Despite his looks," I said, "Tommy seems like a very mature young man. As if there's been some hardship in his life."

Uncle Tinh lifted his hands, palm up.

"Adversity builds character. Look at you."

I was tired of half truths.

"You know that Tommy's brother is Nguyen Tri," I said, making it a statement.

"Of course. Your Anthony and I spoke of just this before I phoned Senator Reed and asked for your help."

Either Beauprix was lying or my uncle was. Beauprix had no reason to lie.

"Why didn't you tell *me?*"

"I thought I had."

Uncle Tinh tried to look confused. But he was not a man familiar enough with that condition to form an expression that rang true.

"An oversight only," he continued. "Certainly, your young policeman said something to you about it."

"No."

"Maybe he thought it didn't matter."

But my uncle, who understood the Vietnamese, would have known that the family connection mattered very much.

"It turns out that Tommy's the nephew of *my* employer, Mr. Yang."

"Yes, I know of Mr. Yang. And the Red Lotus. Good food. Excellent location. When Anthony told me you'd gotten a job there, I was pleased."

Briefly, I thought about the Red Lotus's smashed front window. Lacie was attacked by men wearing bird masks on Bourbon Street. Feathered crimson and black masks were thrown into Squirt's workplace. There were only two people who knew that Lacie and Squirt were the same person. Uncle Tinh and Anthony Beauprix. Not only did my feelings cry out against the possibility that either man would harm me, but I could think of no reason for the terror campaign. There had to be another explanation. So I dismissed my fears about the carrion birds as irrelevant to the business at hand.

"Uncle Tinh?" I said.

"Yes?"

"Would you ever lie to me?"

At the mention of Nguyen Tri, any trace of humor had disappeared from his round face. My latest question deepened that look into a frown and wrinkled his usually smooth forehead. As the limousine pulled into the alley behind Tinh's City Vu and the driver killed the engine, Uncle Tinh examined me with dark, serious eyes.

His driver and bodyguard left the car and stood outside our door, waiting. But Uncle Tinh made no move to leave the privacy of the back seat.

"I would lie only if the truth betrayed the confidence of another. Is there something you fear I would lie to you about?"

I chose my words carefully.

"I know that you have a reputation for being discrete. Perhaps, because of your…connections…you are privy to information denied to others. Maybe you hear or know things of a…sensitive…nature."

I paused, giving him an opening, deciding in that moment not to reveal Uncle Duran's accusations. If Uncle Tinh was to become an adversary, such information could give me an advantage.

"What do you want to know, Lacie?" he prompted.

I pitched my voice to make my theories sound like certainty.

"A shipment from overseas arrived in New Orleans ten days ago. A shipment of illegal immigrants. It was stolen by the Benevolent Society and is now hidden, awaiting documentation, before moving north."

Uncle Tinh lifted his eyebrow, pursed his lips, nodded.

"Important information," he said finally. "From this, it would seem that *you* are the one with connections."

I ignored the gibe, noticed that he hadn't questioned or contradicted anything I'd said.

"Do you know where that shipment is?" I asked.

He didn't lie to me.

"I cannot say."

"Can't say because you don't know or because you'd be breaking a confidence?"

He shook his head.

"I can assure you that the shipment, every piece, is safe. Please, Lacie. Don't be distracted from the *real* problem by hunting for it. Have you found the head of the viper? Do you know who directs the gang that terrorizes Little Vietnam? Have you identified the sociopath who murdered three of our people?"

I blurted out what I was beginning to suspect.

"When I find this monster, this viper of yours, will I also be destroying my uncle's business rival? Who is providing the documentation for the shipment? The Young Businessmen's Association? Or you?"

I wanted Uncle Tinh to be outraged, to hotly deny my accusation, to demand that I apologize. I wanted him to tell me that I was wrong, that he was a good man. That he would never betray my trust.

But he didn't react at all. Except to turn away from me and tap sharply on the window.

At his signal, the driver opened the door.

Then Tinh Vu hesitated. He turned and the expression on his face was one of utter sadness. As if someone beloved had died.

"Only for the most honorable of causes would I place you in jeopardy."

Then he stepped from the limousine.

"Take my niece wherever she chooses to go," he said.

Then, with his bodyguard at his heels, he walked through the door marked Private.

Chapter 19

Tuesday and Wednesday passed like a nightmare. I learned nothing of value throughout the day and saw nothing worth noting that night. And I could think only of a group of desperate refugees, trapped and helpless. Their fate in the hands of strangers.

On Thursday afternoon Vincent came into the Red Lotus with a newspaper tucked under his arm. He opened it to the business section and pointed at a blurb that was just a couple of column inches long. It was an announcement about the grand opening of a new discount store. Instead of braving the traffic into New Orleans, many residents of New Orleans East shopped across the bridge in nearby Slidell. Which was where the store was located.

"What's important here," Vincent said, "is that the manager is going to hire through me. I mean, through the Refugee Center. There'll be at least ten jobs for people living right here in Little Vietnam."

"Nice," I said, trying to sound like I cared. "Congratulations."

"Are you interested in a job there? It'd pay better than this one. I could recommend you…."

I had just finished gathering the small, half-empty soy sauce bottles from along the counter and was using a butter knife to pry off their plastic shaker tops as an excuse to work nearby. I concentrated on lifting a particularly stubborn top as I remembered the drawing I had done of him. Bird mask and all. My subconscious had insisted that Vincent Ngo was not what he pretended to be. But I had no idea what he *was*. The proper response to his offer might help me find out.

I looked around, saw that Mr. Yang was deeply engaged in conversation with the butcher, but still pitched my voice low when I replied. "The Yangs are nice. But waitressing? It's hard. And not much money. I'd like another job. Except…"

I left the word hanging as I finally popped off the lid and waited for Vincent to take the bait.

"Except what?"

I ignored the narrow-eyed look he shot me, flipped off another bottle top and added it to the growing pile on the counter.

"When I left home, I had to take off fast. Because my stepfather wasn't going to take no for an answer anymore. I didn't take my birth certificate. And I don't know what my social security number is. My mom probably called the cops. I figure if I try to get copies, they'll find out where I am. And I'll get sent back home."

I let a little anger creep into my voice as I pulled a heavy gallon can of soy sauce out from under the counter and began refilling the row of bottles.

"So I'm stuck in crummy places like this until I'm eighteen."

"No you're not. I know a man in the Quarter who will sell me a birth certificate. You will have to go by a different name but, with it, you can get a new social security number. And a driver's license, if you want one."

I tried not to react to anything but his offer. The French Quarter was home to hundreds of unsavory businesses. No reason to assume that this was proof.

"How much?" I asked. "I pay with money, not my body. For that, I might as well be back home."

"This man has other women. He's Vietnamese, like us. And he owns a restaurant. So maybe he'll give you a discount. Shall I ask him?"

I let tears creep into my eyes. Genuine tears. To Vincent, they must have appeared to be tears of gratitude. But I knew they were tears of mourning. For everything Uncle Tinh had been to me.

"I'll find a way to save up," I said.

I was still snapping tops back on the small bottles when he left.

On Friday morning, there was no meeting of the Benevolent Society.

On Friday afternoon, the protection money was paid to the Young Businessmen. And the man who counted the money passed Mr. Yang a note.

Near the end of my workday, Mrs. Yang fought with Mr. Yang, their argument ending abruptly when Mrs. Yang stormed from the restaurant.

Mrs. Yang's cousin had been out back smoking a cigarette, so he missed the drama. But when he returned and discovered that Mrs. Yang had left, he assured me that this sort of thing happened often and that Mrs. Yang would probably be back by dinnertime.

Somehow, I doubted it. I had been standing, unnoticed, in the utility room and had overheard their whispered battle.

"The documents are ready," Mr. Yang said in Vietnamese. "The meeting is arranged for Sunday. After Mass."

"Good, then they will be gone. And this will finally be over."

There was silence. In it, Mrs. Yang must have read something in her husband's expression.

"What has gone wrong now?"

"The price has doubled. That is what the note said. We can pay the same amount again and receive the documents. Or we can turn over the women to their *anh hai*. He will sell the tea himself."

My God, I thought. Tea. It was trafficker gang-slang, language I'd learned working for Uncle Duran. Tea referred to a shipment of Asian women, usually illegals, headed for the sex trade.

"We can let them go."

"Whether the shipment arrives at its destination or not, we will still owe the *anh hai* for the documents."

"Then we have no choice," I heard Mrs. Yang say. "There is no more money. Give him the shipment."

"I will borrow the money."

"Against what? From whom? The *anh hai*? Our future is already given away to his thieves."

"I will go to Tinh Vu, beg his forgiveness and ask him for his help. He will not refuse me, I think. That shipment is ours. We liberated it."

Forgiveness for what? I wondered. And I suspected that the Benevolent Society had made the mistake of going to Tinh Vu's rivals for counterfeit documents. I could hear the determination in Mr. Yang's voice.

His tone angered Mrs. Yang. She hissed through her teeth, "Your pride started this. You saw yourself as a soldier leading your comrades into battle. But you are an old fool, leading foolish old men. Now see what you have done!"

And that was when Mrs. Yang stormed from the kitchen, slamming the back door behind her.

* * *

I called Beauprix. Though I had intended to outline everything in some logical manner, when he answered I simply blurted out that which had weighed most heavily on my mind.

"My God, Anthony, they hijacked a tea shipment."

He knew the term and reacted with the same horror I felt.

I abandoned any attempt to protect Uncle Tinh. Too much had happened to shatter the trust between us.

I told Beauprix about Senator Duran Reed's suspicions. Repeated, nearly word-for-word, the conversation between the Yangs. And then told him about Vincent's offer the day before.

"So Vincent is an independent?"

"A middleman, a social worker. Maybe a good Samaritan, though I don't think so. But he offered to get forged documents for me."

"From Tinh Vu?"

"I think so," I said, hesitating. And then I said what I believed. "Yes."

"So you're saying Tinh Vu is the *anh hai*. Number two brother?"

He'd translated the words literally, so I explained.

"It means most-esteemed brother. In a Vietnamese gang, it's the equivalent of a mafia don. And yes, I'm saying that Uncle Tinh is the *anh hai*."

The thought still made me feel ill. Uncle Duran had been absolutely right in his judgment of Uncle Tinh. How was it possible that I had been so wrong?

"Then why did he call you in? Why expose himself deliberately to an investigation?"

I'd thought about that for days, thought about it again after hearing the Yangs argue.

"It's a war, Anthony. A rival gang—the Young Vietnamese Businessmen's Association—moved in and attempted to destroy Uncle Tinh's operation. By killing his forgers, I think.

Maybe that's why Mr. Yang went to the Young Businessmen for forged documents. Against Uncle Tinh's wishes, I'm sure.

"I don't think Uncle Tinh knows who the rival *anh hai* is. So he brought me in. Used me. Pointed me at the protection racket and the murders, hoping I could destroy the competition for him. Both groups, I suspect, specialize in breeder documents. Maybe in human trafficking, too."

We talked for a while about what we would do next and, for a change, quickly reached agreement. On Sunday, if we followed Mr. Yang, we would sooner or later witness the meeting where money and documents would be exchanged.

"I'm sorry, Lacie," Beauprix said before he hung up. "I'm truly sorry."

I went to work Saturday because I wanted to keep an eye on Mr. Yang.

When I walked into the Red Lotus, the elderly cousin greeted me at the door. He was wearing a clean, white apron and setting up tables for Saturday's early lunch crowd. I looked past him through the kitchen door. As I expected, Mr. Yang was busy preparing the day's soups. But to my surprise, Tommy was in the elderly cousin's usual spot, busily chopping onions.

"What's going on?" I asked the elderly cousin in Vietnamese. "Why is Tommy here?"

It seemed that Tommy had somehow been co-opted into helping in this emergency. Only because, the elderly cousin rushed to assure me, it was young Tommy's day off from his better-paying and far-more-important job at a very expensive restaurant in the Quarter. Though the cousin could not at the moment recall what the name of that restaurant was.

I knew its name, though I didn't say that to the cousin. Still, I had no idea what was going on at the Red Lotus that morning and the elderly cousin's meandering explanation hadn't helped.

"What emergency?" I asked, hoping for some information that might help me make sense of the situation.

Mrs. Yang's anger, it seemed, had prompted her to pack her bags and take the Friday train—Amtrak's Spirit of New Orleans—to her sister's home in Illinois. Accompanied by the twins.

Then the elderly cousin waved his hand dismissively.

"No need to worry," he said, self-importantly. "*I* have arranged everything. Today, I will help you wait on customers. Tommy will help Mr. Yang and wash dishes. Of course, it will be very busy, and you and I will have to work very hard." Then he bent in close, dropping his voice to almost a whisper, implying that what he shared next was a little known truth. "But this is an opportunity to earn the undying gratitude of Mr. Yang, who is a very important man in Little Vietnam."

The cousin continued speaking, now in a normal voice.

"Tomorrow, Mr. Yang will go to Mass as he does every Sunday. If he is wise, he will pray for rapid return of his wife and daughters. Perhaps the Holy Spirit will guide him to apologize so that there will be no strike on Monday."

It took me a moment to translate the unfamiliar word from Vietnamese to English and back.

"Strike?"

"Ah, yes. It would not be proper for me to work while my cousin and her daughters languish in Illinois."

Somehow I was missing something and I wondered if chronic fatigue had slowed my comprehension. I gave my head a half shake, trying to clear it.

"But what about today?" I asked.

"Saturday is a very busy day," was the cousin's pragmatic answer. "On Monday, if it is necessary, I will remain at home. Thus I demonstrate solidarity without damaging the family business. On Monday, it will be up to you to help Mr. Yang carry the burden of his stubbornness."

The cousin clapped me on the shoulder as if he were royalty bestowing an honor.

"By Tuesday, I am sure, everything will return to normal."

I envied the elderly man his optimism.

More than twelve hours later, my feet hurt from endless running between kitchen and tables, my head hurt from the constant din of voices and the clatter of dishes, and my face hurt from smiling pleasantly.

By the time the restaurant closed and we'd cleaned up for the night, exhaustion prompted me to join Mr. Yang, the elderly cousin and Tommy eating leftovers at the small prep table in the kitchen. As did everyone, I used my chopsticks to lift morsels of vegetables, seafood and meat from an assortment of larger plates into my small, rice-filled bowl. Except for an occasional brief positive comment, usually about the flavor and quality of the food, the meal was eaten in companionable silence.

Now, all I wanted to do was walk home, soak my feet and try to get some sleep. Tomorrow, Beauprix and I would meet early and follow Mr. Yang through every step of his day.

I detoured into the kitchen, grabbed my denim purse from the hook inside the utility room and unplugged my phone from its charger. I punched in my security code and checked my voice mail. One message. Beauprix's familiar voice.

"I've got some curious information for you. I'm going to spend the afternoon following up on it. I'll call you tonight."

Curious information.

Now that, I thought with a weary smile, was a curious choice of words. His information was apparently important enough that he had called early, anticipating that I'd leave work on time. But there was no urgency in his message, so I was content to wait for his call.

I slid my phone back into my purse, then trudged back through the restaurant to the front door, raising my right hand, waving and calling out "Good night" without bothering to look behind me.

Tommy bounded past me with the kind of energy only a teenage boy could muster at the end of a long day. He tugged open the heavy door one-handed, swept an imaginary cap off his pink-and-blue streaked hair with the other hand and managed an awkward bow. All this accompanied by the familiar tinny jingle of the tiny bell mounted above the door.

"Ladies first," he said.

I was tired and cranky and not feeling particularly youthful. But I smiled anyway at the special attention, as any teenage girl would have.

"I have my car," he offered eagerly. "I can drop you off at home."

I shook my head wearily. I had noticed the way he'd been looking at me throughout the day and I was not in the mood to fend off more amorous advances.

He might not have understood why, but I think he sensed my reservations. As the door closed behind us, he lifted his hands, palms toward me. I noticed the thickened ridges of old calluses and wondered how long he'd worked for Uncle Tinh.

"Hey, no funny stuff," he said, his voice an odd combination of maturity overlaying adolescence, of Louisiana's long vowels overlaying the choppy syllables of Vietnam. "Promise. I was just thinking that you looked real tired. And I have a car."

It was an indication of how truly weary I was that I accepted.

Chapter 20

Tommy had a rusty blue Ford Escort with torn seats, a bad muffler and a loud stereo. Dangling from the rearview mirror were a silver St. Christopher medal and a colorful paper-mâché charm of Ong Tao—the long-skirted Vietnamese kitchen god—flying to heaven.

I slid into the front seat, arranging my feet to accommodate the battered textbooks, glossy cooking magazines and pieces of graph and notebook paper that littered the floor. Just before Tommy shut the door for me, extinguishing the overhead light, I had a look at the open ashtray. It held a handful of quarters, a coupon for half off a large pizza and a flat, unopened condom packet. In case of emergency, I thought.

Tommy got in behind the wheel. He started the car, turned down the radio that blared on when he turned the key in the ignition, and rolled down the windows to let in the cool evening air. Somewhere in between, he managed to slide the ashtray shut. I smiled as I tried to remember if I had ever been that young.

When he asked where I lived, I told him. Though his eyes widened and his studded eyebrow lifted, he made no comment as he pulled the car away from the curb. My house might be just over a mile away, I thought, but it was far removed from the middle-class sensibilities of Little Vietnam.

"Be there in a few," he said, punching the accelerator.

The old car coughed, strained and edged up to thirty. The night was bright and, after the stuffy warm-food atmosphere of the restaurant, the breeze washing in through the open windows was pleasant.

Two thirds of the way to my house, low- and medium-density housing transitioned to a block of multistory tenements that lined both sides of the street. As we drove down that block, we were on the opposite side of the street from the worst of them—three dilapidated, nearly identical four-story buildings of frame construction. Each flat-fronted exterior had an entrance that opened onto a cracked sidewalk without benefit of porch, stoop or overhang. Between the tenements, weedy trees grew tall enough to rub their thick branches against the walls on either side.

From my wanderings, I knew that beyond the three entrances there were foyer doors that had no locks and steep stairwells that led to long hallways on each floor. At the far end of each hallway was a back exit. But the steps and landings at the rear of the building were mostly rotted and someone had padlocked the exit doors to keep the residents away from the hazard.

During one of my late-night surveys, I'd walked through the tenement. Just looking. So I knew that, although there were supposed to be a dozen apartments on each floor, more than half of the units had been subdivided. Unlocked and missing doors along the hallways on every floor led into a maze of short corridors and unpredictable dead ends. At every turn there was a locked door that marked a rented space—a space that had once been part of a bedroom, living room, dining room or kitchen.

Tonight, as we drove past the tenements, the moon was full and very bright. Without it, I would have missed seeing the black smoke drifting up from the building in the middle, creating a veil across the face of the moon.

"Fire!" I cried to Tommy, pointing.

He pulled to the curb.

I snatched my cell phone from my purse, dialed the fire department and gave them the address. As I spoke, Tommy killed the ignition, grabbed his own cell phone, hit the speed dial, said, "Fire!" and gave the street name. Duplicating my call to 911, I thought. Just in case.

I folded my phone, slipped it into my pocket and grabbed the door handle. From the corner of my eye, I saw Tommy do the same. Without discussion, we both bolted from the car, locking the doors behind us, and ran toward the tenement. Tommy was just half a step behind me when we reached the entrance. We entered the foyer and, side by side, raced up the stairs. On the second-floor landing, we paused briefly, catching our breaths.

"I'll start warning people on this floor," he volunteered.

"Sounds good," I said. "Then work your way down to the first floor. I'll start on the fourth, then do the third."

"Got it," he said.

"Be careful, Tommy."

He nodded, looked grim.

"Squirt, there are lots of interior apartments—"

No time to have him explain what I already knew.

"Yes."

He flashed me a smile, then turned on his heel and ran into the hall, started banging on doors, shouting "Fire!" and "Wake up!" and "Get out of the building!" in Vietnamese and English.

I took one last glance at him, then started up the stairs, climbing the remaining two flights at top speed. Somewhere between the third and fourth floor, I could feel the phone buzzing in my pocket. I ignored it, made it to the fourth floor and raced down the hall, detouring into the corridors within the apartments, yelling for people to get out, get out now.

Smoke wafted through the hallway of the fourth floor.

Those who opened their doors took one whiff of the air, looked at my face, and didn't need any more convincing. Some grabbed their loved ones; others ran back inside to snatch up wallets, purses or possessions; some simply ran for the stairs without a look back.

Soon the sounds of shouts and cries and running feet drifted constantly from the stairwell. Tommy, I thought, was successfully rousing the residents of the lower floors.

A middle-aged woman with a café au lait complexion stepped from an apartment into the hallway in front of me. She was tall and lanky, and was dressed in a royal-blue nylon warmup suit with a hooded top that was pushed back to reveal dozens of thin, uniform braids capping her head.

"The building's on fire," I said urgently.

Unlike the others, she didn't look panicked or immediately turn her attention to escape.

"How can I help?" she asked, and her voice was calm and cool.

I pointed past her, down the hall. Two doors hung open and I knew that inside was a maze of tiny apartments.

"Bang on every door," I said. "Don't wait for someone to answer. Not everyone will be home. Then get out of the building as fast as you can."

"Okay," she said.

As I made my way back to the stairwell, I could already hear her behind me, kicking at a door and shouting warnings to the occupants.

I ran down the stairs to the third floor, leaning—half-sliding—on the railing, my feet barely touching each step. As I rounded the corner into the third-floor hallway, I could see a thick layer of roiling smoke hanging at ceiling level. It was much thicker than it had been upstairs. I searched for its source, noticed that the smoke was more dense and hung lower at the far end of the hall.

I decided that there was no longer time to detour into each branching corridor and bang on every locked door. Instead, I screamed "Fire!" repeatedly as I ran down the hall, shouted it until the smoke was so thick that all I could do was manage to breathe. But I'd made it to the most remote pair of apartments.

The doors that should have marked the entry to the apartments were missing. Smoke poured out from the doorway on my left. That one first, I thought urgently.

I pressed my nose and mouth into the crook of my arm and hurried down the maze of a corridor, locating doors more by feel than by sight. I kicked at them, pounded on them, jiggled knobs trying to open them. When the smoke became so thick that I was coughing more than I was inhaling, I backed out into the hallway. The air was better, but not by much. The layer of smoke had dropped farther, now hanging about midway between the ceiling and the floor.

Between me and the stairwell, I heard another voice shouting in the hallway. Another set of feet and fists were banging on doors. For a moment I thought it was Tommy. Then I realized it was the woman from the fourth floor. I continued moving in her direction and our combined warnings echoed up and down the hall.

Finally, we met. Job done, we leaned into each other's arms and supported each other as we began staggering toward the stairs.

That's when we heard the cry.

Behind us.

We both turned. Listened. Hurried back down the hall, coughing and wheezing in the thickening smoke, trying to locate the sound. We heard it again. A wavering cry. Back in one of the cut-up apartments. Together, we turned into the small interior corridor. This time, we didn't pound on doors or yell out a warning. We just listened.

The cry came again. And a single word. "Help!"

"This one!" the woman from the fourth floor said as she rushed to a door where the corridor dead-ended.

The door was locked.

My companion was more than half a foot taller and at least fifty pounds heavier than I was. She shouted an obscenity and threw her shoulder against the door. Once. Twice. The wood around the lock split with a loud crack and the door swung open.

Behind us, flames roared up in the hallway, ate their way down the twisting corridor. Smoke still hung in the air, making breathing difficult. And it stung our eyes. I looked at my companion, saw that she, too, had tears running down her cheeks and was periodically rubbing her eyes with the back of her hand.

There would be less smoke and better air down low. I dropped to the floor, grabbed the woman's sleeve and pulled her down beside me. On hands and knees, we crawled through the apartment's single large room, searching beneath the bed and behind furniture, listening for cries that would guide us.

Nothing. No cries. Nobody, conscious or otherwise.

I glanced around the apartment, looking for another way out. No windows. Walls lined with shelves supporting dozens of tiny statues. Sacred Heart. Madonna and Child. St. Francis. St. Therese. St. Martin de Porres. And votive candles, short and tall. All lit. Dozens of single flames captured within crystal cut containers that glittered red and violet and blue.

Outside, the inferno raged unchecked.

God help us, I thought, which was as much prayer as I had time for.

There were four doors into the large room. One shattered. Three closed.

I crawled to one closed door as the black woman went to a second. Both closets. No one huddled in either of them.

Fire began licking around the broken doorway

We both headed for the third door and I pushed it open.

A bathroom. The apartment's only window was on the wall just above the bathtub. It offered the only possibility of escape.

Inside the tub was a cage covered by a cotton towel. From inside, a green parrot called out.

"Help!" it said, and, "Oh, my!" And then it wailed, "Oh-h-h-h."

We'd risked our lives to save a bird.

I had no intention of dying for our trouble.

I pushed the bathroom door closed, grabbed a towel from a hook on the wall, soaked it in the cracked sink, and packed it around the base of the door. That offered temporary respite from the smoke and fire.

In the meantime, the woman pulled the towel from the cage, soaked it, and put it back in place.

"We've got to get out of here," she said.

The parrot said, "Gimme five!"

"Come on," I said. "Get in the tub."

From there, I pushed the window open, grabbed the bird-cage and dangled it outside. The woman was at my side. Together, we hung our heads, shoulders and arms out over the sill. For a minute, we gasped and coughed and dragged fresh air into our lungs.

The power had gone out in the building, but the moonlight cast long shadows between the two buildings. Immediately opposite us was the blank wooden wall of the tenement next door. And I could hear approaching sirens. Help would arrive within minutes.

Even if we shouted, it would take a few more minutes for them to locate us. I doubted the fire would wait that long. Despite the closed door, smoke was working its way into the small bathroom, already pouring out around us, threatening to choke us.

Safety was three stories straight down.

Between us and the ground was a tree with sturdy branches.

"We have to climb down," I said, coughing.

"I can't," she said.

For the first time that evening, I heard fear in her voice. I turned my head, looked into her face, saw that her eyes were stretched wide.

The flames behind us weren't offering any options.

I still held the caged parrot.

She'd risked her life for it. Maybe it would give her the incentive she needed. I leaned farther out the window and pulled a corner of the fabric away from the cage door.

"I'd better let this little guy go."

"He'll die!"

I doubted she'd see my shrug, so I made sure she could hear it in my voice.

"If we stay here, he'll last longer than we will. But if you think it'd be better, I can drop him. Maybe the cage'll protect him."

The parrot helped my cause by squawking out its displeasure.

"No way!" it cried.

Stupid bird.

"We can carry him down," she said.

I shook my head.

"We need our hands free."

She forgot about how scared she was, focusing instead on saving the pet's life. She was a brave woman. Or, perhaps, a foolish one. But she wasn't going to let the little bird die. Within moments she'd found a solution. I hurried to help her so that we, too, would reach safety.

I dragged the cage back inside the window and she pulled off its fabric cover and smoothed it out. Then she grabbed the bird. It squawked and bit her for her trouble, but she ignored it, hauled it from the cage and wrapped it in the folds of the damp towel. I helped her tuck the bundle deep into the hood of the jacket that she wore. A quick tug on the drawstrings kept the package secure.

I hung back out of the window and tossed the cage so that it would clear the tree and hit the ground. It'd give us a place to put the parrot once we climbed down. Then I turned back to my companion.

"What's your name?" I asked.

"Dolores."

"Okay, Dolores. You first," I said.

Just beneath us was a substantial branch that slanted gently down toward a thick trunk that was no more than six feet away. In between, there were lots of smaller branches to use as handholds. From the trunk, it was an easy climb down to the ground. An easy climb if you didn't mind heights. I could feel the woman trembling as I held her arm, supporting her as she edged out the window.

In my pocket, the phone vibrated. Not now, I thought. Not now.

Dolores, the parrot, and I made it to the ground, one step at a time, one branch at a time, one fear-filled moment at a time. Easy for the parrot who, once confined within the folds of fabric, was silent except for an occasional crackling "chirrup." Difficult for Dolores who, once in the tree, had not miraculously discovered that she had a knack for climbing.

I coached her every move as we inched our way from branch to branch. And she did what she had to do.

She made it down, leaned weakly against the building for a moment, then picked her way through the litter that had accumulated between the tenements. Overhead, smoke and flames poured out through the third-floor window. But she seemed not to notice as she searched the shadows for the cage.

I saw it first, hurried to pick it up for her. It was badly bent but still intact, and I held the door open. Dolores freed the bundle from her hood, pushed it inside the cage, then unwrapped the parrot. It flapped and squawked and managed to bite her.

After Dolores yanked her hand away, I carefully latched the door, then grinned at her.

"After all this, it'd be bad if the little guy escaped," I said.

Dolores stuck her pinched and bleeding knuckle up to her mouth.

"Yeah," she muttered. "Little fucker might kill someone."

By now, more emergency vehicles were arriving by the moment. The sounds of sirens and diesel engines and loud male voices filled the air as trucks pulled into position and squad cars began blocking off the street to traffic. In front of the building, firefighters were swarming from their trucks, dragging hoses and opening fire hydrants, pouring into the apartment building.

Dolores gave me a quick hug before we parted. Then, holding the cage tightly in her arms, she threaded her way between fire trucks to the opposite side of the street.

I paused on the sidewalk in front of the tenement and scanned the crowd for Tommy and his telltale mop of Technicolor hair. I didn't see him and had just started to cross the street when the wind whipped thick, acrid smoke through the passageway between the buildings. Suddenly, I was enveloped in it.

I had taken a breath at exactly the wrong moment. Smoke filled my throat, stung my eyes. My body was racked by another bout of coughing and I couldn't seem to drag enough air into my lungs. Suddenly a firefighter had his arms around me and I half walked, was half carried, to a nearby ambulance. Its stretchers were already occupied by other escapees from the building, so I sat on the back bumper as a busy paramedic slapped an oxygen mask over my face.

"Just breathe," were the terse instructions he gave me, but he followed them up with a smile.

The traffic was blocked in both directions by emergency vehicles. I had a clear view of the burning building, so in between coughing fits I watched the proceedings. And watched for Tommy.

One firefighter was in charge of the scene, orchestrating equipment and personnel with the grace and control of a symphony conductor. The barriers between the buildings had been pulled aside and hoses writhed like snakes through the narrow space. Streams of water from pumper trucks hit the roof and the side walls of the tenement and the adjacent buildings. Helmeted firefighters rushed in and out of the front door and around the sides of the building carrying axes and smaller hoses. Some ended up beside me, faces stained by the smoke, coughing and gasping for oxygen.

Flames licked out the windows and shot through the roof of the building.

Ambulances screamed away from the scene.

Rapidly erected barriers and dozens of uniformed cops kept the curious back from the scene. The tenement's uninjured residents—hundreds of them—were gathered on the near side of the barrier. Ages and races intermingled—young, old, black, white, yellow, brown—reflecting the diversity of poverty. Sitting or standing, in various states of shock and undress, they watched and some wept as their homes and possessions burned. Tonight they were all victims of a color-blind inferno.

The longer I sat, the more anxious I became. From where I sat, it was difficult to see everyone who had escaped the building or who, like me, was tucked in beside an emergency vehicle. Certainly, I told myself, Tommy would have stayed at the scene looking for Squirt. Unless he was injured…

I hadn't coughed for several minutes. I lifted the mask, took a breath of the outside air, didn't cough or gag, so judged myself cured. Then I stood, spotted Tommy's car still parked where we had left it, and began searching the crowd for him.

The distinctive blue-and-pink hair and the assortment of rings and bars that adorned his face should have made him easy to pick out and remember. Even in a crowd, even in the chaos of the fire scene. I walked from one ambulance to the next, talking to anyone who could spare me a moment, looking for him among those who were receiving first aid, wondering if he'd been so badly injured that he had been sent to the hospital.

No one remembered treating him.

I walked the perimeter of the fire scene. The barricades blocked the street and sidewalks at the middle of the block, several doors down from the flaming structure. I walked around emergency vehicles, paralleled the barriers and then walked along the sidewalk to the corner.

People had come from blocks away to view the dramatic fire. As I searched for Tommy, stopping to talk to occasional bystanders and every cop I met along the way, I recognized faces in the crowd. Regulars from the Red Lotus. People from the checkout lanes and aisles at the grocery story. A few prostitutes I'd seen on Old Gentilly Road between Chef Menteur and the railroad tracks. The woman who sold me detergent at the Laundromat on Dwyer Drive. I saw Vincent Ngo in the distance, talking to the driver of a Red Cross van that had just arrived.

Oddly enough, I didn't see any of the Young Businessmen. The apartment building, I knew, was within the perimeter of their patrol patterns. But maybe they were here and I'd simply missed them. Or maybe there were too many cops around for their tastes. Interesting, I thought, to find out if the fire had been arson—a common problem for landlords who were reluctant to pay protection.

I walked around the corner, behind the fire trucks and cop cars parked all over the street, still searching. A fire truck was positioned at the mouth of the narrow alley that ran behind the building. I skirted the truck, peered past the handful of curious on-lookers who certainly hadn't chosen the best seat in the house. Paralleling the alley was a broad drainage canal and then railroad tracks. Away from the streetlights, in the deep shadows beyond the roadway that passed over the canal, beyond the railroad crossing, I saw people moving. Running.

I took a roundabout route to the far corner, hunkered down low, crept along a shallow ditch, then crawled through the broken glass and overgrown weeds between a boarded-up tattoo parlor and a discount bakery that was closed for the night. I lay flat, peering through the darkness at the scene unfolding a dozen yards away from me.

I picked out Tommy's hair right away.

He was standing at the edge of a group of more than twenty people that included a handful of men. But judging from the shadowy outlines—from their figures, long hair and dress— most of the group were women. And a few were adolescent girls.

They moved mostly in silence and what conversations they had were murmured so low that I couldn't make out any words.

The men, including Tommy, were helping the women climb into the back of a panel van. Their body language made it clear that the situation was urgent; they needed the women to hurry. The men grabbed the women's arms, helping them, or perhaps hauling them, up into the van. The smallest of the women, or perhaps those who were not cooperating were picked up and deposited inside.

Occasionally, I would catch a glimpse of a face. Those being loaded into the van looked distressed. But it was impossible to tell for sure if they were going willingly or being coerced. Undoubtedly, though, they had come from the burning tenement.

One by one, I picked out the faces of those who aided them, or held them captive. Seven men, including Tommy. I saw only profiles and shadowed faces as they glanced furtively around. Still, it was easy enough to recognize them, their features, their postures. Mostly because I knew them so well. The membership of the Little Vietnam Benevolent Society. All of the men except for Tommy carried a weapon. Handguns, except for the sawed-off shotgun that the butcher carried cradled in an arm.

Protecting their shipment, I thought, for undoubtedly that was what it was. The hijacked shipment. The fought-over shipment. The one that required documents to move up north. A shipment of women who, from their looks, had probably traveled on board a container ship from the East. They might be Vietnamese, Thai, Chinese or Malay.

I remembered Tommy's phone call. Not to 911, I realized. But to one of the men who held the women captive inside the tenement. Or to someone on the outside who could bring help and transportation. He knew exactly where they were being held, I realized. On the second floor.

I shook my head, continued to stare, still not believing that any of these men—and now Tommy—could have become involved in such a business. I'd misjudged people before, but never so badly. But I watched as Tommy lifted a girl of no more than twelve into the back of the van. And the others— they were men that most would characterize as responsible, hardworking and kind. As family men. Didn't they know what awaited these women? Didn't they care? The youngest would likely be sold outright to sexual predators, the others would spend years working off debt-bondage contracts in brothels across the United States.

I moved my hand toward my pocket, intending to call Beauprix. The area was crawling with cop cars. I'd give him the van's description, the license plate numbers, and the dispatcher could broadcast it. With sirens screaming, they could stop the van, arrest the bad guys, free the captives.

Assuming that everything went right.

But if anything went wrong, if they were chased and escaped, if they decided to fight the police for possession of their valuable shipment…

Mr. Yang was the link between the money, the documents and the shipment. And tomorrow, all of those things would come together. At the meeting, we would have not only Mr. Yang, but someone with documents. Odds were, the Benevolent Society would be holding the shipment somewhere nearby. We'd follow Mr. Yang to the women. Squeeze the guy with the documents until he gave up his boss. I'd cut the head from Uncle Tinh's viper. And then I'd use Mr. Yang to go after Uncle Tinh.

I watched the last of the passengers cram into the back of the van. Within minutes the doors were closed and locked. As the seven men stepped away from the boxy white vehicle, I saw that the back door panels were emblazoned with a winged Mercury and the logo of the florist shop next door to the Red Lotus.

The men scattered, Mr. Yang and the elderly cousin jumping into the front seat of the florist's van, the baker and the butcher getting into vehicles that were parked farther up the street. They pulled away, leaving Tommy standing alone on the sidewalk. He turned and began jogging back in the direction of the fire.

I followed him, but detoured around the emergency vehicles so that I could approach his car from the direction of an ambulance.

He was leaning against the fender, and rushed forward when he saw me.

"My God, Squirt, where have you been? I've been wandering all over the place looking for you."

He was a good liar.

So was I, but I stuck to a variation of the truth.

"I inhaled lots of smoke, so they made me sit with an oxygen mask on."

He asked if I was all right now, and I assured him I was.

"Then I'd best get you home."

The fire was under control and barricades no longer blocked his car in. I had no ready excuse to avoid riding with him.

We rode in silence, except for me occasionally coughing and Tommy drumming his fingers on the steering wheel at every red light. A habit he hadn't demonstrated before we'd run into a burning building.

As he rounded the corner onto my street, my cell phone vibrated again, its buzzing audible in the confines of the car. Tommy, too, heard it.

"Probably my mom," I said. "She calls every night at about the same time, begging me to come home."

Tommy said, "Oh," as he pulled the car to the curb.

I said good-night. Stood in my driveway, fairly close to the porch, and talked to Lucky as I watched the taillights disappear in the distance.

"You're a good boy, aren't you, Lucky?" I said, mostly from habit.

He pushed his angular muzzle up near the railing and his pink tongue lolled out from his open mouth, displaying a wet canine smile lined with big pointy teeth.

He didn't bark or growl.

Progress, I thought, comforted that there might be one relationship in my life that I could be absolutely sure of.

Lucky snarled at me as I walked away.

Chapter 21

I arrived home, let myself into the dark kitchen, and immediately pulled my phone from my purse. My phone had buzzed three times and I had three voice mails from Beauprix. All with the same content, each sounding a little more concerned than the one before.

"Call me. I have news."

"Why haven't you called me?"

"Damn it, where the hell are you?"

I called Beauprix. My call rolled over to voice mail.

"I'm back at home," I said. "Call me when you get this."

Then, though my taste buds would have preferred a pot of chicory-laced French roast and my nerves voted for a stiff drink, I boiled water on the gas stove and made myself a soothing cup of tea. Sweetened with honey. With just a slop of whiskey from the bottle that I'd discovered a week earlier in the back corner of a kitchen shelf. And I hoped it would help soothe the rawness in my throat.

I was too tired even to walk upstairs. For a few minutes I sat on one of the tall chrome-and-black stools, resting my elbows against the glossy kitchen counter as I alternated sipping my tea and resting my head in my hands. I reeked of smoke. My chest hurt. My eyes stung. And my feet hurt.

"Stop your whining," I said out loud. But the words that emerged were little more than a hoarse croak.

A shower would help, I thought. And some sleep. And talking to Beauprix, finding out what information he had. And telling him what I'd seen that night.

Wearily, I rubbed my hand over my face. And caught another whiff of smoke with a strong overlay of damp parrot.

You need a shower, I thought. Right now.

I fixed myself another cup of tea, this one without any whiskey, and left the kitchen. Carefully keeping to the narrow path I'd cleared for myself through the first-floor construction zone, I made my way upstairs.

At the top of the landing, I juggled purse, flashlight and a cup and saucer to open the bedroom door. I stepped through the doorway, pushed the door closed with my foot, and was attacked. My entry had apparently disturbed a large bug who was making its way across the ceiling. It lost its footing—all six of them—and landed in my hair.

The noise that came from my sore throat was little more than a croak. It's only a bug, I told myself. With deliberate calm, I put the saucer down on the nearest flat surface, making a point of not spilling the hot liquid in the cup. Then, in a movement that would have made my self-defense instructor proud, I leaned forward, knocked the roach to the floor with a swift sweep of my hand, and stepped on it. All in one smooth motion. The roach made a satisfying, if somewhat nausea-producing, crunch beneath my foot.

I'd been trained well enough that I didn't allow silly disruptions to jolt me from important routines. So I shot the heavy iron bolt to secure the virtually indestructible cypress door, hung my purse on the doorknob as I did every night, took my cell phone and put it on the nightstand beside the bed. After that, I walked around the room lighting candles and stood the flashlight in its spot on the dresser next to the cypress door.

Only then did I focus on the silly disruption.

I wiped up the remains of the roach with a wad of tissue and deposited his corpse in my wastebasket. For good measure, I pumped hand-sanitizer from a bottle on the dresser onto another wad of tissue and wiped the bottom of my shoe. Then I discarded that tissue and pumped another glob of sanitizer onto my hands.

The irony of the moment was not lost on me.

"Oh, you're a tough one, Lacie Reed," I muttered under my breath. "Murder. Betrayal. Raging fires. No problem. But let a stupid bug drop on you…"

I shuddered. And then I told myself that the smell I carried into the room with me, not the thought of the roach's journey through my hair, made the shower a priority. I opened my battered blue suitcase, pulled out clean underwear, sweatpants and a sweatshirt, closed the suitcase and latched it carefully, then opened the door to the bathroom.

Halfway along the narrow balcony, I remembered that my cell phone was still on my nightstand. I looked back over my shoulder. Behind me, as it was ahead of me, the balcony was dark. Clouds had covered the moon and it was beginning to drizzle again. The streetlight at the corner, which cast inadequate light anyway, had been broken several nights earlier. But it wasn't as if you could get lost on the route between the bedroom and the bathroom, even in the pitch dark.

I was tempted to backtrack, to fetch my phone from the bedside table, to carry it to the bathroom with me. Just in case Beauprix called while I was in the shower. But in the moment I stood thinking about it, the breeze tickled my hair and I could almost feel six tiny feet…

I'd make it quick, I thought, lengthening my stride. Worst case, Beauprix would be pissed when I didn't answer again and would smoke another cigarette or two.

At the end of the balcony, I grabbed the knob, pushed the bathroom door open, took a step inside and closed the door. The door's tiny hook-and-eye latch was ridiculous as a security measure, but I latched it every time I entered the bathroom. The long ingrained habit of locking a bathroom door for privacy was uncomfortable to break even when I knew I was alone. Closing the door left me in darkness only slightly more impenetrable than that outside. But I was in familiar territory.

Immediately inside the door to my left was a waterfall-fronted vanity, veneered in a ruddy-colored wood, topped with a round mirror that was at least a yard in diameter. An assortment of lemon-scented pillar candles and a single butane lighter rested on a mirrored tray.

A free-standing tub was opposite the vanity, in the center of the room. Directly above it was a metal hoop, suspended from the ceiling by chains that supported the generous folds of a billowy shower curtain. On the wall beyond the bathtub, two narrow open cabinets stacked with books and towels reached almost to the ceiling.

I hadn't yet kicked off my shoes, so there was no risk of stubbing my toes, and I walked confidently the few steps to the vanity. My fingers encountered the vanity's rounded front and I turned to stand in front of it, running my hand over its surface until I located the butane lighter. I flicked it on, lifted it to the wick of the tallest candle. The slight breeze coming in from the bathroom's tiny louvered window caught the twin flames, made them flicker.

In front of me, the vanity's thick, round mirror reflected the lighter and the candle. As I moved my hand to light a second candle, the flickering light illuminated my chin, my cheeks, my nostrils, and the upper ridge of my eye sockets.

Shadows cast upward created a dark mask over my forehead and around my eyes.

Behind me, the pale shower curtain moved with the breeze and the flames in the mirror flickered. For a moment, my eyes traveled past the wavering mask on my face. Beyond the curtain, at the height of a man, the shifting curtain briefly revealed the edge of another mask. Glossy, black, and feathered.

Then the breeze abated and the shower curtain fell back into place.

But I already knew that a man, darkly dressed, stood with his body tucked between the two narrow wood cabinets on the opposite wall. His shoulder was to the room. And I had glimpsed the bare, glinting blade of a stainless-steel knife he held down beside his leg.

Lingering terror from the last attack urged me to run, to escape. Urged me to panic.

But I didn't.

I held my breath, then exhaled rather than screamed. I kept my hand steady, trying not to throw shadows around the room, shadows that would let him know that something had startled me.

He was being cautious, I told myself. Otherwise, he would have risked ambushing me downstairs. Or in the bedroom. But those places offered many avenues of escape. Here, he'd waited patiently, knowing that eventually I would come into the bathroom to go to the toilet or step naked into the shower.

If waiting removed risk of failure, I reasoned, he was prepared to wait. So he wouldn't attack, I reassured myself, until I moved away from the room's only exit and deeper into his trap. He wouldn't attack unless I panicked and ran to the door. Where he could see me clearly. And come after me.

It would take me just a moment, I thought, to disengage that token lock on the bathroom door. And in that moment, if he was fast, he would be on top of me.

There was no other way out. So I needed to buy myself some time.

I carried on with my original task, lighting the pillar candles on the mirrored tray.

The breeze ruffled the curtain again, but I concentrated on touching each wick with the lighter. Though fear twisted my guts and a cold sweat dampened my body, I didn't look over my shoulder. I started humming softly to myself, keeping the melody slow, predictable, reassuring.

I lit all the candles, watched them flicker in the breeze. Unbuttoned my shirt, took it off, laid it beside the tray. Watch me, I thought. Savor the idea that I don't know you're there. Enjoy your guilty pleasure, I mentally urged him. No need to rush.

As I felt the breeze begin to wane, I moved my hands behind my back, fingering the clasp on my bra.

The breeze died down again.

I looked at the reflection of the shower curtain in the mirror, knowing I'd taken a risk by teasing him. He might be tempted to attack sooner, might grow thoughtless, might lean too far to peer around the curtain to leer at a naked female body. And then I wouldn't be able to pretend that I didn't see him.

But I'd gambled that he wasn't the type, that he hadn't waited so long and been so careful and thought it out so carefully to act prematurely, to risk his plan over one impulsive act.

I looked in the mirror. And saw no mask.

If I couldn't see him, he couldn't see me.

Let him keep imagining me vulnerable and half naked, I thought as I dropped my hand away from my bra. Let him picture me standing in front of the mirror, undressing. Just for him. I began humming some sweet little nothing loudly enough to reassure him that he needn't look, that I was not moving.

And I prayed that no breeze would stir the curtain until I was ready.

I held my shirt in my left hand as I slipped my right beneath the tray that held the candles. Palm flat, fingers splayed to support the weight, I slowly lifted the tray upward, pausing as the candles flickered and sent shadows dancing across the room.

I kept humming as I prayed again and watched the reflection over my shoulder. He didn't move. So once the flames were steady, I lifted the tray again, this time ever so slightly. Then I held it balanced. I dropped my shirt into the candles' midst. And I waited.

The shirt caught fire.

The candles flared.

Three steps to the door.

And as I took them, I flung the tray across the room at the carrion bird, who was moving.

I reached for the latch and flicked it upward.

The candles hit him squarely in the middle of his chest. He dropped his knife, beat his body and bellowed with shock and pain as hot wax poured over him. It set his shirt on fire, threatened the mask that covered his face.

It slowed him down.

I ran through the door, pulled it shut behind me, wished that I could lock it, consigning him to a fiery death.

Nothing is that simple.

I'd almost reached the door to the bedroom when he emerged from the bathroom. No longer on fire. Now carrying his knife. And madder than hell.

He screamed an obscenity as he rushed toward me.

I yanked open the door, ran through the bedroom.

The heavy bolt on the cypress door slowed me down, and then he was just a few feet behind me.

But in the house beyond the bedroom, the darkness was on *my* side.

I counted six steps down to the landing.

Then ten steps to the first floor.

I crossed the room, keeping to the path I'd made for myself and had practiced for weeks. A quick detour around the shattered interior wall and the adjacent heaps of broken plaster and splintery lathe. Through a split in the plastic sheeting that divided one room from the next. And across the second room.

He must have had eyes like a cat's. Behind me I heard only a single crash, one muffled curse, and then he was running again.

I pushed through the swinging wood door into the kitchen. Considered grabbing a butcher's knife from the block on the counter and making a stand. But I was no knife fighter, and he had the advantage of size and reach.

Instead, I ran for the kitchen door and let myself out.

He was right behind me.

It was not a race I could win. Not tonight, after the toll that the fire and smoke in the apartment building had taken on my stamina. I was physically drained. And I knew that the adrenaline that now drove me wouldn't keep me ahead of him for very long.

My screams, if they were heard, would most likely inspire only closed windows and locked doors. Doubtful that anyone would call the police. Not that the police, if called, would arrive in time to be of much help.

For the second time that night, I gambled.

I raced along the driveway toward the front of the house, ducked to run close to the bottom branches of the oleander hedge and stayed close to the rail as I ran up the six sagging steps to the porch. My pursuer outweighed me by at least a hundred pounds, so perhaps I could use his weight to my advantage. His weight and, perhaps, the time I'd spent befriending a stray.

The dog pack fled the porch. All of them. Except for

Lucky. The muscular, three-legged red dog emerged from the shadows, his single eye glinting as he stood squarely in the center of his territory.

My pursuer was fast on my heels.

I didn't try to cross the rotted section of floor between the steps and the front door. I picked a similarly rotted section on Lucky's side of the porch, trying to stay to the edges where the wood might be stronger, praying that weeks of food bribes and chatter had paid off.

"Good dog," I said breathlessly, hoping that he was.

My pursuer pounded up the stairs behind me, took two steps onto the porch before a board cracked and sagged beneath his weight. He was overbalanced, but he lunged in my direction as he fell. I had already turned to run, but as he sprawled flat onto the porch floor, he hung on to his knife with his right hand and managed to grab my left leg with his left.

Before he could organize himself enough to pull my leg out from under me, I twisted around, used my free right foot and kicked his knife hand as hard as I could. Kicked *through* it, rather than *at* it. For maximum impact. Just as I had been trained.

He yelped and the knife went skittering across the porch, falling into a gaping hole. But I hadn't injured him badly enough. With his now-empty hand, he grabbed my other ankle and yanked my feet out from under me.

I landed hard. And cried out in pain.

I think it was my cry that did it.

Lucky, who'd begun pacing and growling, launched himself at my attacker. He landed with his front legs on the masked man's back and grabbed the man's arm in his broad slash of a mouth.

The carrion bird let go of my leg. He screamed for help. Not something he was going to get from me.

The carrion bird was flailing his captive arm, lifting Lucky off his feet, beating at the dog's head and shoulders with his free hand. But the feisty little dog was hanging on.

I concentrated on skirting the battle, intent on making my way back to the porch steps. I stepped carefully to avoid the holes I had miraculously missed stepping into when I'd run up onto the porch. But I hadn't gone very far when I slammed to a stop.

Between the straight branches of the oleander hedge, I'd caught a glimpse of the street. A car was there, its passenger side door hanging open, the interior dark. The second carrion bird had arrived wearing a red-feathered mask. Drawn by the cries of the first man, he was running up the front sidewalk. And he had a gun.

He stopped at the base of the steps.

I stood almost immediately above him, hidden from him by one of the porch's support pillars and an overgrown oleander. Immediately behind me was one of the pots that was clipped to the railing. As I'd stepped back, it had jammed me in the small of my back.

The first carrion bird screamed again as Lucky found a moment of footing and used the leverage to shake the man's arm.

"Damn it, Dave, hold still," the second man yelled, "so I can shoot the fucker."

I wasn't going to let him kill my dog.

I twisted, lifted the heavy, red clay pot from its hook with both hands. I stepped out from behind the pillar and cast it downward at the second man.

It smashed against the side of his head.

He dropped his gun. Stood for a moment as shards of pot and clumps of soil showered onto his shoulder and the ground. Then his knees folded beneath him and he fell.

Stunned or unconscious, it didn't matter. I wanted his gun.

I scurried down the steps, intent on grabbing it. As I bent over to pick it up, the guy was moving, groaning his way back to full consciousness.

In the midst of it all, I'd heard another car roar up into the yard.

Reinforcements, I thought. And, for no more than a heartbeat, I flashed on the image of carrion birds gathered around their prey, tearing bloody pieces from my body.

The fallen gun was my best defense against the present threat. And the new one. Though I didn't often carry one, I knew how to use a handgun. And, at this range, it wouldn't matter if I was a sharpshooter or merely competent. Aim at the chest, I reminded myself. It offered the largest target.

I wrapped my hand around the gun, slid my index finger into the trigger guard, began to straighten, readying myself to turn, aim and—if necessary—

"Police! Freeze! Hands in the air!"

Beauprix's voice. Hard and mean. All business.

I froze. Let go of the gun. And put my foot squarely on top of it as I slowly straightened and raised my hands. I waited, knowing that only two men knew both of my identities *and* knew where I lived. One of those men was coming up behind me, undoubtedly armed.

He put a hand lightly on my shoulder, and I tensed.

"I didn't want to startle you, little girl," he said softly. "Figured you'd look first, shoot second, but I couldn't take the chance."

That left only one man—Uncle Tinh—Tinh Vu—who could have directed the attacks.

"You can put your hands down," Beauprix suggested gently.

I did as he said.

"If you like, I can step back so you can pick up his gun," I offered.

"Yeah, why don't you just do that for me?"

I took a step backward, then another, and Beauprix put himself between me and the fallen man.

The crimson mask had been knocked nearly off the second carrion bird's face and it hung, tilted, covering one cheek and most of his chin. It was covered with soil.

Beauprix kept his own gun trained on the man as he bent to retrieve the gun. Then he backed away a few feet, taking me with him. In one smooth motion, he expelled the clip, checked the chamber and put the gun on the sidewalk behind him.

Then he moved forward again.

"Flat on the ground," he ordered.

He gave the carrion bird a push with his foot to help him into the correct posture, pulled his arms behind him and secured his wrists with handcuffs.

On the porch, my attacker screamed again.

"Think you can call your dog off?"

I didn't think I could, but I gave it shot. I stepped away from Beauprix, and went around to the railing on Lucky's side of the porch. I tapped the bars, trying to get his attention.

"Lucky, come here, boy. Come on, Lucky."

Amazingly, the dog stopped mauling the man on the porch, turned his head in my direction and tilted it as I called again.

"Come on, Lucky!"

The dog trotted over to the railing and I told him what a good boy he was. As he wagged his tail, I told him that I owed him my life. Or a raw steak. Or maybe just an extra few pork-filled steamed buns.

And as I babbled relief inspired nonsense to a one-eyed red dog, a well-chewed carrion bird stumbled off the porch, down the stairs and into Beauprix's waiting arms.

Other cop cars arrived, apparently called by Beauprix before he'd left his car. At some point, early on, someone had draped a blanket around my bare shoulders and, though I hadn't realized I was cold, I appreciated its warmth.

Headlights, Mars lights and flashlights lit the scene. But, unlike the fire, no curious neighbors had arrived to witness this particular show. And I imagined the few there were peering out from behind torn curtains, sagging blinds and through cracks in boarded-up windows.

An ambulance arrived, adding red lights to the blue, and I watched a medic put a pressure bandage around my attacker's arm. I moved my eyes away from him and looked over at his accomplice. Another medic had put a thick pad over the man's ear and was securing it by wrapping gauze bandage around his head.

No doubt these two were the same men who had attacked me on Bourbon Street. That, I had told the police. And now that it had happened twice, the investigating officer agreed, there was no question that I was the target. I'd given them my real name and age, and left it to Beauprix to explain whatever needed to be explained about my living situation or appearance.

What I hadn't told the police, because they didn't need to know, was that the carrion birds' faces had plagued my sleep nightly. That their last attack had inspired unpredictable thrusts of terror in the middle of the day that compelled me to glance anxiously over my shoulder. But without their masks, my attackers looked unremarkable, the kind of people that one passed on the street every day. The pair who lay handcuffed to the gurneys as they were loaded into the ambulance were nothing more than thick-necked, middle-aged white men. As common as the brown mutts that roamed the streets with Lucky.

My attackers would be interrogated, a uniformed black cop had told me. His muscular arms and shoulders suggested that he lifted weights, and he had, unconsciously, clenched his fists as he assured me that New Orleans cops didn't much like men who terrorized women. Especially for no reason.

I had smiled and thanked him. But the men who were in custody struck me as hired muscle. Brutal, brainless muscle. Nothing more. And I doubted they even knew the identity of the man who was paying them.

It had to be Uncle Tinh. But why? I asked myself repeatedly. Why? Had I stumbled too close to a secret with the very first drawings I showed him? Perhaps discovered something that he hadn't expected me to find?

Between answering questions from Beauprix and his cronies, I continued reassuring Lucky, warning everyone else away. Lucky didn't seem inclined to move from the privacy of his porch. Which was just as well. There were too many guns, too many cops in the yard, walking up and down the driveway, going in and out of the house. The cops would, very rightly, react quickly to a perceived threat. Even if that threat came from a dog who had saved my life.

As Beauprix ventured up onto the front porch with a flashlight, I stood and spoke to Lucky again, actually sticking my fingers through the porch rail and stroking his head. My fingers encountered something sticky on the dog's muzzle. Blood, I realized. Beauprix picked up the battered mask, looked down at it, then put it in a plastic bag. I noticed that its feathers were also clumped with blood.

Thankfully, the blood wasn't mine.

"You said you kicked the knife out of the guy's hand and it fell through a hole," Beauprix said to me. "Can you tell me where?"

Slowly he played the flashlight's beam over the shattered boards of the porch floor, moving from gaping hole to gaping hole.

"There," I said.

Lucky remained calm, ignoring Beauprix, wagging the stump of his tail and the back half of his body as I continued to pet him.

Beauprix flattened himself out on the floor, dangled his head and an arm into the hole, and lifted out a knife using two fingers. It looked as nasty as I remembered it. Long, slim and sharp. A filleting knife, I thought, shuddering. This time there'd been no camera. This time, they'd meant business.

As Beauprix bagged the knife, I thought I was lucky that my blood wasn't on it, either.

Only when the other vehicles left taking the carrion birds with them, only when Beauprix and I were the only humans left near the house, did Lucky come off the porch. He trotted down the front steps, paused for a moment, then walked directly to me. Ignoring Beauprix, who was again standing by my side, he butted his thick forehead against my hand. I patted him, reached to scratch his muscular neck. He turned his head, gave my hand a quick swipe with a warm, wet tongue. And then he walked away. His bouncy, three-legged gait carried him across the street and into the cover of the neutral ground.

Chapter 22

On the way back up to the second floor, I apologized to Beauprix for not returning his calls.

"I was...distracted...by a fire," I said. "I'll tell you about it...after. Okay?"

Beauprix already knew there was something more urgent on my mind, something I needed to do first. And then, I had promised, I would give him the details of my day.

"Okay," he said as he used his flashlight to pick his way carefully along the path through the front area of the house. "Though it's just as well you *didn't* answer the last time I called. That's when I started worrying. And decided I'd better drive over here, find out what was going on."

"Good thing you did," I said.

We started up the stairs with him in the lead. He was wearing jeans and a maroon dress shirt and, without being told, stayed carefully to the middle of every step.

"Yeah, good thing." Then Beauprix chuckled softly. "On the

way here, I kept telling myself how paranoid I was being. That you'd be pissed as all get-out that I was being so over-protective."

"Hey, Anthony?" I said.

He half turned to look down at me, keeping the flashlight on the steps in front of him.

"Next time I get pissy, you just remind me of this little incident."

He grinned.

"You can be sure of it."

I didn't want to go back to the second-floor bathroom. Ever. But I forced myself to do it. Because I knew that the irrational fear I now felt—the fear that was simply a reaction to a trauma—could, unless confronted, be crippling.

I was in no danger I told myself.

And, in the more rational part of my mind, I knew it.

But the trip down the narrow balcony was, anyway, enough to make me start trembling. To clutch the blanket that covered my shoulders closer to me. To hesitate when I put my hand on the doorknob.

"I can go first," Beauprix said.

He was standing just behind me and I could hear sympathy in his voice.

Right now, sympathy was the last thing I needed. This was no time to back away, to give up. I needed to confront my fear, to control it. Needed to prove to myself that the stuff of nightmares no longer lurked in the shadows.

This was the best way for me to do it.

I took a deep breath, pushed the door open and stepped inside. Then I waited until Beauprix had cleared the doorway and asked him to shut the door. And lock it.

Trapped! my fearful, exhausted mind wailed.

I ignored it.

I had borrowed Beauprix's flashlight and concentrated on keeping the beam steady as I played it against every corner of the room. Lingering in the space between the two tall, narrow sets of shelves on the far wall. Showing myself that what I feared was no longer there.

Another cop had taken my statement, gone to check out the bathroom. So this was the first time Beauprix had been on the second floor of the odd little house. He'd followed me silently through the bedroom. And now he stood silent again, lingering near the doorway, allowing me to view the room unimpeded for as long as I needed to.

But when I stopped moving the light around the room, he stepped in close behind me, close enough that I could feel the heat of his body against my back. He reached around me to put his right hand over mine, so that we both held the flashlight. Then he guided the beam to the floor, used its light to examine the path from my attacker's hiding place to the door.

He saw the broken tray, spatters of cooled wax, broken candles scattered across the floor. Then he saw the charred remains of my shirt. And I felt, as much as heard, his quick intake of breath.

Then he moved our hands so that the light shone through a gap in the shower curtain, into the deep bathtub. And it revealed...absolutely nothing. But still we stood there, staring at the tub.

I couldn't help myself. I imagined what would have happened to me if I hadn't noticed the man who'd been waiting for me, knife ready. If I hadn't found a way to escape his trap.

Beauprix's thoughts seemed to follow a similar line. He shuddered, folded his arms around me, pulling me against him. The flashlight's beam bounced uselessly against a wall as he pressed his lips to the top of my head.

"If anything had happened to you—"

He didn't finish his sentence, just hugged me tighter.

At that moment I wanted nothing more than his arms around me. I wanted him to hold me forever, to protect me, to keep me safe. And that, I was sure, was exactly what he wanted to do.

He held me for another moment, leaned to brush his lips against my cheek, then tucked his face in close to my neck and shoulder as he spoke.

"I saw you tonight. Half naked. Unarmed. Outnumbered. And still fighting."

His voice cracked, and he took a deep breath. Exhaled slowly. Then he straightened and stepped back. Just a little. But he kept his arms around me.

When he spoke again, he almost managed to sound irritated.

"Damn it, little girl, you just don't know how to give up, do you?"

I turned in his arms, looked up into his handsome face and smiled mostly because he was such a lousy actor.

"That really pisses you off, doesn't it?" I said lightly.

Then I put my hands flat against his chest and gave him a little shove in the direction of the door.

"Get out of here," I said. "Go smoke a cigarette if you have to. And let me take my shower."

"I'll wait right outside the door."

He said it like it was a question.

And though I knew the shower was safe, I didn't argue.

Not much later, I was warm and clean and dressed in the sweats I'd taken into the bathroom with me during my first attempt at showering.

Beauprix and I sat on my bed, talking. With candles glowing on the nightstand. Terrifically romantic, except that I was under the covers with my back propped against the headboard and was wearing sweatpants and a sweatshirt. And Beauprix was sitting cross-legged on top of the blankets, facing me, still fully dressed in jeans and a dress shirt.

The conversation was anything but romantic.

"I ran all those prints from off the teacups. Nothing surprising about the ones belonging to the Young Businessmen—every one of them had a record. Petty crimes, mostly. Coupled

with the license plates you gave me, we have current ad-
dresses on all of them. None of them have outstanding war-
rants. But when this is done, we'll pick them up anyway. For
questioning. Who knows, maybe someone in the Benevolent
Society will be willing to testify against them in exchange for
a reduced sentence on the trafficking charges. Without that,
we only have your account of the extortion incident at the Red
Lotus, and if no one else will admit it happened…"

He paused for a moment, frowned, then shrugged. That
bridge, apparently, would be crossed when we came to it.

"Anyway, the big surprise was Vincent Ngo. When we ran
his prints against the FBI's database, we got back the kind of
result that sets off red flags, probably in any local P.D. in the
nation. The kind of non-information that is a clear sign that
some *federal* agency is mucking around on your turf."

I nodded, understanding, idly wondering what kind of information a local police department would get if they queried
my prints.

"So I set Remy on our little problem—he hates the Feds,
by the way—and by the end of the day, he'd come up with
something. Your boy was somehow connected to the FBI."

My eyes widened, but he lifted a hand to stop any questions.

"There's more. I know a gal who works for the FBI here,
in their local office. She has a weakness for one of the more
interesting recreational activities that New Orleans has to
offer. She got herself caught in a raid about a year back—
wasn't doing anything illegal herself, but there were reporters outside and that kind of publicity would have been
career-ending. So I let her slip out the back door. Today, I
called in that favor. Based on your assessment of his personality, I figured Vincent Ngo for a snitch. I was wrong."

He paused dramatically, leaned back on his elbows as he
stretched out his legs so his stockinged feet were near my hips.

I pinched his big toe.

"Give," I said.

"Turns out your Vincent is an FBI agent, working under-cover."

Later—when the candles had burned down to nothing—Beauprix moved his head onto the pillow next to mine. With his gun on the nightstand, ready to fend off any attack, he lay on his back on top of the blankets.

Earlier—when the last candle still flickered—I'd looked around my bedroom at all the sketches I'd hung on the wall. Faces of enemies and of friends. Faces of people I didn't trust. And those that I did. Faces of people that I'd liked and loved and respected.

Then that flame died, leaving me in darkness. Tears that I'd fended off all night slid, warm and silent, down my cheeks. And in the cover of darkness, I was finally able to tell the only person I knew I could trust what I'd been thinking for hours.

"Tinh Vu, who has loved me like I was his own blood, sent those men after me," I said, and I struggled to keep my voice from betraying my tears. "And Vincent Ngo, who my every in-stinct tells me not to trust, is one of the good guys. And Tommy, Mr. Yang, the others—my God, Anthony—how could so many decent, hardworking people be trafficking human cargo?"

He lay very still.

"You're exhausted," he said. "Forget about it for now. We'll think about it tomorrow."

Unbidden, my stepmother's favorite movie flashed to mind. But in this Beauprix-inspired remake, he'd said Scar-lett's lines. And the image prompted the faintest of smiles.

I rolled onto my side, moved my hands beneath the blan-ket so they were tucked in next to Beauprix.

"G'night, Anthony," I said.

I let my body relax. Encouraged my breathing to become slower, deeper. Began to drift.

He must have thought I was soundly asleep.

"Don't worry, little girl," he whispered. "I'll keep you safe for as long as you'll let me."

Sleep had become more urgent than talk. But my drowsing mind insisted that I make one thing clear.

"I'm not a child," I muttered.

I felt him shift and his lips brushed my forehead.

"Yes, Lacie. I know."

I awakened after no more than two hours of sleep. Sleep that had been plagued by fragmented dreams—scattered images, really—which now I couldn't recall. But beyond vague feelings of frustration, I felt refreshed. As if I'd had a full night's sleep—an event that I had experienced so rarely of late that it, too, was hard to remember. Obviously, I was developing a teenager's resilience, I thought to myself with a smile, and I hoped it would persist when I went back to being my twenty-something self.

Beauprix's eyes had snapped open the moment I stirred, and I'd taken a moment to stroke my hand along his cheek. And to think a few lust-driven thoughts, which I promptly dismissed in favor of a shower. I didn't at the moment need the complexities of a new relationship. Even with a man as tempting as Anthony Beauprix.

"Go back to sleep," I said. "I'm just going to the bathroom."

He was just tired enough that my announcement set off no alarms, and he closed his eyes again.

So I gathered my clothing and, without an escort, walked along the balcony to the bathroom. I searched the lingering darkness for anything that might indicate a threat, but saw only birds and the dog pack wandering the empty lot next door. Not a surprise. Despite his concern over my remaining in the house last night and his insistence that he stay to protect me, Beauprix and I had both agreed that it was unlikely that another attack would be organized in the space of a few hours. I had a day, I thought to myself. Perhaps two. And then, until Uncle Tinh was behind bars, I would constantly watch my back.

Chapter 23

Beauprix and I drove to the Yang residence at dawn and followed Mr. Yang to church at noon. By tonight, I suspected, I would be able to abandon my alter ego. But, until then, I would stay in character. Much to Anthony's surprise, I spiked my hair that morning and added glitter, then dressed in flare-legged jeans and the most modest of Squirt's tops, which happened to be synthetic raspberry shot through with pink.

I carried my denim purse, too. But today it was weighed down with a Ruger revolver—a .357 Magnum with a two-and-a-quarter-inch barrel—compliments of Anthony Beauprix. He spent a few minutes reviewing its features for me, then told me just to point and shoot. I didn't bother telling him that I could do a damned sight better than that.

Beauprix remained in the car, but I went inside, intending to watch the proceedings from the choir loft. The enclosed, narrow staircase that led to the loft was in the vestibule just inside the entrance to the church. Casual entry was discouraged by a thick velvet cord clipped across the doorway. And by ushers, who seemed to be constantly vigilant for mischievous schoolchildren and wandering toddlers bound on scampering up the stairs.

I arrived for Mass early, went into one of the rest rooms that was also located near the back of the church, waited and listened. Catholic Masses, no matter what country or language, followed the same ritual every Sunday. And I had been raised with those rituals. In Vietnamese and English.

From my seat inside a rest room stall, I could hear drifts of the service. The beginning of the Mass was marked by singing, the wandering voices of the faithful augmented by a pianist, a guitarist, a flutist and a female vocalist.

I knew, from my past visits, that the priest and the servers would be entering the altar area from a door that opened in from the sacristy, where the priest prepared for the service and put colorful vestments on over his plain, dark robes. At the far end of the sacristy was an exterior door. From there, a flagstone path led across the lawn, paralleling the parking lot behind the church and ending at the rectory next door.

The priest's amplified voice—the words unintelligible from my hiding place—carried into my hiding space. It alternated with the more generalized rumbling of the unenhanced voices of the faithful.

Fifteen minutes into the service, as the time for the reading of the gospel approached, I left the stall and watched the vestibule by opening the rest room door just a crack. Arriving late to the last Mass of the day seemed to be a ritual, too, conducted by members of the faithful throughout the United States. And, perhaps, the world. The latecomers would congregate at the rear of the church. And the ushers would scramble to move the stragglers into the few vacancies in the pews, to find them places to sit before the sermon began.

Easy enough, during that time, to slip from my hiding

place, walk nonchalantly across the vestibule, duck beneath the velvet cord and walk as quietly as possible up the steep, winding stairs.

The choir loft was a remnant of a bygone era, when booming organ music and formal choirs were more common even among smaller Catholic congregations. Now, most of its space was consumed by an imposing pipe organ whose keys were layered with dust and seven pews, elevated like theater seating. I ducked low as I walked down the seven shallow steps and then settled behind the low wall separating the loft from a fifteen-foot drop to the floor below.

"And this is the word of the Lord."

The sentence, spoken in Vietnamese, was a signal for the standing congregation to be seated. And the sermon began.

As the elderly French priest spoke of the power of forgiveness, I peered into the church, using my tiny binoculars to scan the congregation. Picking people out by looking at the backs of their heads, then waiting for them to turn briefly to confirm their identity was a slow process. Except for the absence of Mrs. Yang and the twins, who were still, I supposed, in Chicago, I eventually found all of the people I'd expected to.

And several more.

Uncle Tinh was there, flanked by his bodyguard, his chauffeur, his personal cook and even the unfortunate Odum who had been demoted for splashing soup on Lee Leng's dress. All uncharacteristically wearing suit coats. And, I suspected, they were armed.

At the very front of the church, in the pew that was nearest to the altar, was Vincent Ngo. Sitting alone.

Why, I wondered, was the FBI here? Had he caught wind of the same transaction that Beauprix and I were waiting for?

This Sunday, I knew, was not going to be like the others.

As I sat in cramped silence through the rest of the service, I thought about Beauprix. He was parked just down the street from the church's front steps. Waiting and watching, as I was.

Earlier, we'd agreed on that strategy. Then Beauprix had called his captain and given him the broad outlines of what we suspected. And what we knew. He mentioned no names, but still made a convincing argument. The captain had thought so, too. A district's worth of unmarked cars and plainclothes officers were now only a phone call away, though the implication was that Beauprix had damned well better be right.

"Go in peace to love and serve the Lord," the priest intoned, bringing the service to an end. Then, led by a white-robed Vietnamese boy carrying a crucifix, the priest and the servers began walking to the rear of the church along the center aisle. That was the signal for the congregation to sing an enthusiastic if significantly off-key recessional hymn.

Before the first verse ended, many of the parishioners began following in the priest's wake—intent, perhaps, on the refreshments in the social center. But the female vocalist, who should have been discouraged by what she was hearing and obviously wasn't, urged the congregation into a second verse. It was delivered with far less enthusiasm and continued off key.

Inside my jeans' pocket, my cell phone vibrated. There was enough noise down below that I risked answering it.

"Heads up," Beauprix said. "You've got six guys heading *into* the church. They look just like your sketches. Young Businessmen, each and every one of them. It's a safe bet they're armed. I'm going to follow them in."

"No. Stay there. If this blows up, we're going to need more than one cop to stop it. Vincent Ngo's here. So's Uncle Tinh, accompanied by his own little militia. But I doubt they're planning to shoot it out in the church."

I disconnected as the last sour notes of the recessional drifted through the church.

After the service ended, the elderly priest returned to the church to escort a few straggling parishioners out the door. As if it had all been arranged in advance. And I wondered by whom.

Mr. Yang had left with the rest of the congregation.

The priest was just below me, still talking with one of his parishioners.

"There's coffee waiting for us," the priest was saying. He and the parishioners were out of sight, but his clear, strong, French-accented voice carried up the twisting stairs from the vestibule. "Do I understand correctly that your son has joined the navy? You must be very proud."

I took that opportunity to call Beauprix again.

"Don't follow Mr. Yang. The action's still here."

Only Uncle Tinh and his bodyguards, Vincent and Tommy Nguyen remained inside the church.

Why Vincent? I asked myself.

The priest and the proud parents left the church.

The silence seemed to stretch into minutes.

The members of the Businessmen's Association remained out of sight, but I suspected that they were beneath me at the vestibule doors. Standing guard.

I began to hear movement in the back of the church. Suddenly the location of the Businessmen didn't matter. Because I knew exactly what one of them was doing. He was climbing the winding stairs to the choir loft.

I flattened myself onto the waxy wooden floor and half slid, half scrambled into hiding beneath the nearby pew. My back ended up against the step that supported the pew behind me. Between me and the short wall, there was no more than eighteen inches of space.

The footsteps ended at the top of the choir loft, near the organ.

I lay very still, kept my breathing shallow, and waited. My eyes were fixed on the wall across from me, where dozens of black scuff marks marred the yellowing paint. It would be unfortunate, I thought, if that was the last thing I ever saw.

He walked down the steps, pausing at each one, and as I counted to keep track of his movements, I imagined him glancing across each empty pew. There were no lights in the loft, but enough light flowed through the church's tall, stained-glass windows that no lights were needed. He had only to make an effort, I thought. If he bent down and looked beneath the pews, he would inevitably catch a glimpse of bright raspberry fabric.

He reached the bottom step and stood beside the wall. From my hiding place, I could see that his black leather shoes were well polished and that his dark trousers had neatly pressed cuffs. His heels lifted slightly as he put his hands on the wall and leaned out into the church.

Then I heard one quick sentence. With the loft's acoustics, he didn't have to speak all that loudly.

"Clear up here," he said in Vietnamese.

And then I followed the rapid, echoing sounds of his footsteps as he went back down to the first floor.

I slid out of hiding and peered back over the wall.

Uncle Tinh had left his pew and was standing in the shelter of the alcove that held a red-robed statue of Jesus. Beside him was a square, black briefcase. And Tommy.

Uncle Tinh's bodyguards had also moved, spacing themselves out and facing away from my uncle and Tommy. Ready to meet any threat. They no longer attempted to hide their guns.

Uncle Tinh picked up the briefcase and gave it to Tommy.

Tommy had dressed in uncharacteristically form-fitting clothes and it was easy to see that he was unarmed. I thought it was likely he'd dressed as he had for just that reason. He wore a black turtleneck shirt and a pair of black, straight-legged jeans. Conservative, except for the hair and the piercings.

Under the watchful eyes of Tinh Vu's bodyguards and, I assumed, the men of the Businessmen's Association, Tommy walked to the front of the church.

Vincent Ngo had remained sitting there. He faced constantly forward, his back squarely to Uncle Tinh.

I suddenly realized it was a symbolic gesture. Vincent was totally confident that he was in control. He was protected by the men at the rear of the church. The undercover assignment must have placed Vincent Ngo in charge of the Young Vietnamese Businessmen's Association. Had an FBI infiltrator managed to become *anh hai?* I wondered. What better position could there be to take apart organized crime, to bring someone like Tinh Vu to justice.

Tommy gave Uncle Tinh's black briefcase to Vincent. Vincent laid it on the pew, opened it briefly, and nodded. The money that Mr. Yang had asked for. Delivered in person by Uncle Tinh.

Vincent handed Tommy a large, padded envelope in return. It was stuffed to bulging. He held it flat against his chest, his arms crossed protectively over it, as he returned to Uncle Tinh's side.

The documents, I thought, that Mr. Yang had begged Tinh Vu to buy from a rival.

Transaction apparently complete, Vincent walked confidently down the center aisle, carrying Uncle Tinh's briefcase at his side. Beneath me, I could hear his men leaving their posts at the door to accompany him outside.

Then Uncle Tinh and his bodyguards left the church, too.

Only Tommy remained.

He crossed the width of the church, cutting between the pews, and went to the vestibule on the far wall. The one with the crowned statue of a blue-clad woman with Asian features. After picking up a taper and lighting one of the candles, he knelt and made the sign of the cross. Bowed his head in silent prayer. Then he stood, walked up the aisle to the front of the church, genuflected briefly as he crossed in front of the altar, and walked through the door into the vestibule. The door that provided a private exit from the church.

I hit speed dial as I ran down the twisting stairs and through the church.

"Vincent and Uncle Tinh made an exchange. Money for an envelope full of forged documents. I don't know what the FBI is up to, but I say we proceed as planned. Follow the documents to the tea. Tommy Nguyen's gone out the back door. If he gets into his car—a rusty blue Ford Escort—he's yours. If he stays on foot, I'll follow him."

Beauprix said enough that I knew he understood me.

I jammed the phone back in my pocket as I raced through the altar area and didn't take the time to genuflect. Ten steps through the sacristy and I was out the door. In time to see the pink-and-blue hair on the crown of Tommy's head. He walked toward the church parking lot, but then he turned to cut through the backyard of the rectory. From there, he cut across another yard and onto the adjacent street. And then through another yard, over a back fence and around a corner. But it wasn't as if he was trying to avoid being followed. His pace was fast, but he wasn't running. And he never looked over his shoulder.

Finally, I began to discern the direction that his route was taking us. And it wasn't too long before we rounded a corner onto the sidewalks of the Vietnamese business district on Alcee Fourtier.

In Little Vietnam, Sunday was a day for tourists. They wandered the streets in droves, many of them a head or two taller than the Vietnamese residents. They came individually, in pairs, and by the busload. They filled the sidewalks and crowded into the stores, buying expensive jade bracelets and flashy trinkets, silk fabrics and stuffed toys, candy and medicinal herbs. They stared in the windows at whole pigs' legs and smoked ducks, and nibbled at delicacies purchased from bakeries and restaurants and ice-cream parlors. Their cars filled every parking place and traffic clogged the streets.

I followed Tommy along the bustling street. Intent upon his errand, he walked steadily, which made him easy enough to follow through the shifting crowd. He passed the Red Lotus with its Closed sign, in Vietnamese and English, hanging in the window. He passed the adjacent florist shop, which was also always closed on Sundays.

Just beyond the florist shop was the busy souvenir shop. Owned by a member of the Benevolent Society.

Tommy walked into the shop, which filled the front half of the long, narrow building. I followed him through the busy store and hid from the owner's sight by a round rack of New Orleans postcards.

The owner finished ringing up a customer, then slipped from behind the counter and preceded Tommy to the warehouse door. They were talking but the store's intercom, as usual, was blaring Vietnamese music and the sound muffled their voices.

I'd been in and out of the shop often, chatting with the owner, who seemed to find Squirt amusing. Each time, the door to the back warehouse was opened or unlocked. But this time, the owner used a key to let Tommy into the room. What better place to hide the women than the warehouse?

The shop's owner turned to help a woman who was juggling a stack of lacquered rice bowls. There was no way I was going to get past him and into the room beyond. And, besides, I didn't want to barge head-long into a room protected by other, armed members of the Benevolent Society.

I backtracked, hurrying past the wall-to-wall buildings that lined the street, and went around the corner, making my way into the alley that ran behind the Red Lotus. On the opposite side of the alley was an eight-foot-tall chain-link fence surrounding the parking area of a block-long office complex.

About halfway down the alley, I passed the Red Lotus's Dumpster and the battered chair where the elderly cousin took his breaks and smoked his cigarettes. As I continued on past the florist's shop, I saw that her delivery van was now parked in its usual spot by the back door. I came around it slowly, using it as cover between me and the back of the souvenir shop. There was no one there, so I walked behind the building to take a closer look.

Beside a pedestrian door with a peephole in its center, a short flight of poured-concrete steps led up to a narrow loading dock. Access to the dock was protected by a solidly closed overhead door. And the steel-clad pedestrian door was also shut.

I had the tea shipment, the documents, Tommy and at least one member of the Benevolent Society. Probably more. It was time to call in the cops.

Beauprix answered his phone immediately. So quickly, in fact, that I wondered if he'd been holding his phone in his hand.

"Beauprix here."

"It's me."

"Where are you?"

I thought that he sounded more relieved and then more anxious than the situation warranted. The downside of emotional involvement, I diagnosed.

"I'm in the alley on the west side of Alcee Fortier, behind the Viet My Souvenir Emporium. We've got them." I couldn't keep the triumph from my voice. "The shipment's inside the warehouse. Guarded, probably."

"Any chance they'll take them out through the front door?"

"Too risky. There are lots of tourists, so if one of the women tried to run or screamed for help... My bet is that they'll load the women through the warehouse door."

"We'll take them as they're loading up."

I shook my head, not liking it, and let my concern touch my voice.

"Between the tea in the warehouse and the tourists in the

store, you could end up with a nasty hostage situation. Besides that, I want to be absolutely sure the women are here before you commit your guys."

Beauprix thought about it for a heartbeat.

"Are you somewhere out of sight? Where you can safely watch the warehouse?"

"Yeah," I said.

"Hang on."

I heard him talking on the unmarked car's radio. Then he came back on the line.

"I'm heading over to meet my guys, brief them about the situation, then position them nearby. We can tail the transportation, stop them somewhere away from the tourists."

"I'll give you a description of the vehicle—or vehicles— and let you know when the shipment is on its way."

I'd just tucked my phone back into my pocket when I heard a vehicle turn into the alley behind me. I glanced in that direction and saw a bright yellow rental truck of a size that would accommodate a small apartment's worth of furniture. Or twenty women.

My first thought was that they'd arrived faster than I'd anticipated. My second was that I should get out of sight. But I was too far from the florist's van to duck behind it and there was nowhere else in the alley to hide.

Then I realized that there was no reason Squirt *shouldn't* be in the alley. So I simply began walking in the direction of the slow-moving van. By the time it drove past, I was near the Dumpster behind the Red Lotus, and I saw that the ugly butcher was driving. I lifted my hand in casual greeting, but he didn't seem to notice me. He rolled past and parked parallel to the loading dock. As he was maneuvering the truck, I slipped back behind the florist's van.

He turned off the engine, stepped down from the driver's seat and went to the pedestrian door. After tapping on it, he stepped back so he could easily be seen through the peephole.

The door swung open.

"You're early," Tommy said.

The butcher nodded.

"I figured I could help you distribute the documents."

"Cool," Tommy said as he turned away to walk back inside.

But instead of going with him, the large man stood solidly in front of the door. Blocking it open.

For a moment, I wondered why. Then the back door of the truck slammed upward and six armed men jumped out. The entire membership of the Young Vietnamese Businessmen's Association. Minus two.

At the same time, Vincent jumped down from the truck's passenger side door. He, too, had a gun. The men stormed past the butcher and swept into the building. The butcher stood for a moment, then followed them inside.

As I pulled out the gun that Anthony had given me, I heard the muffled cries of several women. The tea shipment, I thought, and I was certain that those cries wouldn't be heard inside the noisy store at the front of the building.

Even armed, rushing into the warehouse would be foolish. With the gun in my right hand, I pulled my phone out with my left. And hesitated. For just a moment, I wondered if Vincent— the FBI agent—was actually trying to rescue the women.

But then he returned to the back door. He held Tommy in front of him.

Tommy was sagging, weak-kneed and barely conscious. He looked as if someone had pistol-whipped him. His nose was bleeding, probably broken, there was a nasty abrasion on one cheek and blood was pouring from a wound on his scalp, staining his bright hair with a third color.

Vincent had a gun pressed to Tommy's temple.

"Lacie Reed," he shouted. "I saw you as we drove past. Show yourself. Now. Or the kid dies."

My hesitation had lost me my chance to phone Beauprix.

I quickly tucked my cell phone under my shirt where my bra crossed my breastbone. Perhaps later there would be an opportunity to use it. In the meantime, I could only hope that when Anthony didn't hear from me, he'd call, get no answer and then come running.

I stepped from behind the florist's van, holding my gun up where Vincent could see it. And I wondered how he knew my real name.

"Toss the gun away, Squirt," he said, going back to the name he knew me by. "And the purse, too."

I did what he said. And I realized that he was the *third* person who knew both of my identities.

"You're the one who sent the carrion birds."

That stopped him for a moment. He looked confused.

"The guys in the bird masks."

"Yeah. That was me. Before you arrived in New Orleans, the senator—your Uncle Duran—told me about your awkward relationship with Tinh Vu and sent me photos of you. He asked me to keep an eye on you, not to let you screw up a *federal* operation, and to watch your back. As necessary."

I was hoping to buy enough time for Beauprix to start worrying.

"Then why?"

"Just playing with you. Now quit stalling or I'll shoot young Tommy. Come on up the steps. Slowly. And keep those hands raised."

I did just that, and tried to walk without bouncing. I stopped halfway up.

"Why the photo?"

He shrugged.

"Why not? I needed proof they'd done their job. Better, I think you'll agree, than asking them to bring back your severed finger. Hurry up. Inside."

The brick through the Red Lotus's window, I thought, was another attempt to scare me.

"And Saturday?" I asked as I walked past him.

"You were getting too close. You'd become an impediment. But even then, they had orders not to kill you. Just to do a little cosmetic work. I just wanted to send Senator Duran a little something to remember me by. But this is even better."

And then something hard slammed into the back of my head.

Chapter 24

I was in a boat, escaping Vietnam. Beneath the deck, where it was dark, the sounds of the sea were drowned by the roar of the diesel engine.

I felt queasy. And my head hurt.

Seasick, I told myself.

Maybe I would feel better if I went up on the deck.

I lifted my head, intending to stand and do just that.

The world shifted. Up, down, forward and back were suddenly indistinguishable directions.

I shut my eyes again, watched as pinpricks of light exploded behind my eyelids, and blacked out again.

When I came to the second time, the world made more sense.

I was moving again, but this time I knew I was riding in a vehicle on a well-paved road.

I smelled soil and rubber and diesel fuel. There was a

ridged surface beneath my right cheek and the metallic taste of blood in my mouth.

I opened my eyes and it took a moment for me to figure out that I was in the cab of a truck, not its trailer. I was on the floor, in front of the passenger-side seat. And we were moving fast.

A pair of feet, tied with nylon rope at the ankles, rested beside me. My face was to the bench seat, my knees were bent, and the bound feet were tucked in somewhere in the vicinity of my stomach.

My own feet, I realized, were touching the door. I tried to move them, succeeded, and realized that my ankles were not bound. But my hands were tied behind me. Tight.

I twisted my neck far enough to see another pair of feet, right foot on the accelerator.

"Hello, Vincent," I said quietly.

"Ah, good company at last," a mocking voice replied.

I heard him strike someone.

"Where are your manners, boy? Lift your head and say hello to your little girlfriend."

"'Lo, Squirt," Tommy said, and though his voice was weak, the bound feet that rested next to me moved slightly. Tapped me lightly in the stomach.

I managed to roll halfway onto my back, tipped my head to look up in Vincent's direction. Rediscovered my headache and saw nothing but a cloudy sky moving past.

I had no idea where we were or how long I'd been unconscious.

"Where are your buddies?" I asked, wondering how talkative he was feeling.

"They're going to meet us in Miami. I'd gotten a phone call from one of my bosses a few days ago. Seems like someone was nosing around, and suddenly he's got questions about my ongoing undercover investigation. And the way you were sniffing around…

"I decided it was time to move our operation. In Little Vietnam, I ran a nice little neighborhood protection racket and sold counterfeit documents. That was enough for me and my little organization to get our feet wet. Now we can move on to bigger and better things. Our equipment is all in the back of the truck. Computers. Copiers. Cameras. Paper. Everything. But a move's expensive. So I upped the price of the documents. And stole the shipment the Benevolent Society hijacked."

"You delayed the documents on purpose."

"Hell, no. Damned computer got a virus. Then there was some software incompatibility...."

Vincent's sudden anger twisted his mouth, whitened the knuckles on his hands. He stepped down on the accelerator, hard.

Where, I wondered, was a traffic cop when you needed one? And I prayed that suddenly I'd see lights flashing in Vincent's side-view mirror.

Vincent must have had the same thought. He took a breath, slowed back down. I was sure he was, once again, keeping carefully to the speed limit.

And he was smiling again.

"Usually, we can provide superior customer service," he said matter-of-factly. "Birth certificates from all fifty states. And Puerto Rico. Social security cards. Drivers' licenses. Occasionally, for special customers, a U.S. passport or two. We're computer literate and extremely entrepreneurial. I don't much care who we sell papers to. The folks in Little Vietnam wanted to hijack tea shipments and I said, more power to them. But anyone trafficking humans through the Port of New Orleans buys their *documents* from me."

He was a compulsive talker, I thought. And I was certain he'd prefer to have his audience looking at him. To be able to look at his audience.

"Would you mind if I sat up?"

"Help the girlfriend, why don't you, Tommy?"

Tommy managed to tuck his feet beneath my shoulders and lifted as I sat up. My head hurt and now my back was to Vincent. But there was enough space on the floor of the truck that I was able to shift myself around. I pulled my knees up in front of me, leaned back against the door and discovered an extremely sore bump.

"You hit me with your damned gun," I said, cursing softly.

Vincent laughed.

"Seemed like a good idea at the time. Made it a lot easier to find that phone you stashed. You have such soft little breasts."

I shuddered at the thought.

Tommy threw himself against the seat belt that bound him, made a noise in his throat that sounded like outrage.

Vincent dealt him a backhanded slap.

"My God, boy. Don't you learn? I think the kid's in love with you, *Squirt*. Tried to protect you earlier from a little friendly petting."

Then Vincent grew silent, concentrating on the road as he slowed to take a sharp curve. As he did, I tugged at the ropes that bound my wrists, then turned my head to look at Tommy.

"Thank you," I mouthed.

When I'd seen him last, he'd looked bad. But now… His lips were split, one eye was swollen completely closed and the eyelid had turned a dark, angry purple. Blood was smeared across his face, its source a broken nose and a tear in his right eyebrow where a piece of silver jewelry had once been. His ears were also bloody and there were small, ragged wounds where his many earrings had been torn away. Somehow, the ring that pierced his left nostril remained, and it glinted gold when the sunlight hit it. A grubby ballcap was pulled down over his bright hair. Its billed cap, I suspected, kept any passing drivers from getting a good look at his face.

He now looked just like his brother, I thought, whose

slashed and battered body I'd examined at the morgue. But this young man was no lifeless corpse. He angled his head slightly so that Vincent couldn't see his face, then dropped his left eyelid in a slow, deliberate wink.

Good boy, I thought. Don't give up.

I shrugged my shoulders to relieve their cramping, stiffened my elbows and gave the bindings on my wrists another tug. Then I shifted so that my head and back were leaning against Tommy's legs.

Vincent was staring at the road.

I tried to start him talking again.

"So you moved into Little Vietnam and took over."

There was an edge of madness to his sudden bray of laughter.

"Imagine Tinh Vu having to buy forged documents from me. For a while I thought I'd put him and his Vietnamese soldier buddies out of the human trafficking business. They didn't like buying their documents *retail*. But they ended up paying sixty-thousand dollars for documents that I'll sell again.

"Tinh Vu didn't like coming up with all that extra cash, did he? But this time he didn't have much choice. I killed all his forgers. Smashed the very hands that Tinh Vu used to defy me. It was easy enough for my people to track them down. Use the right pressure and people betray almost anyone and do anything they're asked to do. Take the butcher, for instance. All I had to do was grab his little florist girlfriend, cut one of her fingers off, and show it to him. After that, he told me everything I needed to know. And he betrayed his friends. Fortunately, a missing finger won't affect her resale value."

My stomach roiled, as much from the thought as the lingering feeling of concussion. Uncle Tinh's business rival was, indeed, a sociopath. When I brought Uncle Tinh the drawings of the victims, told him about the pattern I'd seen, he already knew that the message was for him. I had simply shown him the reality—the brutality—of those deaths.

At the mention of his brother, Tommy had struggled violently against the seat and lap belts that held him tightly in place, struggled to somehow free the hands that were tied behind his back.

Stop it, I thought. Save your strength. Sooner or later, there will be an opportunity to use it. Wait for it. But when finally he sagged against his bonds, he wiggled his feet, and I realized that he'd shifted them beneath my bound hands.

"You bastard," Tommy muttered. "I'll kill you."

I braced for Vincent to hit the boy again. But he didn't.

"There's nothing wrong with a little family loyalty," he said. "But that's the last I want to hear from you, Tommy."

And then, without warning, he slammed him in the face again.

Tommy made a small, strangled noise and went very still. I turned my head to look at him, saw that his undamaged eye was closed. I wondered if he was sleeping. Or unconscious. Or simply playing possum.

After that, we rode for a while in silence.

I lay back against the seat, staring at Vincent, working my fingers through the knots that bound Tommy's ankles. And I tried to think of what good it would do if I actually managed to free him. Especially if he was unconscious.

I kept working at the knots.

"The tea shipment, it's in the back of the truck?"

"You *are* good," he said sarcastically. "Yeah. The tea shipment, with the pretty little florist thrown in as a bonus. By now, her boyfriend's gator food. But I wouldn't do that to our young Tommy. There are people who'll pay well for him, even in his slightly bruised condition."

Vincent spent a moment enjoying the thought.

I tried not to be sick.

"I hadn't planned it," he continued, "but we had all this extra space. And you can be sure that I won't be wasting this opportunity like Tinh Vu and his buddies did. I'll sell my merchandise."

"I don't understand," I said. And I didn't.

Beneath my probing fingertip, I felt a knot ease, just a little. I worked my fingertips into the next knot.

"Tinh Vu has contacts. He'd tell one of his old soldier buddies, who happens to be the chairman of the Benevolent Society, about arriving tea shipments. Then the Society and a few of their trusted friends would steal the shipments and hide them…"

Another piece of the knotted rope moved easily through my fingers.

"…arrange for documents, and send the women up north."

He wasn't telling me anything I hadn't already guessed.

"So what. They're sex traffickers."

"I've been told for most of my life how *smart* you are," he said. "Don't you understand? They steal the women, give them papers and money, and set them free. What a waste."

He set them free! I felt a surge of joy that even the current situation couldn't dilute. Uncle Tinh was the man I'd grown up believing him to be. He was not a brutal exploiter like Vincent.

And as for Uncle Duran's suspicions, his evidence… Then I remembered what Vincent had said just before knocking me unconscious.

"Is Senator Duran Reed in on this?"

Vincent giggled. It was a sound more terrifying than his laughter.

"Hell, no. Senator Reed had the FBI send me to New Orleans to investigate Tinh Vu. There was a rumor—nothing more—that he was trafficking in humans. And supplying counterfeit documents. I was feeding the senator bad information, trying to get rid of Tinh Vu. And using the opportunity to bring in my people."

I slipped my fingers beneath the ropes that bound Tommy's ankles. One more knot, I thought, and his feet are free.

"He asked me to call him Uncle Duran, too, you know,"

Vincent continued. "*My* family was wealthy, but they sent me away anyway. For my own good, they said. And they put me on a boat. I ended up in Thailand. You were in the camp at Songkhla, weren't you?"

"Yes," I said.

"I was at a larger camp—Sikhiu. For two years. I'd almost given up the dream of coming to America. No American family would want to sponsor a thirteen-year-old camp rat. Then along came Uncle Duran. Do you remember the tests they gave us?"

He stared at the road ahead.

I began working on the final knot as I thought about the Americans who'd visited the refugee camp. It was one of the best memories of my young life. They played games. Gave me toys, candy and hugs as rewards. Told me I was *pretty*. And there had been a special game. They showed me photos, took them away, then asked me to tell them what I'd seen. I remembered showing off a little—I described what I saw to the interpreters, but then I drew pictures for the Americans.

"Everyone took those tests," I said. "IQ. Aptitude. Psychological evaluations."

Vincent shook his head.

"No. Only a few. Prescreening, you might say, before being selected for the senator's version of the American dream. I'd been in America for three months when he told me that my job, if I didn't want to be deported back to the refugee camp, was to infiltrate the Born To Kill gang."

I was genuinely horrified. I knew from the reports I'd read that around the time Vincent was talking about, the BTKs were just organizing. But its members were already notorious for their brutality.

"But you were just a child!"

Vincent nodded.

"Unlike you, I didn't need nurture and education to bring out *my* skills. I was young, male, Vietnamese, and a survivor.

And I was willing to do whatever it took to maintain my perfect cover, to please Uncle Duran. Robbery. Rape. Beatings. Extortion. Murder. But, eventually, I gave the authorities the foothold they needed. I *earned* the bright future the senator promised me."

Then he fell into a deep silence.

I watched the side of his face, saw the muscles working beneath his cheeks, saw the way he clenched the steering wheel.

I finished untying the last knot, but I left the rope around Tommy's ankles. He hadn't moved for almost fifteen minutes. I looked up at him, watched his chest rise and fall. Alive, at least, I thought. And then I felt his foot move, a quick tap against my fingers.

"There's a place I know just up ahead," Vincent said. "We'll stop there."

The truck jounced as we pulled off the road. I caught a look at a wrecked neon sign. It was covered in corrosion and the remnants of the long bulbs hung from bits of wire. I could make out the word "motel."

"Lots of these places along I-90. Always for sale. Never selling."

He drove back to a place where tall, moss-hung oaks crowded the sky.

Vincent took off his seat belt, reached over and hit Tommy's face.

I flinched from the sound of the impact, but the boy only whimpered.

"He's not going anywhere," he said.

And then he leaned over, grabbed my ankles and attempted to drag me from the truck.

I kicked his hands away. Managed to roll up onto my knees and almost stand up. When Vincent grabbed for my ankles again, I fell backward against Tommy, scrabbled against his seat belt. Tommy slumped sideways, unresponsive.

Vincent pulled me from the truck.

He dropped me to the ground and kicked me onto my stomach. Then he picked me up, wrapped his arms around me so that my hands were trapped between my body and his, and carried me toward a cabin. Its roof was swayed, its door hung open and was supported by a single hinge.

I fought him all the way, kicking, screaming, twisting.

But it didn't matter. He was stronger than I was.

There was no furniture in the room. Simply a floor that was wet with moss and rot. And a torn, badly stained mattress in a corner.

He threw me onto the mattress, leaned over me, breathing hard.

I sat there, trapped and gasping, but I tried to put a foot in his gut.

He shifted aside and laughed at me.

I'd never heard a more chilling sound.

As I glanced around, searching for escape, I saw the blood spatters on the wall. And knew that Vincent had killed here before.

I was undoubtedly next.

Then Vincent began shouting.

"You were the favorite, the brilliant one, the brave one. The one who could do no wrong. My family was wealthy and you were nothing but *bui doi*. Still I heard about you from the day I set foot in this country. But look at you now."

Rage twisted his face as he slapped me. Unprepared for the stinging blow, I bit down hard on my tongue and tasted blood. Tears welled in my eyes.

He snapped his mouth shut, gave his head a quick shake, and then used his fingers to wipe away the warm trickle that escaped the corner of my mouth. He spent a moment looking at his reddened fingertips, then pulled a handkerchief from his pocket, wiped them off, and dropped the hanky on the mattress.

"I've always been jealous of you," he said.

Abruptly, his tone had become moderate again. At exactly the wrong time.

Past Vincent, through the broken door, I could see Tommy. He was wobbly on his feet, but he was moving, staggering toward the cabin. He'd been tough enough to take Vincent's blow without reacting and smart enough to lay still during our fight in the truck.

I'd unclipped his seat belt as I was being dragged from the cab.

"Sibling rivalry is a bitch, isn't it?" I said, trying to goad Vincent into another rage. "Especially when we're not even related."

I braced for another blow.

Instead, he stripped off his shirt.

His arms, golden-brown chest and flat stomach rippled with well-defined muscles. A complex, jewel-toned tattoo of a dragon wrapped itself around his left biceps. The crimson heart it held in its claws was torn in two. On his left breast, another tattoo. An American flag, consumed by flames. And from its center, a phoenix rose, undefeated. It, too, clutched a crimson heart in its claws. But this heart was intact and the droplets of blood that flowed from it seemed to be feeding the flames.

My God, I thought.

Tommy was almost to the cabin. But his hands were still bound behind his back. As were mine.

Vincent's trousers remained on.

"Do you see this?" he said, pointing to the dragon, which was more faded than the other tattoo. "I earned it by pistol-whipping a shopkeeper. And raping his wife. Afterward, they took me to a tattoo parlor in Chinatown and told me I was one of them. A *sai low*—a little brother—in the Born To Kill gang.

He slapped his right hand over his heart, briefly covering the phoenix with the bloodstained beak.

"This tattoo, I chose for myself ten years ago. My work had helped destroy the BTKs. But it was their impatience, their greed, that brought them down. I began planning then, knowing that someday I would use the senator, just as he used me. And now it's left only to tie up a loose end."

He stared at me as he unbuckled his belt, slipped it smoothly from its loops and held it with the buckle end dangling. Suddenly, he snapped his wrist, swinging the belt at me.

I flinched aside and the buckle whipped past my cheek.

He was smiling now. His hand was poised for another blow.

"You'd be worth more undamaged, but I think I deserve this…."

I widened my eyes, stretched my mouth, allowed my face to reflect my fear. I used my feet to push myself away from him, cowering….

Tommy was almost to the doorway.

Vincent swung his belt.

I turned, deflecting the blow with my shoulder, and screamed in pain.

Vincent stepped in closer, enjoying himself.

"No, please," I begged.

He swung again as Tommy came into the room.

I flattened myself onto the mattress and kicked upward with all my strength. Vincent clutched his crotch as he dropped to his knees. The belt still dangled from one of his hands.

"You bitch," he whispered as the blood drained from his face.

Tommy took advantage of the moment and landed a kick squarely on the back of Vincent's neck.

I rolled aside as Vincent fell forward onto the mattress. He lay beside me, momentarily stunned.

This was our chance. Our only chance. If Vincent recovered, Tommy and I would undoubtedly die slow deaths at his hand. And the women in the truck would be sold into slavery.

"Put a knee between his shoulder blades," I cried to Tommy. "Use your weight to hold him down."

I turned and grabbed Vincent's belt with my bound hands. Worked frantically, clumsily to loop it around his neck.

He groaned, began moving.

I grasped the ends of the belt tightly in my hands, gave them a half twist and threw all of my weight away from Vincent.

He fought us.

He struck out with his fists and bucked his body, tried to work his fingers between his neck and the belt, tried to reach me, to dislodge Tommy. But we held on, fighting for our lives as desperately as he fought for his.

The loop tightened around his neck.

Vincent choked, gasped for breath, then was silent.

We held on until he wasn't moving anymore.

Later, I walked along the highway until I found a gas station. Dialed a familiar number. And asked Anthony to please come get us.

Chapter 25

Uncle Tinh and I sat opposite each other at a table on his balcony. The day was sunny and the morning light cast a heavenly glow on the trio of alabaster statues on the lawn below us. Appropriate, I supposed, for the saintly Ursulines. Our conversation had more to do with manmade hells.

We had finished breakfast and were both sipping a second cup of coffee.

After a few minutes Uncle Tinh put his cup down, straightened his shoulders and lifted his chin, and began providing long overdue explanations.

"I don't believe in slavery," he began. "So when some…contacts…who own ships that dock in New Orleans asked me to…organize…counterfeit documents for them, I sent them away. My mistake, though I did not know it at the time. I opened the door for the gang who invaded our community."

He spent a moment looking at some gulls wheeling overhead, then met my eyes again.

"After that visit, I began thinking about the people who would be coming here. Who would end up as slaves. As you know, information is the commodity I trade in. I asked a few questions, paid a little money, talked to some trusted friends. And soon the hijacking of tea shipments began. Selective hijackings, only of cargoes that originated in Vietnam. To save our people from bondage. As for the rest—" He shook his head slowly. "Even my resources are limited.

"I didn't know until you almost met your death that Vincent was the *anh hai* of the gang that invaded Little Vietnam. For a time, they were content to profit from the many other shipments moving inland from the Port of New Orleans. Our illegal activities suited them. They built their protection racket on our reluctance to go to the police.

"Then a message was given to Mr. Yang. The hijackings could continue, but the forged documents were to be purchased from the Young Vietnamese Businessmen's Association. For a short time, we thought we could ignore them. Then came the killings. The deaths of people I knew and cared about."

He stopped speaking, picked up his cup of coffee with a shaking hand, and took a sip. Then another.

I sipped my own coffee, idly watched a group of tourists walking through the convent's grounds, and considered the NOPD's findings as I gave my uncle the time he needed to control his emotions.

The police were now convinced that Vincent had murdered all three residents of Little Vietnam as part of his gang's intimidation of the community. His name now cleared, the unfortunate husband of the second murder victim had been released from prison. The NOPD also concluded that Vincent and his gang were solely responsible for trafficking the tea shipment—the warehouse of the souvenir shop had been used against the owner's will and the butcher had been killed because he had unwittingly stumbled onto the scene. Nothing that Beauprix or I said contradicted any of their conclusions.

Even Remy had acknowledged Beauprix's persistence.

"Maybe Anthony is not so crazy after all," he had said to me.

Uncle Tinh put the cup down with a steadier hand.

"And so, now, you know everything."

Almost, I thought. But one question still weighed on my mind.

"After three murders, why didn't you just quit hijacking the tea shipments? Why rescue this last group?"

He shook his head, his lips tightening with frustration.

"Mr. Yang learned secondhand of a shipment that supposedly contained a cousin among the women. Fearing that I would not approve the venture, he convinced the others to help him without my knowledge. Maybe, under those circumstances, I would have done the same. But, as it turned out, there was no cousin. I wonder, even now, if the shippers set up the situation, hoping to eliminate those who had stolen their shipments in the past. But they underestimated the skill and determination of the Benevolent Society."

We sat silently for a few minutes, enjoying the warm day and the peaceful surroundings, each entertaining our own thoughts.

"You should have gone to the police," I said finally.

"And said what? We carry guns. Steal shipments of human beings. Provide forged documents. And then we say to the police, please make those bad men leave us alone? I did not think I could trust any policeman—not even Anthony—to ignore *our* activities. And this same secret—shared by many honorable people in Little Vietnam—meant that I could give you very little guidance. I judged it necessary to distance myself from my friends so that you would not suspect them."

I looked back out at the statues. They looked peaceful, I thought. Satisfied that they'd done their job, opened their schools and hospitals in the backward, fever-ridden bayou.

I was still a long way from feeling like that.

"So Mr. Yang and the Benevolent Society hijacked another shipment without your permission and collected money to buy documents from Vincent. But then the price went up and Mr. Yang went to you for the money he needed."

"I could not abandon my friends," he said simply. "Or those women."

I sighed.

"Perhaps not. It was a generous gesture. But you realize that there were few good outcomes. More people died. Tommy was badly hurt. Anthony doubts that we'll ever find Vincent's accomplices. The INS is returning the women to their countries of origin. And the money you paid is gone. I don't think you want to tell the FBI that the money they seized from the Ryder truck was yours."

Uncle Tinh shook his head slowly.

"I grieve for the women. And I am so sorry, *chère*, for what I put you through. Had I known how badly it was to go wrong…"

I looked at my uncle, whose face was also lit by the sun and whose eyes were sad. He was less than saintly. But I loved him. He was my family.

"It's done," I said. "And forgotten."

He smiled, looked relieved.

"But Uncle Tinh?"

"Yes, Lacie?"

"The hijacked shipments—no matter whose people—must stop. Do I have your word on this?"

He wouldn't lie to me. So he answered my question by not answering it.

"Everyone deserves a chance to live in America," he said.

It took me almost six weeks to do what I needed to do in Washington, D.C. But I had a flight booked for later that evening and had only one stop to make before I returned to New Orleans.

It was the first time since I'd returned to Washington that

I'd visited the Right Honorable Senator Duran Reed. An hour had passed since I'd walked through the door into his suite of offices. And now, just as I had when I first left my adopted uncle's office to go to New Orleans, I found myself standing behind the tall back of a visitor's chair and digging my fingers into its expensive tapestry upholstery. This time, there was a briefcase at my feet.

Once again, my uncle's expansive desk was just in front of me. And the emotions I felt as I looked at him across the desk were the same as they had been. Anger. Frustration. Disappointment. Pain. But a report, written by me, now lay stacked neatly in the middle of his desk. It was what I had come to talk about.

The report followed the format of dozens of other reports I'd turned in to him over the years and contained a similar level of detail. A description of the operation. What I knew going in. What I'd encountered. The people I'd met. The mistakes I'd made. Relevant conversations. Outcome and conclusions. Irrefutable evidence and unsupported conjecture. And the official positions and unofficial accommodations made by any agencies I'd interacted with.

I'd come into his office complex without an appointment and asked his secretary to carry an envelope containing the report and a short note from me into his private office. I waited in his reception area and tried not to think too closely about what I was going to say when I saw him. Or what I was going to do.

The secretary showed me into his office within sixty minutes. Enough time, I thought, for him to read, reread and digest the report's contents. Enough time for him to become furious.

The report was facedown on his desk. Beside it, in his expensive crystal ashtray, his inevitable Cuban cigar was not just chewed. It had been broken in two. And, as I'd walked in, Uncle Duran had swung his leather-bound chair around so that he could study what remained of the postcard view outside his picture window.

Winter had come to the capitol city. Beyond the expansive sheet of glass, the fall colors were long faded. Rain had stripped the leaves from the cherry trees and cast them, brown and rotting, to the ground.

"Corruption can crop up anywhere," the senator said without looking at me.

I stared at his aristocratic profile, his impeccably groomed hair, at the perfectly tailored suit jacket that lay across his broad shoulders.

"And in anyone," I murmured softly enough that he didn't hear me.

He swung his chair around to face me and narrowed his cold, gray eyes.

"Who has seen this?" he asked.

"You. Me."

"That's all?"

I nodded.

"For now. But there are sealed copies in safe places, held by reliable people. If something should happen to me—"

Outraged, he slammed his hand down on the sheaf of papers, and his rich, baritone voice echoed off the office walls.

"Read your own report, damn it. I'm not a criminal. Or a murderer. There's nothing that connects me to Vincent Ngo or his investigation. Except for your speculation and what you say a dead man told you."

"There are people well placed in the INS who could testify about your involvement in Operation Wounded Dragon. A rather melodramatic title, by the way. Your idea?"

The senator scowled at me, an expression I'd seen before.

"You can't hold me responsible for what he did."

I smiled, and found within myself a certain surprising malice.

"I am holding you responsible for what he *was*. For what you made him. For what you forced him to become."

He shook his head, retreated behind a wall of righteousness.

"I did nothing illegal. I found homes for dozens of children. War orphans. Street urchins. Half-breed throwaways. *Bui doi.*"

He spat out the old insult, intending it to hurt me.

It didn't.

"I'm grateful to you, Uncle Duran," I said calmly. "You gave me my parents, my life in America. You gave *me* choices. Which is why I'm here."

The spiderwork of purple veins across Uncle Duran's fleshy cheeks were in stark contrast to the angry flush that touched his face.

"Who are you trying to kid? You came here because you have no proof."

I laughed, but I doubted he heard any humor in the sound. None was intended.

"You forget," I said, "that *proof* is one of the things I do best."

He simply stared at me.

"The dates that you visited the refugee camps in Thailand are part of the public record. And I remember that you had reporters with you, always, when you visited Songkhla. They took pictures of you holding me. I thought that there must be other pictures, other stories. And I was right. The newspapers and magazines from that era are full of your activities. The great humanitarian. The senator with a heart. And a conscience."

I paused, but still he had nothing to say. And I tried not to remember how often, as a child, I'd heard his voice on the phone, calling to ask me if I'd received his gift or to congratulate me because I'd gotten good grades. And I tried not to feel pity for this pitiless man.

"The list of dates narrowed my search through immigration records and international adoption agency records. I cross referenced that with lists of men and women employed by government agencies.

"I looked at a lot of lists, Uncle Duran. Fortunately, I have a good memory."

I leaned over to pick up the briefcase I'd carried in with me. Opened it and pulled out a single sheet of paper. On it, thirteen names.

I put the list on the desk in front of him.

"I haven't talked to them. And, I'd rather not."

He shrugged.

"So I helped a few needy Vietnamese kids get jobs. What of it? As you said, I'm the senator with a heart."

"When I've finished interviewing the names on this list, I'll start looking beyond Vietnam. And I know I'll find more children just like me, just like Vincent, who were brought in on the coattails of Honorable Senator Duran Reed. From how many of them did you demand an impossibly high price for the American dream?"

Of course, he didn't answer me.

I hadn't expected him to.

"What do you want from me?" he said finally.

"Absolutely nothing," I said. "Except your retirement from public office."

He leaned forward on his desk, trying to intimidate me, and he reminded me of nothing more than a carrion bird. With its mask torn away.

"You can't—"

"Oh, yes, Uncle Duran. I can. And if I ever hear even the slightest whisper that you intend to run for President, I'll send these names to every newspaper in the country."

Then I turned on my heel, kept my back straight, and walked away.

And I knew that I had just gained a powerful enemy.

Epilogue

I went back to New Orleans.

The late-night flight was uneventful, except that the stewardess assumed that I was nervous about flying. She'd asked me just that after takeoff, her eyes fixed on the many small paper packets that I'd set on the table-tray in front of me. I told her that, in fact, concentrating on sorting tasks worked better for me than medication. Which didn't seem to reassure her at all.

By the end of the flight, I had cleared the tray and folded it back into its upright position, tucked two quart-size plastic bags back into my carry-on, and discarded a wad of emptied packets into the trash bag that the stewardess had walked through the cabin with. As the passengers exited the airplane, she actually flashed me a nervous smile.

Before I'd left for Washington, I'd promised Beauprix that I would return. But I had made no promises as to when. I had some business I needed to wrap up, I'd told him.

And some thinking to do, I told myself.

He hadn't asked me for details.

"Damn it, little girl," he said, "you go and do whatever you have to."

Then he'd pressed a house key into my hand and briefly taken me into his arms.

In the end, I hadn't called to tell him I was coming back. I'd simply gotten onto a plane bound for New Orleans.

It was past midnight when I took a taxi to the Beauprix house in the Garden District. This time, I didn't use the servants' entrance.

Beauprix had given me permission to let myself in.

"I'm not the kind of cop who sleeps with a gun by his bed," he'd assured me before I left. "You're always welcome in my home. Day or night. The guest room is upstairs, first door on the right." Then he'd paused, adding, "You already know where my room is." And his voice had been husky with invitation.

I didn't need his key.

After retrieving the less bulky of the plastic bags from my carry-on, I hid my suitcases behind a rose trellis near the front door. Then I tucked the bag into my blouse and walked quietly around to the side of the house.

I went into his bedroom the same way I'd left it weeks earlier.

I climbed up the vine-wrapped drainpipe to the second-floor gallery, pulled up on the guillotine window. It slid silently open and I let myself inside the bedroom. The long, tangerine-colored sheers framing the windows moved gently with the cool evening breeze. And the moonlight flooded in.

Beauprix was sprawled in the center of his queen-size bed. He was on his back, arms flung wide, a soft blanket in a shade of dark chocolate draped across his belly. The corded muscles on his lean body glistened faintly with perspiration.

For a while I stood watching him, listening to the deep rhythm of his breathing. Even at rest, the body reflected the soul of the man. Beautiful. Intense. All strength and symmetry and passion.

I imagined myself nestling in against him, skimming my fingers along the angle of one of his rough cheeks, pausing to touch his full lips, trailing my fingers downward until I was stroking his chest. And then my fingers would continue their journey until I'd pushed the blanket down past his muscular belly.

Looking without touching quickly became too much to bear.

I pulled the plastic bag from my shirt.

"Hello, Anthony," I said.

With a start, he opened his eyes, turned his head.

That's when I tossed the bag.

It landed, as I'd intended, right next to his pillow.

He sat up and swung his legs off the bed. Picked up the bag, saw what it contained. And he began laughing.

His deep, soft laughter continued until he was across the room and had his arms wrapped around me. His bare skin was warm, and he smelled deliciously male.

I could feel the weight of the plastic bag resting against my back.

"That's payment for a foot rub," I said as I nuzzled his chest.

"A foot rub," he murmured. "And much, much more."

Then he pressed his mouth to mine. And before too long, he had better things to do with his hands than hold on to a bag filled with blue M&M's.

ATHENA FORCE

Chosen for their talents.
Trained to be the best.

Expected to change the world.

The women of Athena Academy
share an unforgettable experience
and an unbreakable bond—until
one of their own is murdered.

The adventure begins with these six books:

PROOF by Justine Davis, July 2004

ALIAS by Amy J. Fetzer, August 2004

EXPOSED by Katherine Garbera,
September 2004

DOUBLE-CROSS by Meredith Fletcher,
October 2004

PURSUED by Catherine Mann, November 2004

JUSTICE by Debra Webb, December 2004

**And look for six more Athena Force stories
January to June 2005.**

Available at your favorite retail outlet.

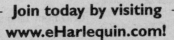

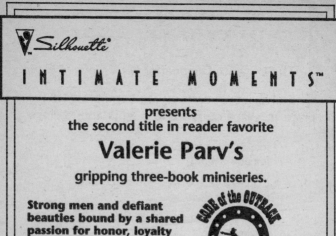

like a phantom in the night comes
a new promotion from

HARLEQUIN®

INTRIGUE®

GOTHIC ROMANCE

Beginning in August 2004, we offer you
a classic blend of chilling suspense and
electrifying romance, starting with....

A DANGEROUS INHERITANCE
LEONA KARR

And don't miss a spine-tingling Eclipse tale each month!

September 2004
MIDNIGHT ISLAND SANCTUARY
SUSAN PETERSON

October 2004
THE LEGACY OF CROFT CASTLE
JEAN BARRETT

November 2004
THE MAN FROM FALCON RIDGE
RITA HERRON

December 2004
EDEN'S SHADOW
JENNA RYAN

Available wherever Harlequin books are sold.
www.eHarlequin.com   HIECLIPSE

Silhouette
BOMBSHELL

COMING NEXT MONTH

#13 STELLA, GET YOUR GUN—Nancy Bartholomew

Stella Valocchi left home a mousy girl with a broken heart.
Now she was back as a sexy blond cop on a mission.
Her uncle had been murdered and her ex-boyfriend—still
undeniably tempting—was the main suspect. With the
help of her quirky cousin, a fishnet-wearing lawyer, and
one trusty dog, Stella was out for justice...and revenge!

#14 DOUBLE-CROSS—Meredith Fletcher

Athena Force
Desperate to bring down her friend's killer, fearless undercover agent Samantha St. John got sidetracked when she
was accused of betraying her country and was thrown into
jail. Now she'd have to prove her innocence by taking on
her most dangerous assignment yet—finding an archene-
my with a shocking resemblance.

#15 PRIVATE AGENDA—Natalie Dunbar

CIA agent Reese Whittaker was having a hell of a year.
She'd lost her partner and husband to a rebel camp, and
now her brother was suddenly missing and presumed
dead. Suspicious that the CIA was keeping information
from her, Reese immersed herself in the dangerous life of
a spy, determined to see that justice was served....

#16 KILLER INSTINCT—Cindy Dees

She didn't work with partners. And tracking down stolen
diamonds with a wet-behind-the ears rookie agent wasn't
covert operative Amanda McClintock's idea of the perfect
last mission. But circling the globe with the enemy hot
on their trail forced her to face the facts: her partner had
brains as well as brawn, and the two of them had to work
together or they'd never come out of this mission alive....

SBCNM0904